*There, in the garden, he stole a kiss.
One quick brush of the lips and a bond
existed between them, forbidden,
secret and exciting…*

Leah's baby was nestled protectively in the crook of Devon's arm.

In the golden firelight, his expression appeared grim. The neck of his shirt was open, the sleeves rolled up. With a soft gasp of mother love, Leah reached for her child. But Devon's deep, silky voice stopped her.

"Who is the baby's father? And do you love him?"

She froze. Her mouth went dry. Her heart pounded in her chest.

He waited.

A part of Leah wanted to run. But she'd never been a coward. Through sheer strength of will, she raised her chin in defiance, her gaze not leaving his.

"Where is he now?" he demanded.

There was an edge to his voice. One she'd not heard before. One she didn't trust. "I want my baby."

"And you shall have him, *when* my question is answered."

She could have challenged him, told him she didn't owe him explanations. But in truth, she did. . . .

Other Avon Books by
Cathy Maxwell

BECAUSE OF YOU
FALLING IN LOVE AGAIN
MARRIED IN HASTE
WHEN DREAMS COME TRUE
YOU AND NO OTHER

CATHY MAXWELL

A Scandalous Marriage

AVON BOOKS ◆ NEW YORK

AVON BOOKS, INC.
An Imprint of HarperCollins*Publishers*
10 East 53rd Street
New York, New York 10022-5299

Copyright © 2000 by Catherine Maxwell
Excerpt from *Almost Home* copyright © 2000 by Barbara Freethy
Excerpt from *A Scandalous Marriage* copyright © 2000 by Catherine Maxwell
Excerpt from *Rules of Surrender* copyright © 2000 by Christina Dodd
Excerpt from *Never Love a Cowboy* copyright © 2000 by Jan Nowasky
Excerpt from *Baby, Don't Go* copyright © 2000 by Susan Andersen
Excerpt from *What the Heart Knows* copyright © 1999 by Kathleen Eagle
Inside cover author photo by Glamour Shots
Published by arrangement with the author
Library of Congress Catalog Card Number: 99-95330
ISBN: 0-380-80832-3
www.harpercollins.com

First Avon Books Printing: February 2000

AVON TRADEMARK REG. U.S. PAT. OFF. AND IN OTHER COUNTRIES, MARCA REGISTRADA, HECHO EN U.S.A.

Printed in the U.S.A.

WCD 10 9 8 7 6 5 4 3 2 1

To my friend Bonnie Tucker

I Dreamed

I dreamed I held
A sword against my flesh.
What does it mean?
It means I shall see you soon.

LADY KASA

PROLOGUE

1815

Devon Marshall, viscount Huxhold, rode hell-for-leather across the frozen fallow fields, bound for London and his grandfather's deathbed.

Overhead, swift-moving clouds promised a storm. The air was already damp and heavy. He'd be cursed if he didn't beat the bad weather. His trip could not be delayed.

Suddenly, Gallant stumbled, almost tossing Devon over his head. The horse recovered his footing but limped.

"Damn." Devon's single word echoed in the winter silence. He slid off Gallant's back, his booted heels uneven on the frozen, overturned earth. The accident was his fault. He'd taken a shortcut, turning off the main road and urging his horse across pasture and farming lands. Now, he stood in the middle of Yorkshire without an idea of exactly where he was.

1

It was a wickedly cold day in February and no time to be traveling the North Country. Sensible people would be huddled around their fires. Then he remembered it was Sunday. The pious would be in church. He searched the surrounding tree line for a tower or steeple rising above the bare limbs. Nothing.

Gallant stumbled a step on the uneven terrain, and Devon reached for the bridle. This horse was his pride and joy. The knock-kneed black boasted a great flat head and a tendency to trot with his tongue hanging loose. More than once, the sight of Devon on Gallant's back had been compared to that of a drunken sailor winding his way home from the pub.

Devon didn't care. He had no need for grace and beauty in a horse or even in people. He valued intelligence, loyalty, and heart—qualities Gallant had in abundance. Better yet, the animal was as fiercely independent and ill-mannered as Devon himself. Gallant might be ungainly, but he had won more than his share of races and could travel with the perseverance of a camel.

Grimly, Devon picked up Gallant's hoof and took a look.

The shoe was missing. No surprise there. Gallant should have been shod the week before, but Devon had been too busy warming himself in front of his friend McDermott's fire to see to the matter. He hadn't expected to be called to London in such haste.

Taking a penknife from his pocket, Devon

cleaned the hoof, flicking out a number of small rocks.

"There you are, boy. Not much better." He patted the horse's muzzle. "You're a damn nuisance," he whispered with affection. In answer, Gallant nudged him back.

He had to find a farrier.

He had to reach London.

You're never prepared, Devon. A wise man is always prepared. His grandfather's words rang clearly in Devon's mind, almost as if the crafty old bastard were standing by his shoulder, saying them aloud.

Devon drew in a deep, shuddering breath. He could recall his grandfather's exact tonal inflection, even though the man hadn't chided him for his shortcomings in years. They'd seen each other, but never for long enough to start an argument. Devon's choice. Especially since all the bitter words they'd hurled at each other still haunted him.

Now it no longer mattered. Seeming indifference and polite platitudes came down to this: Devon was the marquess of Kirkeby's heir. Past differences were to be set aside because the marquess was not expected to live beyond the week.

Beyond the week. Those were Brewster's words in his curt message.

Devon could curse the man his terse note. So many questions had crowded his mind that he'd barely been able to take his leave from McDermott with any civility. He was still in a state of shock.

How could his grandfather, whose political power had few limits, whose personality engaged all who entered his sphere, who had proven time and time again to be larger than life itself, how could this man die . . . as simply, and as quietly, as all other mortals?

Now, away from friends, society, all that he knew and held familiar, Devon could not escape one unassailable truth— In spite of their differences, he had loved this man who had raised him after his parents' deaths.

He had to set things right between them.

And that's what had brought him to this point, stranded in a farmer's field, the victim of his own unpreparedness and haste.

Buttoning his heavy greatcoat and setting his beaver hat lower on his head, Devon spied a path leading from the field through a line of trees.

"Come, Gallant. Let's see what we can do for you." There had to be a farm cottage close by.

Gallant followed, his breaths coming out in puffs of frigid air.

The path wound its way through a small wood. As Devon walked, he realized this area was not totally unfamiliar to him. The seat of his good friend the earl of Ruskin was hereabout. Having his bearings made him feel better. He'd get a horse off of Rusky if he didn't find a solution sooner.

Either way, he was determined to make London and the family home, Montclef, if he had to crawl to the place.

Around a curve on the other side of the wood,

Devon caught sight of a picturesque farm less than a quarter mile away. Smoke curled from the chimney of the whitewashed cottage, while a rooster crowed from somewhere around the stone shed.

Gallant's ears picked up and then laid back. He nickered in protest. Devon sniffed. The wind carried the pungent scent of pigs. The pen must be located on the other side of the barn. It was just Devon's bad luck he was downwind from the buggers. He hated the smell of pigs. Gallant obviously did, too.

As he drew closer, the door to the cottage opened. A portly woman wobbled out and made her way across the yard toward the barn. In each fisted hand, she carried a heavy bucket with the strength of a woman accustomed to hard work. A heavy wool shawl tied around her hat and shoulders protected her from the cold. Unfortunately, the wind kept blowing the straw bonnet's floppy brim down in her face. She had to toss her head to let the wind blow it back up, allowing her to see. Consequently, her path toward the shed with the heavy buckets was a zigzag of frustration.

Devon shouted out, "Hey, there."

The wind must have carried his words away, because the woman didn't break stride. Instead, she disappeared behind the shed. A second later, Devon heard the ear-piercing squeals of hungry pigs.

Wrinkling his nose, Devon gave Gallant's reins a tug. "Come on, lad."

In the barnyard, a milk cow stuck its head out

beyond the round sandstone columns supporting the shed's roof. A pair of oxen munched contentedly, watching Devon and Gallant with seeming disinterest.

He didn't bother with the pig girl but tossed the reins around a stone posed in front of the cottage for that purpose. He knocked on the door. It swung open.

"Hello?" Devon listened for an answer.

The room was neat and homey, with rush-bottomed chairs and colorful rag rugs on the floor. Freshly baked bread was set out on the hearth.

But no one was home.

He wished now that he had sent a message telling Brewster and the members of his family he was on his way, but he'd been certain he could travel faster than any courier. Obviously he was wrong.

Doggedly, he followed the smell of the pigs. No dog barked a greeting. Even the chickens were wise enough today to roost instead of scratching the yard for food. He turned the corner of the shed and found himself on the opposite side of the pig-pen from the woman.

She was busy trying to make sure the two larger pigs gave the runt his fair share. Her soft, cajoling words were ignored by the pigs . . . but Devon did notice she was younger than he'd first surmised.

She hadn't noticed him.

Over the noise of grunting pigs, he said, "Excuse me."

Pig squeals drowned him out. The earth was soft

and warm here, and his boots sunk a bit into the muck. He tried not to think what it was he stood in.

He raised his voice. "Excuse me!"

This time he caught her attention. The woman looked up, startled to discover she was not alone. Holding the slop bucket protectively away from the pigs, she lifted the brim of her hat, the better to see him—and then gasped in surprise.

Devon was no less shocked himself. He knew those brown eyes. They had once fascinated him with their ability to be innocent and seductive . . . naïve and worldly . . . honest and deceitful all in the same moment. A temptress's eyes.

This was no simple pig girl.

It was Leah Carrollton, a London debutante who only months ago had been the reigning belle of Society—until she had abruptly disappeared.

When she'd first vanished, her family put it about she was visiting relatives out of the city, but gossip and speculation among the ton had run rampant. Devon had heard the whispers even in his self-imposed exile from London. He had tried not to pay attention. He'd told himself that Leah Carrollton's whereabouts or grand doings were no longer his concern . . . but on those nights when he had no companions but a lonely fire in the grate and a half-empty bottle of brandy, he'd thought of her often. He hadn't been able to prevent himself.

Now, in the whisk of a second, he no longer saw himself standing by some yeoman's pigsty but back in London almost a year ago when he'd been

badgered into attending a ball. He usually avoided
such affairs. But this one was sponsored by
McDermott's aunt, a laughing, Junoesque woman
whose company Devon enjoyed, and he'd good-
naturedly agreed to make an appearance. Of
course, he'd been determined to escape the affair
as early as possible . . . that is, until he had laid
eyes on Leah Carrollton.

*She had been standing a step apart from a
group of other debutantes. They'd all worn pastels
and smelled of rose water. Their conversation con-
sisted primarily of self-conscious giggles. She was
one of them, and yet alone.*

*He instantly recognized a kindred soul. He un-
derstood. She wanted, no, had to be accepted by
the group but exerted her own independence.*

*She sensed him staring at her. She turned,
searching, and then looked straight at him.*

*In that moment, time halted. He even stopped
breathing, knowing he still lived only because his
heart pounded in his ears, its beat abnormally fast.
Cupid's famed arrow had found a mark.*

*For the first time in his adventurous life, he felt
the sweaty palms and the singing in his blood of
a man smitten beyond reason by the mere presence
of a woman. The poets had been right!*

*Oh, she was lovely to look at. Petite, buxom,
rounded. He could have spanned her waist with
his two hands.*

*Her heavy black hair, styled in a simple, elegant
chignon held in place by gold pearl-tipped pins,*

emphasized the slender grace of her neck. He imagined himself pulling those pins from her hair one by one. It would fall in a graceful, swinging curtain down to her waist. Her eyes were so dark and exotic that they reminded him of full moons, Spanish dancers, and velvety nights.

But it wasn't her beauty that drew him. No, it was something deeper. Something he'd never felt before. He wasn't a fanciful man, but he could swear he'd been waiting for her to walk into his life.

She smiled. The most charming dimple appeared at the corner of her mouth, and his feet began moving of their own volition. He wasn't even conscious that he was walking until he stood in front of her.

"Dance with me." He held out his hand.

Carefully, as if she, too, understood the importance of her actions, she placed her hand in his. It was a magic moment. He felt changed in some indefinable way.

He raised her gloved fingers to his lips. "Do you feel the draw? The pull between us?"

She nodded. "My heart is pounding against my chest."

"As is mine. Tell me your name."

"Leah—"

He cut her off. "Leah." He loved the sound of it. "I'm Devon. Do you know what I think, Leah?"

"That we were destined to meet?" She smiled shyly.

Her answer reinforced his belief that something

greater than both of them was at work.

"Come." He led her out onto the dance floor.

Devon rarely danced. He thought men who enjoyed dancing were little different than peacocks preening for women. But tonight, he would not let her from his sight. He was staking his claim to her. Here, on the dance floor, all the world would see that she was his. No other man could have her.

The dance they took their places for was the pavane, the sort of ritualistic promenade he usually hated. But not tonight; as the musicians struck the first chord, he was transformed. Him! A man who had sworn that one woman was as good as another and had sampled most. Colors were suddenly brighter, the music sweeter, the world full of possibilities.

In her presence, he discovered something had been missing in his life—

A rough hand grabbed his arm.

Devon whirled on his attacker, ready to defend her. Before him stood Julian Carrollton, his face red with anger, his fists clenched.

Devon almost laughed. Julian was more bluster than bully. The man was a shiftless gambler, just like all the members of his family.

The Marshalls and the Carrolltons did not mix. Especially since Devon and his grandfather blamed Richard Carrollton, Julian's father, for the tragic accident that had claimed the lives of both Devon's parents.

"Take your bloody hands off my sister, Huxhold."

Carrollton's sister? Then Devon noticed the straight black hair, the midnight dark eyes common to them both.

The floor seemed to disappear beneath his feet.

Devon didn't look at her. He didn't want to see her face and the damning confirmation. She must have felt the same. They both turned and walked away from each other like two magnets suddenly repelled from each other. Devon left the ballroom without looking back.

But he'd never forgotten her or those precious, magic moments . . .

Now here she stood in the middle of nowhere, slopping pigs, and looking more lovely than he had remembered her. For a moment, all he could do was gape, drinking in the sight of her like a thirsty man reaching for water.

And then he realized that she'd changed.

She was pregnant. Very, very pregnant.

The jolt of jealousy was staggering. A cold numbness spread through his body.

Her lips silently formed his name.

He'd kissed those lips.

Surprisingly, he found his voice first. "Miss Carrollton," he said tersely, frigid air rising around him with the words. It took all his strength to speak.

She didn't answer. She seemed horror-struck by his presence.

Good.

"I'm certain my appearance here has caught you

by surprise," he continued stiffly. "My horse needs a shoe. Point me in the direction of the nearest farrier and I'll be on my way." He was proud that his voice was steady. He could have been talking to a stranger rather than the woman he loved. No, whom he had *once* loved, he amended.

She still didn't answer. Her stare was unnerving. It irritated him. What did she fear? That he would go rabid with jealousy? Bay at the moon? Or wear his heart on his sleeve?

Oh, no, he had too much pride for that.

"Come, *Miss Carrollton*," he said, infusing all his anger and scorn into the syllables of her name. "Certainly you know who I am. Lord Huxhold? Or has pregnancy addled your brains?"

He immediately regretted the words, but he couldn't call them back.

Bright spots of color appeared on her cheeks. And then she hurled the slop bucket at him with surprising force.

Devon ducked just in time, knocking the empty bucket away with his arm.

Miss Carrollton didn't wait to apologize but lifted her skirts and attempted to run from him.

Devon watched her. Her run was more a lumbering trot. She didn't go toward the house but headed for the woods. She looked almost comical, her petite figure practically swallowed whole by the baby she carried.

Another man's baby.

He should let her go.

After all, he had his horse to see to and his

grandfather's summons. He told himself all this even as he took the first step around the fence in her direction. By the time he'd traveled the length of it, she'd almost disappeared past the tangle of still green holly and winter-bare shrubbery. He caught a flash of her red shawl. Where the devil did she think she was going? To her husband?

"Miss Carrollton, wait!"

As he expected, she didn't slow her step. Leah had always been stubborn. Stubborn and willful and proud. But she would have an accident charging off the way she was willy-nilly. Then it would be on his conscience. Or so he told himself as, with a heavy sigh, he set out after her. He was a knave, a jealous fool. If her husband had any sense, he'd call him out.

Worse, Devon would welcome the opportunity to run the man through. He hated him without even meeting him.

Leah ran as if the very hounds of hell nipped at her heels—or as well as a woman nine months with child could run. Her shawl fell down around her shoulders. The gathering wind of the threatening storm blew her hat off her head. It bounced on her back, held by the frayed ribbons tied in a knot around her neck.

Meeting Devon Marshall was her deepest fear come to life.

She'd been dreaming a lot lately, vivid, disturbing dreams that the village women assured her were common to all pregnant women. But it wasn't until she saw *him* standing there that she realized he'd been the dark, menacing figure in those dreams.

In that moment of recognition, she'd been transported to another time, another place. She'd been at Lady Trudgill's ball, and a man more handsome than sin had swept her off onto a dance floor. A man who had commanded her with his presence and with something more, something she couldn't explain and had not felt since. Not even with David Draycutt.

She should have run to the cottage for shelter from him. She could have locked the door, but she hadn't been thinking clearly. Her every impulse had been to escape, to fly.

Devon called her name. He was closer than she'd imagined.

Panic surged through her. She ran now. He was her past, her personal demons come for a reckoning.

Two steps. Three. And then her foot caught a root. Her feet were suddenly yanked out from under her, and she fell to the ground. Her hands, fingers splayed, reached out to save herself—but she was too late. She fell on her belly.

Pain ripped through her. *The baby!* She doubled over on the cold, damp earth trying to protect it. The ground was hard and rough beneath her cheek. Her stomach roiled with a will of its own.

What had she done to her baby?

Devon was by her side in a blink. "Leah!"

Tears came to her eyes at the concern in his

voice. She wanted to shout at him to leave her alone. She didn't deserve his worry. She'd wronged him. She'd wronged everyone she'd ever loved, and now her baby was paying for her sins.

Oh, God, help my baby!

Cramps rolled through her, even as she felt her water break.

Strong hands lifted her from the ground. "Talk to me. Tell me what is the matter."

She reached for Devon, clenching the woolen material of his all-too-fashionable-for-Devon greatcoat in her fist. He'd lost his hat, and his black hair, always overlong for style, hung over his brow.

"My . . . baby . . . you must . . . help my baby."

"I will, Leah. It'll be all right. I promise, I will make it right."

He slid his arm under her legs and rose to his feet, carrying her with him. She cried out as she felt another rush of warmth between her legs. This time, the pain vibrated through her like the dull thud of a drumhead being pounded. *It was starting!*

She hadn't expected it to be like this.

"Leah, your skirt . . . it is wet," he said. "Is it blood—" he started to ask anxiously, but didn't seem to want an answer. He pressed his lips together, his expression grim as he tightened his hold . . . and she realized that he didn't understand. How could he? She had just learned the stages of labor herself. Then, again, maybe she *was* bleeding. Her body no longer felt like her own.

"Leah, what have I done? Dear God, what have I done?"

She wanted to say, "Nothing, Devon. You did nothing." But the words wouldn't come. The baby was consuming her, just like in her dreams. And the nightmare lover—the one she now knew was Devon—began carrying her through the woods. She didn't know where. She didn't care.

All she knew is that it hurt. Her baby was coming, and she was going to die. Her every woman's instinct told her this was so. She'd given up everything she had for this child, and now both of them would die.

"I'll find help, Leah. I will." His voice shook slightly. Funny, she'd never thought Devon would be afraid of anything. Not strong, handsome Devon with the devil-may-care attitude.

Then another contraction began building inside her. Devon was taking her to the cottage. She realized that now. She buried her face in the folds of his coat. It smelled of him and fresh air and rain and the spices he loved. It smelled of safety. Yes, Devon would help her. Devon would know what to do. Devon would save her baby.

A litany started in her head. She began praying, not knowing if she talked to God or Devon. *Take my life, but don't let anything happen to my baby. Please save my baby.*

Part One

London, 1814

CHAPTER 1

Devon's friends thought it a grand joke that he had been about to dance with Carrollton's sister without realizing it. They claimed he had to be the only person in the world to not know the gossip swirling around the chit's London debut.

The Carrolltons were bad ton if there ever was any. That they had the audacity to not only present their daughter at Court but also expect her to marry well had Society reeling. Yes, she was uncommonly beautiful, but a line had to be drawn somewhere. Numerous hostesses had vowed to snub her.

And although the little scene on the dance floor resurrected all the rumors concerning the circumstances of Devon's parents' deaths over twenty years ago, Miss Carrollton ironically became somewhat of an overnight sensation—as did Lady Trudgill, the ball's hostess.

Suddenly, Miss Carrollton and Devon were on everyone's guest list. Ambitious hostesses smelled

scandal. They knew that just the mere speculation
of the couple meeting again was enough to ensure
the success of their party and a mention in the
following day's papers.

Of course, Devon never honored those invitations. He didn't care what Miss Carrollton did, and
to prove it he carefully avoided her company.

His circle of friends—all scapegrace rogues and
out-and-out bounders to a man, no matter how
loyal—couldn't help but sing the praises of such
a beautiful young woman who quickly became the
Toast, and the talk, of the Town. They ribbed
Devon mercilessly, comparing his family to Mon-
tagues and hers to Capulets. He pretended it didn't
matter.

But it did. It irritated him beyond rationalization.

Especially when he received a terse note from
his grandfather:

Brewster says you made a cake of yourself at
Trudgill ball over Carrollton chit. I am displeased, but not surprised. A Marshall has
never been nor will be the subject of gossip.

Kirkeby

It had been almost two months since he'd last
heard from his grandfather. Another time when
he'd been displeased. Devon wadded up the note
before tossing it in the rubbish bin.

Unfortunately, a week later, in the Parson's
Knot, a club known for high-stakes games, Devon

crossed Julian Carrollton's path. He ignored Carrollton until he overheard Carrollton receiving the same sort of harsh teasing that Devon had received. Carrollton was deep in his cups, but in spite of that fact, his snarled, colorful answer damning all Marshalls to hell, "especially that bastard Huxhold," infuriated Devon.

He'd been called names before, but not by the son of Richard Carrollton.

Something inside Devon snapped.

His parents would still be alive if Richard Carrollton had not cheated in that long-ago carriage race. Some claimed the broken lynchpin had been an accident, nothing more. Richard had always maintained his innocence—but Devon's grandfather had known differently.

He said his son always took care of his rigs. Someone had broken the pin on purpose. And to his mind the only person who had stood to gain by winning the race had been Richard.

Anguished beyond reason by the death of his only son, Devon's grandfather had protested to the authorities, but there had been no proof, and Carrollton had walked away a free man. Carrollton had refused to accept the winnings from the race, but that had not consoled Lord Kirkeby.

Now, his son dared to call Devon a bastard.

It made Devon furious. Especially when Julian declared in a voice that carried above the sound of the rattling dice cups that his sister would rather "lie with dogs than dance with a Marshall."

Everyone in the room heard him. McDermott,

Leichester, Ruskin, all gathered around Devon, silently siding with him and waiting for him to take action against his enemy.

Devon sat quiet. He did not have a hot head. He'd ignored Julian's drunken whining in the past. He could do it again.

Or, he could call Julian out, put a bullet in him, and rid the world of his pretentious bragging. Devon's reputation for pistol and sword was famous. His skill was one of the few things his grandfather admired about him. Better yet, his grandfather would be pleased to have justice finally served.

Instead of what he could have done, what people expected him to do, Devon accepted Julian's words as a challenge.

So he thought his sister would rather lie with a dog than dance with a Marshall? Devon knew that wasn't true. Leah Carrollton was not immune to him. He'd sensed her attraction to him immediately.

He would prove it by seducing her.

Devon rose and left the club, content to let Carrollton believe he'd scored a small victory while in truth the game was just beginning . . .

Only much, much later would Devon admit to himself that he'd chosen that course of action not for revenge but because in spite of himself, all common sense, and all reason, he had secretly wanted to see her again.

*   *   *

Contrary to popular opinion, Devon had never considered himself a rake. A rake was a reprobate, a man beyond redemption, a man with no moral fiber.

Devon was none of those things, at least not in his own mind.

In his opinion, his only vice was that he adored women. That wasn't so much of a sin, was it?

He liked women in all their guises—the old, the young, the middle-aged, the rosy plump, the slender, the laughing, the soberly sedate. His cronies thought only of a woman's face or her breasts or what she had between her legs . . . and those things were important to Devon, too. But he also admired their intelligence, their spirit, their sense of humor.

He loved the mysteries of their sex: their intuitive powers, their supple strength, their fanciful whims, their serene wisdom. Oh, yes, and their generosity. God bless their generosity. Their bodies and their minds were his altar of worship.

Consequently, they, in turn, adored him.

He never lacked for bed partners, although it was his custom to take only one lover at a time. Part of the reason was his own caution about sex and disease, but he also believed that a man didn't have the ability to concentrate fully on more than one task at a time . . . and when Devon was with a lover, he always "concentrated" very hard.

His partners appreciated him for it. And when he parted company with them, they remained friends, friends that he valued.

Over the years, a few had even claimed to love

him. He didn't understand how. Love was the emotion of poets and dreamers—and Devon was firmly rooted in realism. Many of his lovers had touched his mind, most had found a place of friendship in his heart, but not one had ever reached his soul.

Nor, he discovered to his own surprise, had he ever seduced one. Women had always come to him willingly.

He didn't realize this gap in his worldly education until he started to mull over the fate of Leah Carrollton. How did one seduce a debutante? An innocent. A guarded treasure.

He had an extensive acquaintance of villains, sailors, and blackguards who might have experience in such a thing, but he shied from quizzing them. He didn't want anyone to guess his intentions or examine his motives too closely. He wasn't certain of them himself.

He also had to be careful. He couldn't meet her through her usual activities, balls and routs and the such. He was a gentleman, after all. If Society watched him seduce her, he'd be honor bound to marry her—and a Marshall would never marry a Carrollton. Ever. It was the Unthinkable.

The answer to his dilemma presented itself one morning, when he was coming home at half past ten. He'd spent the night at a particularly lucrative card party. The cool, sunny March day was one of those rare harbingers to spring, and he decided to take a stroll around the block to clear his head of brandy fumes before heading for his bed.

It was Sunday, a day of rest, and the usually bustling streets were respectfully quiet.

He'd just rounded the first corner when he almost collided with Leah Carrollton. She was accompanied by a maid who had to be close to six feet tall and looked like she boiled fish heads for a living.

Rearing back just in time, he imagined he'd conjured Miss Carrollton from thin air. She was dressed in yellow, the color of jonquils, from the brim of her charming straw bonnet down to the hem of her dress, but no flower of spring had ever had such an impact on him. He was struck dumb.

Miss Carrollton wasn't. Her back straightened, her nose took a haughty tilt. "Come, Mae." She stepped around him, carefully pulling her gauzy skirts aside lest they inadvertently brush against his leg.

"Pity a fine lady can't walk down the street without being practically run over by these young bucks," Mae grumbled. "High and mighty in the instep they are just planting themselves in our path!"

"Yes, they are," he heard Miss Carrollton agree. "And for no reason." She added emphasis to her words with a sniffing glance over her shoulder.

His tiredness vanished. He had just been given the cut direct by a Carrollton.

The gauntlet had been thrown down. He accepted the challenge.

With a hunter's instinct, he followed in the wake of the two women.

They turned at the corner. His pace leisurely, Devon approached the corner and then hesitated when he realized where they were headed.

Miss Carrollton and her maid had started up the steps of a church to join a number of other ladies and gentlemen, dressed in their Sunday finest, who already greeted the curate standing at the door.

Catching sight of Miss Carrollton, the ruddy-faced young churchman welcomed her enthusiastically as though the two were not strangers. And was it Devon's imagination, or did the fellow hold her proffered hand just a tad too long for politeness?

Then the two women disappeared inside.

Devon stood in indecision on the walk below. Several other churchgoers passed him, nodding a good morning. He smiled and pretended he felt perfectly comfortable. The walls of the church would probably come crashing down if he stepped foot in it, something he hadn't done since mandatory services during his school days.

And yet, where else would he be able to make contact with Miss Carrollton? Studying the people entering the church, he did not recognize anyone.

He climbed the steps.

The curate glanced in his direction and then completely ambushed Devon by greeting him by name. "Why, Huxhold! This is a surprise!"

Devon frowned at the lanky man wearing

glasses. "You have the better of me, sir," he said uncertainly.

A smile spread across the curate's face. "We were in school together. Geoff Rodford. They called me Roddy." He waved a dismissive hand. "You may not remember. We did not travel in the same circle, but good God! To think Huxhold is walking into my church."

Devon didn't recall a Roddy. Worse, he would be damned to even name the school they'd attended together, since he'd been asked to leave more than a few in his misspent youth.

Several people overheard Roddy's remarks and began whispering Devon's name to each other. Raised eyebrows and knowing expressions were directed his way.

Devon couldn't turn tail and run now. "Well, very good to see you again, Roddy. I look forward to your sermon."

As he entered the cool darkness of the building, Roddy called out, "Oh, it won't be me doing the service, but the Most Reverend Highgate."

Devon nodded, already searching for his quarry. Crossing the alcove's stone floor, he moved into the church sanctuary. The air smelled of incense and candle wax. The white beadboard pews with their dark walnut railing were not crowded. He scanned the backs of heads. He'd never realized how all bonnets look alike from the rear—and then he saw her. Or rather, she saw him.

She glanced over her shoulder, a cursory look,

nothing more—and then her eyes widened in disbelief.

Devon grinned at her, enjoying the moment.

Her disbelief turned to anger. Very deliberately, she gave him her back.

Intrigued, he walked up the aisle until he came to the pew directly behind hers. If she was conscious of his approach, she gave no sign . . . and yet, he sensed she was aware of his every movement. Very aware. Especially after he squeezed past a rotund man guarding the aisle to sit directly behind her.

He could almost see the hair stand up on the back of her neck.

Her maid, lost in her own prayers, was oblivious to his presence. For whatever reason, Miss Carrollton didn't raise the issue after the woman shut her prayer book and waited for the service to begin. A moment later, the Most Reverend Highgate started the service, but Devon didn't hear a word he said.

Leah. He rolled the syllables of her name around in his mind as he watched her bow her head in prayer. The curve of her back fascinated him, as did the graceful tilt of her head. He wondered what it would be like to place his lips against her neck, to feel the pumping of her heart, to taste her skin with his tongue.

Her back straightened. Her head turned slightly, and a spot of color burned each cheek as if she could read his mind.

He sent her a knowing look, one that he knew

from experience made women's knees weak as jelly. I want you.

Almost as if in answer to his thought, she shifted, the gesture restless, impatient. She then slid down onto the kneeler. Bowing her head, he could feel her shut him out.

One hour passed, then a second. It could have been a decade. Devon no longer considered time important. Not when he was close to her.

His senses were full of her—the sound of her clear voice raised in song, the tendril curls at the nape of her neck, below which thick hair was tucked into her bonnet, the smooth perfection of her skin. She smelled of the rose water that seemed common to debutantes, and of powder, and of a lusher, more verdant scent that was uniquely her own.

He barely registered the fact the service had come to an end until the parishioners around him were up and moving. Miss Carrollton slipped out of her pew and made a beeline for the church door, the maid hurrying to keep up.

Devon was anxious to follow, wanting another opportunity to speak to her—even if she did shoot daggers from her eyes at him. Unfortunately, his way out of the pew was blocked by his overweight neighbor, who had decided to visit with another gentleman in the aisle. By the time Devon had excused himself and squeezed around the man, Miss Carrollton had disappeared.

Damn, he'd lost her. He could have punched the air in frustration.

Then, to his surprise, she walked back into the sanctuary. Her maid didn't follow her. She paused, looking directly at where Devon had been sitting. Her gaze shifted until she honed in on him. She made her way toward him.

Devon waited, uncertain.

She stopped, a hand's breadth between them. Her dark eyes burned with outraged pride. "I know what you want, Lord Huxhold. I know what you think you are doing. And I will tell you now, you will never receive anything other than scorn from me."

She turned and walked away.

Devon watched her, admiring her bravado and the sway of her hips.

He shoved his hands into his breeches pockets and smiled. Silly girl. Her confrontation only made the chase more interesting.

It was with a lighthearted step that he left the church.

Leah had known Lord Huxhold had been watching the twitch of her skirts as she'd marched out of the church. She'd felt him watching, just as she'd been so aware of him during the service.

She'd had every intention of informing her family of his audacious behavior. It would serve him right for Julian to call him out.

However, walking home, she changed her mind. No good ever came from inflaming her brother's quick temper. In her head she could hear her mother admonishing her to be prudent with what she said in front of Julian and Father.

So, Leah decided to keep the incident to herself. Her parents didn't need more worries. Her maid was completely loyal and wouldn't murmur a word, although she must have known who Lord Huxhold was. Mae had joined the family when Leah was born, shortly before the "tragic accident" that had brought so much misfortune upon the Carrolltons.

Besides, Leah knew she could make short shrift of a rake like Huxhold. In fact, she found herself anticipating their next meeting and making plans to give him a proper set down.

There was no doubt in her mind that she would be seeing him again.

CHAPTER 2

"A virgin!" The words burst out of the Baroness Charlotte de Severin-Fortier accompanied by a peal of delighted laughter.

Devon quickly hushed her. "Charlotte, not so loud. Remember the servants." He frowned. "Besides it is not that astounding."

Her expression said it clearly was. With her head of silver hair and sparkling eyes, Charlotte was a woman of indeterminate years. Tall, striking, and very French, she numbered among her lovers monarchs, Turkish pashas, Cossacks, dukes, and Devon. Theirs had not been an affair of passion as much as good-humored friendship.

Over the years, they had come to each other for various favors. He'd always valued her wise counsel, although this was the first time he'd discussed a matter concerning another woman. But then, she was the only one he trusted to hold her tongue.

She sat up from the silk pillows she had been lying on as supple and graceful as a cat. The gold threads of her caftan shimmered in the candlelight as she set aside the mouthpiece of the hookah she'd been smoking.

"Who is this young woman, *cher*?" she asked in her accented English.

He saw no reason to hide her name. She'd hear of it sooner or later. "Miss Leah Carrollton."

"Carrollton?" The name did not sound familiar to her. She repeated it once more, then recognition struck. "These Carrolltons, have I not heard that your families are enemies?"

"No. Well, yes," he admitted. He had told himself that he'd started this venture because of Julian Carrollton's bragging. But he was also honest enough to realize that his wanting to be near Leah had nothing to do with her brother. "Our families have feuded for centuries. The Carrolltons think we robbed them of an estate and title that should have been theirs. We say we didn't. I doubt if anyone remembers the source of the argument."

"Ah, yes," she agreed, and then added thoughtfully, "but there is also the race that cost your parents' lives. That was not so long ago. Was not Richard Carrollton driving against your father?"

Devon shrugged. He shouldn't attempt to disassemble in front of Charlotte. She was too shrewd. "Yes."

"Are you seeking revenge, *mon ami*?"

Was he? Devon had to consider the question a moment. "No."

"Then explain yourself."

Devon capitulated. He had no choice. "I saw her

one night at a ball. I can't shake the memory of her."

"You, *cher?*"

His good humor vanished. "Is it so amazing? Does everyone believe me completely beyond redemption?"

Her lips curved into a generous smile. "No. It's just sad."

"Why do you say that?"

She reached over and brushed an errant lock of his hair off his forehead before saying, "Because a man like you only falls in love once."

Devon rose from the cushions, dismissing her words as foolishness. "I'm not in love. Especially with a Carrollton. I mean, she is the last person I would want to involve myself with."

"But you are interested?"

"I have been interested many times before."

"Like this?" she delved.

No, not like this. The words almost leapt to his lips. He bit them back. "It is not what you think."

"I'm certain," she answered soberly, but her eyes were alive with Gallic conjecture. However, she did not press the issue. Instead, she came to her feet and crossed to a wine table. She poured two glasses of wine and handed one to him. "*Tiens.* The problem is that you wish to pursue this girl but you do not want to go to the balls and affairs where others will observe you."

Wise Charlotte. She understood his dilemma. "Her brother has already made a scene that had people gossiping. Besides—" and he couldn't help smiling as he said this "—she hates me."

Charlotte raised her eyebrows. "She might as well have waved a red flag in front of a matador's bull."

"I admit to being challenged. By the by, I must also keep my interest from my family. My aunt Venetia would relish any opportunity to further blacken my name to my grandfather."

"She still wishes to see you disinherited?"

Devon frowned. "She would dearly love such a thing. Then her son Rex would inherit the title, the money . . . but it would never happen. Grandfather will not disinherit a legitimate heir no matter how much he disapproves of me."

Charlotte sipped her wine, her mind mulling over the problem at hand. "What is it this Miss Carrollton wants? If we offer it to her, she will come to us."

"The only thing Carrolltons ever want is money. They are in over their heads in debt."

"You have plenty of money," Charlotte answered. In fact, she was one of the few people who knew that contrary to the negligent way he knotted his neckcloth, or the plain cut of his jacket, or the scuffed toes of his boots, Devon was a canny investor. She'd followed his advice and made quite a tidy fortune from it.

Devon remembered the fire in Leah's eyes when she had confronted him. "She won't ever come to me for money, even if I offered marriage—which I would never do."

"Then your title holds no attraction either."

He grinned. "Though the Carrollton complaint is we stole it from them years ago, I imagine Leah has too much pride to chase after it now."

"Then she must be convinced to want you for yourself."

"Is that bad?" he asked, laughing at himself.

"I think you are prize, but your best qualities are not something a virgin would be knowledgeable enough to appreciate. Think, *cher*. What else do these people want?"

Devon sank down on the pillows, holding the wine glass on one bent leg. He thought of Julian boasting, basking in the attention of anyone who would listen to him. Of Leah's head bowed in prayer . . . and the straightness of her back as she sat in church . . . and the way she stood a little apart from the other debutantes.

"They want to be respected," he said slowly. "They feel they should travel in the highest circles."

"And do they?"

Devon frowned. "Of course not. Few people accept the Carrolltons since the racing accident, even though it happened two decades ago. The courts may have claimed there was no evidence, but enough people agree with my grandfather that Richard Carrollton caused the accident."

"Then this Miss Carrollton would find an invitation to an exclusive soirée given by none other than our friend the imminently respectable Lady Dorchester irresistible."

"Of course!" Devon agreed with growing elation. "Lady Mary would be perfect." He used the nickname Lady Dorchester adored. "She's so romantic she won't be able to resist helping me. And Leah's mother would jump at the bait."

"Bait?" The baroness's eyebrows raised in mild disapproval. "*Cher*, this girl is an innocent. I do not want her to come to harm."

"I would never harm a woman," he answered, irritated that she would even think him able to do such a thing.

"Every man is capable of hurting a woman . . . sometimes they can't help themselves," Charlotte said softly, her dark eyes sad. She gracefully sat on the cushions next to him. "If I did not believe this was more of an affair of the heart than you wish to let on, I would not help you. A broken heart can be more painful than any physical harm."

"It won't come to that," he answered, dismissing her concerns with a wave of his glass before he drained it. His mind was already too full of plans to heed warnings. Besides, women worried incessantly. "I think it best we have a masquerade," he answered. "And invite everyone of importance."

"Ah, Devon," Charlotte said with a sigh. "Do you know—really know—what you are doing?"

He laughed. Charlotte needn't worry about him. He was going to see Miss Carrollton again.

Lady Mary leapt at the idea of helping star-crossed lovers caught in the grip of a family feud. She embraced Devon's plea for help with passion and planned a masquerade so elaborate and exclusive that everyone who was anyone would be there.

It was an invitation the Carrolltons would not refuse—and they didn't. The acceptance of Mrs. Carrollton and daughter were among the first to be delivered.

Devon wasn't much for masquerades, but it was the only way he could woo Leah without her recognizing him.

The night of the ball, he was the first to arrive. Lady Mary met him at the door with a gruff "Where's your costume?"

He held up the snowy white ruff he had yet to fasten around his neck and the midnight blue domino. "I'm Sir Francis Drake."

She snorted her opinion before turning to the baroness. "Charlotte, look at him. His neckcloth isn't even starched. What shall we do?"

The baroness took a moment to right the botched knot of Devon's neckcloth with a skilled hand before pronouncing, "Never mind, Mary, he appears his usually masculine self. Although, Devon, you might consider spending money on a decent valet."

Devon gave a mock shiver. "I prefer being my own man," he answered as he walked into the empty ballroom, where the servants were moving flowers and performing the last finishing touches.

Lady Mary made a disgusted sound and hurried off to give orders to her butler. Charlotte watched him from the doorway. "Nervous, *cher*?"

"No, excited. I haven't felt this sense of anticipation since I was a boy and Grandfather promised to take me hunting for the first time."

She laughed. "An apt comparison. May you have a successful hunt." She toasted him with her wine glass. At that moment, there was a knock on the door, and the first of a crowd of guests arrived.

Devon kept to himself through the first part of the evening. He decided not to wear the silly ruff and stashed it behind a potted palm before putting on his domino. With each guest, the costumes seemed more and more elaborate. Everyone was delighted with the silliness of pretending to be someone else. Music and laughter quickly filled the room.

Waiting impatiently from his vantage point, where he could see the entrance to the ballroom, Devon decided Mrs. Carrollton obviously understood the importance of arriving late. He was absolutely certain that Leah couldn't enter the room without his recognizing her.

And he was right. Almost two hours into the party, Leah Carrollton and her parents arrived.

Her costume was no disguise at all. She'd dressed as Titania, Shakespeare's Queen of the Fairies. The spangles on her dress caught the light and sparkled with her every movement. Tiny paste jewels had been glued around her eyes, and one had strategically been placed at the corner of her mouth—close to her dimple. Already, before she could enter the room, she was surrounded by a bevy of male admirers. She laughed at what one gentleman said to her, the sound ringing with joie de vivre. In that moment, every man in the room fell in love with her.

Devon cursed his own cleverness, especially as Lord Redgrave took Leah's hand and led her to the dance floor. He knew Redgrave. The older man had come to town looking for a wife. He stared down at Leah as if she were a piece of almond marzipan he'd like to gobble up—or marry.

Devon couldn't waste time.

Worse, there was a line of gentlemen forming to claim the next set the moment Redgrave walked her off the dance floor. Devon was in danger of losing her before he had a chance to even speak to her!

He stepped out onto the dance floor just as Leah and Lord Redgrave circled each other in the pattern before skipping off to their respective lines. With a daring that would have done Sir Francis proud, he stepped in front of Leah and whisked her off in another direction before Redgrave or the others in the set knew what was happening.

She felt incredibly light in his arms. He could have picked her up and carried her. Instead, he twirled her out through a side door and onto a private terrace.

He glanced back. He'd moved so swiftly that few knew his path. Redgrave stood comically in the middle of the dance floor, searching for his partner.

"Let me go back in there," an indignant voice said. He looked down at his captive. She jerked her arm out of his hand as ready to hiss and spit as an angry kitten.

It was dark here, the only light coming from the ballroom through the glass doors and the quarter moon above.

Devon leaned his back against the door, his hand on the handle, thankful for the domino that hid all of his face but his mouth. "I will," he assured her. "If you will grant me a few moments."

Her mouth curled with pride. "You are wasting your time, Lord Huxhold."

That caught his attention. "You know who I am?"

She gave a ladylike snort. "Of course. Your costume isn't very good."

"I'm supposed to be Sir Francis Drake," he answered.

She laughed as if he were to be pitied. "And you have pirated me away." She craned her neck to see in the windows of the French door. "Lord Redgrave will be upset. I must return and give my apologies."

He did not move.

She showed no fear. "Why are you doing this? You know I would rather kiss a pig than spend a moment longer with a Marshall. Besides, if my father or brothers, especially Julian, were to discover what you've done, they would call you out."

Her obvious disdain pricked his male vanity, especially when he was so completely aware of her. "And you would like that, wouldn't you?" he snapped back with uncharacteristic peevishness.

"To see blood on the ground over begging a moment of your time."

Hands on hips, she answered, "Well, the idea does have merit if it's *your* blood. But then that priggish cousin of yours would inherit. Julian says that would be worse than seeing you as Kirkeby." She referred to his grandfather's title, the one that would be his someday.

"Well, if I ever decide to disappoint Julian, I know how to do it," he said dryly and surprised a laugh out of her.

For a second, she stared at him with her diamond-bright eyes, and then she said softly, "I must return. This is not good."

Devon held up a finger. "All I'm asking is one moment. One."

"Lord Huxhold, you are wasting your time."

"Do you think so?"

"I know so."

"Hold out your hand."

"Why?"

"So young and yet so suspicious." He tisked softly.

"I have been kidnapped off the dance floor by one of London's most notorious rakes and you believe I am behaving in a suspicious manner?"

"I am not a rake."

"You are not a choirboy, either."

Devon was charmed. "Julian should be so lucky to have your wits."

"My brother is very well respected," she shot back, revealing her Achilles heel. "But then," she countered with a condescending smile, "you wouldn't understand loyalty, since the Marshalls can't stand each other."

"I think family loyalty is a good thing," Devon protested. "I just don't practice it often. You said yourself my cousin is a prig."

"I think family is the only thing worth valuing," she replied stiffly.

Devon shrugged. "Perhaps, but then, I'm the one with the prig for a cousin. You can only value a prig so much."

Her small, even teeth flashed white in the night. "I should not laugh."

"Yet you can't resist my charm."

She disagreed. "You are completely resistible. Especially since Julian will have your head if you don't let me return."

"Julian isn't here this evening."

"But he will find out."

"It may be worth the risk."

She sighed with exasperation. "Lord Huxhold, I am very serious. I will give you a count of three, and if you don't open the door, I will scream." She said the words almost pleasantly.

"Miss Carrollton—"

"One."

"All I want is—"

"Two."

"Will you listen to me? Just one moment—"

"Three." She opened her mouth and would have screamed except for the fact that he took complete advantage of the circumstance and kissed her, an effective muzzle if ever there was one.

That caught her by surprise.

Her body tensed. He braced, waiting for her to strike him with her fists or kick him or the dozens of things ladies do to express indignation. He had no doubt that in spite of her petite size she could deliver a smarting blow.

But the blow never came.

Instead, with lightning speed, the kiss between them took on a life of its own—and Devon was suddenly questioning who was in charge.

Leah Carrollton could kiss. Their mouths meshed together perfectly. Her kiss was chaste, but there was a seductive quality to it. Their legs brushed, and Devon hardened. A need, the likes of which he'd never felt before, welled up inside of him for more. More, more, more, more, more.

And he would have asked for it, too. His common sense had fled. Every muscle, every fiber of his being urged him to lift her in his arms, raise her skirts, and bury himself deep inside her.

But from the garden came a sound. It could have been a servant or a rabbit. Whatever, it brought her to her senses. Their lips broke contact. She pulled away, and he wisely released her. She escaped the few feet to the opposite side of the terrace.

Devon stood rooted to the spot. Dear God, his heart was racing. He had never felt desire of that force.

She pressed her gloved fingers to her lips, which were already rosy red and slightly swollen from his kiss. "This is madness. If Julian finds out what just happened, he will kill you."

Madness. Yes. He took two steps toward her until there was only a foot between them. "Hold your hand out."

"Why?"

"Just do it," he said patiently.

She glanced at the door. He waited. This was a moment of truth. She could leave if she wished, but he was willing to wager all he owned that she wouldn't.

Leah held her hand out.

"Palm up. Like this," he instructed, holding his own hand up in the air as if taking an oath.

She rolled her eyes but did as he said. Their hands were mere inches apart.

Devon watched her, holding his hand steady. Already he felt the almost magnetic pull, but would she?

Slowly her expression changed from one of skepticism, to uncertainty, and then wonder. "What is it?" she whispered.

He let his hand move forward. It pressed against hers. The kid leather of her gloves was warm with her body heat. "It's something between us. Did you not feel it the other night at Lady Trudgill's ball? I sensed it the moment I walked into the room that evening."

She stared at their hands pressed flat against each other. "I grasped that there was something different in the air that night. A sort of heat. I turned and you were looking at me. I even knew you were here this evening." She smiled shyly. "You about drove me wild in church the other day."

"It was all I could do to keep my hands from you. I wanted to touch you, to hold you." He pinned her with his gaze. "To kiss you."

Leah snatched her hand away as if she'd been burned. "We can't."

"Yes, we can."

"It's not right."

"Leah." He used her given name, and it sounded sweeter than music. "I didn't ask for this. I don't know why it is happening between us. But I do know that I must see you again or I will be ready for Bedlam."

"We can't. Julian will—"

"Julian won't know. Meet me tomorrow at Whitney's. It's a small bookstore on Dobbins Street. Do you know the location?"

"No, no." She took a step toward the door.

He didn't know if she meant the bookstore or if she was still denying what was between them. "Meet me there at eleven. The store is very private that time of day, but we'll still be in a public place."

"I don't—"

He stopped her protest by covering her lips with the tips of his fingers. Almost reverently, he ran the pad of his thumb across her full lower lip. "Perhaps we are mad. Tommorrow. At eleven."

He stole a kiss. One quick brush of lips, and then he jumped over the terrace balustrade into the night garden. Taking a post in the shadow of a pear tree, he waited for her to return to the party. She hesitated a moment, then quickly turned and opened the door.

He could leave now. Inside, Leah would be mobbed by admirers and would probably dance until dawn. Men would argue over her and vie for her favors.

But Devon no longer felt jealousy.

A bond existed between them. He hesitated to put a name to it other than forbidden, secret, and exciting.

Furthermore, he was not the only one of them caught up in this strange new emotion . . . because the next day, she met him at Whitney's.

CHAPTER 3

"Julian said no woman should trust you."

"Why were you and Julian discussing me?" Devon asked.

He and Leah stood in the back stacks of Whitney's, Book Proprietor, hidden by shelf after shelf of dusty books from the view of anyone in the front of the store. Few people ever visited the shop, especially at this time of day, and Whitney himself was an octogenarian who spent his time napping at his desk in the front of the store. Devon found the shop alternately stifling or charming, depending upon his mood.

But when Leah was present, it was paradise.

They'd been meeting in secret for the past week. Sunday had seemed to stretch forever because the shop had been closed and Devon had not been allowed a moment with her.

To their good fortune, Leah's maid, Mae, had a cousin who lived nearby. Apparently Mrs. Carrollton rarely gave the servants time off, and Mae had been so overjoyed at Leah's suggestion she visit her relatives that she hadn't questioned Leah's sudden interest in books too closely.

From the beginning, conversation had flowed easily between them. They talked about everything and about nothing. They debated, argued, and teased. He learned she hated peas. She lamented his lack of appreciation for a trained voice and never-ending arias. He promised to quote Shakespeare if she would quit praising Shelley. They both discovered they held similar values and beliefs.

Devon may have begun this endeavor with seduction on his mind, but he was quickly falling in love. It surprised him, delighted him, frightened him.

However, in spite of their candor on other subjects, this was the first time either one of them had mentioned their families.

She traced the binding of a book of poetry with one gloved hand and took it off the shelf. "I mentioned that one of my friends thought you attractive," she replied coyly.

"Testing the waters, hmmm?"

"Yes." She opened the book and pretended to peruse the contents.

"I don't expect Julian to approve of me. What is more important to me is what you believe."

"I don't know what to think," she answered. "Julian is my brother and cares for me. He is right in saying you have a certain reputation."

He took the book from her, his fingers covering

hers. "What reputation would that be?"

She raised her dark eyes to his. "As a lover."

The last word lingered in the air. It shot through Devon like an arrow. He reshelved the book, leaning close to her ear to whisper, "Perhaps Julian is correct. I would like to be your lover." *I would like to make love to you right here this moment, in fact.*

She drew in a shocked breath as if she'd heard the unspoken as well as the spoken, but she didn't run. Her nipples had tightened, pressing against the sky blue material of her sprig muslin dress. His Leah was a seductive mixture of innocence and temptation. He longed to bend down and cover one of those proud, sensitive points with his mouth, to suck and wet it right through the material of her dress.

Her lips parted as if she knew the train of his thoughts. Suddenly, she turned and slipped around the corner of the stack. Her soft kid shoes barely made a noise as she moved away from him.

Devon followed at a more leisurely pace. She was leading him to the back of the store where it was most private. Rounding another corner, he was stopped by the palm of her hand flat against his chest. Did she realize what her touch did to him? Already, his heart beat double time.

"This is madness," she whispered, her expression bleak. "I can never be yours. It can never be."

"Because of the past? Because of incidents and quarrels that neither of us have anything to do with?"

"Because I don't know if I can trust you. How else to strike out at your enemy than through the weakest member of his family?"

Devon almost laughed. "You are anything but weak. Julian's weaker because of his love for brandy and cards. William—" He broke off with a shake of his head. What could he say that was good about Leah's youngest brother? And he'd better not discuss either of her parents. For a second, he almost agreed with her: His attraction to her was madness.

"I know their faults," she said softly, "but they are my family. Someday, I'm going to see everyone's fortunes restored."

Her loyalty to them sparked sudden jealousy. "How? By selling yourself in marriage?"

She gasped as if surprised by his harsh words. Her temper flared. He caught her hand in midair before she could slap him. The movement brought their bodies close. He could feel her heat and breathe the scent of her skin. Her lips were only inches from his.

He spoke. "The idea of you giving yourself to another is like a sword going through my heart. I care about you, Leah."

She was not mollified. "You are the one who doesn't understand. My father was unjustly accused of your parents' deaths and has paid the price every day of his life. Every time I meet you, I am being disloyal to him."

"And yet, you come."

"I shouldn't."

"Neither should I." He released her hand. "I can never sit at the same table with your father. Whether he engineered my parents' deaths on purpose or it was an innocent accident, I would be disloyal to their memory to honor him."

"He was not responsible! You don't know him. If you did, you would know he would never have done such a thing as damage another's rig to win a race."

"I know he expects you to save his reputation through marriage. What sort of man does that to his daughter?"

"Every one of them," she countered cynically. "There isn't a debutante in London who isn't expected to marry above her station for the sake of her family." Her tone turned conciliatory. "If I don't help my family, who will? Father was always a gambler, but he drinks more than he should now. My brothers are only following his example. But Mother and I know that if I marry well, everything will be made right. We'll all be happy."

"Your marriage wouldn't solve anything. It won't make them better men."

"My marriage is the *only* solution. But then, how can I expect you to understand? Your family is the one who has persecuted mine."

"Your father is the man who killed mine," he retorted with surprising heat.

She physically flinched at his words. The color drained from her face and Devon stood paralyzed, unable to move or think. His charge lingered in the air around them.

When she spoke, her words sounded disjointed, distant. "I don't think we need see each other again." She turned and walked away.

He watched her move toward the front of the store, his mind numb. She didn't even look back. Then, suddenly, against all sanity, he had one thought: *Don't let her go.*

In three giant steps, he caught her arm at the elbow and swung her around.

She resisted, hissing under her breath for him to release her.

Devon tightened his hold. He took her by both arms. "Listen," he ordered. *"I love you."* The words, new feelings that he'd not had time yet to explore, were out of his mouth before he'd even given them a second's thought—but once said, he did not call them back.

He loved her.

He barely knew her. Her father had murdered his, and yet . . . he loved her.

His declaration caught her by surprise, too. Openmouthed, she stared at him.

Devon released his hold and took a step back, self consciously shoving his hair from his forehead. He was in a devil of a fix. What did one say to a woman after he'd just announced his deepest feelings?

She closed her mouth. "It can never be."

"You've said that already. It hasn't stopped me."

"The man I marry must assume my family's debts."

"I have money."

She shook her head sadly. "It would call for a fortune."

Devon regained his equilibrium. "I have a fortune."

"Oh, Devon. What you've earned from gaming wouldn't be enough."

"You make it sound like I'm impoverished."

"Everyone knows your grandfather cut you off years ago," she said gently. "Besides, I have only to look at the cut of your coat to know you don't have blunt to spare."

He defended himself. "I don't need my grandfather's money. I have my own, but I don't waste it on servants I don't need or in paying overinflated prices on coats. And be fair, Leah," he said, tugging his sleeve, "my careless style is aped by all manner of young bucks. I'm considered a Corinthian of the first stare."

"But look how rounded your heels are."

"These are my favorite boots. I wear them because they are the most comfortable."

She laughed as if she felt on firmer ground. "A Pink of the Ton would never value comfort over fashion."

"I'm my own fashion. Unique. Singular. Brazen."

She smiled, but then her expression turned bittersweet. "You are truly different than any man I expected to meet in London, but we are pretending to ourselves. We can never be together. Not publicly."

Practical Leah. Usually he was known for his practical business sense, but now he wanted her to believe that anything was possible.

"I must go," she said. "Mae will be here shortly. Perhaps we shouldn't meet again. It is not wise."

He caught her hand. "Leah, I don't care about what is wise. When I'm with you, the world suddenly makes sense. I must see you again."

"Devon, you have probably said that to a good many women."

"But I've never said 'I love you' to a woman before." There. He had said it again. And this time, it didn't shock him. This time it felt more right than it had the first time.

In fact, she was the one who needed to be convinced. Suddenly, he knew what he should do. He laced his fingers with hers and started walking toward the front of the store. She had to skip to keep up with him.

"Devon, what are you doing? Devon? Wait, if we go up there together, Mae may walk in and see us."

"I don't care," he threw over his shoulder. "In fact, I'm willing to risk it. I'll risk anything if it will make you see that I'm serious about us."

He woke Whitney by rapping soundly on the book-covered desk. The old man blinked and frowned his objections at being forced from an enjoyable snooze. His overlong, silver gray hair stuck out every which way.

"What is it? Oh, it's you, my lord."

"Whitney, I need paper and pen."

The bookseller blew his nose in a large kerchief before saying, "There it is. Corner of the desk." He looked up at Devon expectantly, struck by an idea. "Are you going to buy something?"

"Um, yes, but first my friend needs to write a note to her maid."

"What are you going to buy?"

"I left it on the shelf. I'll fetch it." He drew Leah back, away from Whitney's hearing. "Write a note to your maid. Tell her that you ran into a friend unexpectedly and are going to spend the afternoon with her."

"Devon, I can't."

"I want a fair chance, Leah. I have something to show you, and you owe me an afternoon of your time to judge for yourself what kind of man I am."

"What do you have in mind?" she asked suspiciously.

"I'm not going to ravish you, if that is what you suspect . . . although the idea does have some merit." He leaned close. "I'm going to show that I am not what people think me. A few hours. That's all I ask, Leah."

She studied him a moment. Then . . . "Help me with the note."

"That's my girl." He bent his head closer to hers. "Tell your maid that you have run into an old friend—"

"Which friend?"

"Does it matter?"

"Of course it does. Mother will ask questions."

"Well, then, whom would your mother most like you to spend time with?"

"I don't have many friends that I can trust."

"Certainly there is one. Think." He pulled three books off the shelf and took them up to Whitney. "Wrap these up and have them delivered."

"Yes, my lord. Thank you, my lord."

Devon returned to Leah. "Have you thought of a name?"

"Yes, I will say I ran into Tess Hamlin and she asked me to luncheon."

"The heiress?"

She nodded. "Mother will be ecstatic and not question too closely. After all, we do not belong to the same social circles as the Hamlins, although since Lady Dorchester's ball, I have been receiving many invitations."

Devon didn't like hearing he was orchestrating her social success. However, if he convinced her, she would soon be his and no other's. "Put down Tess Hamlin's name then. I know her brother. He will vouch for us if it comes to that."

Still writing, she said, "What are we planning to do?"

"You'll see." When she finished, he blew on the ink to dry it as he approached the bookseller. "Whitney, my friend," he said, slipping the old gent a coin, "give this to the maid when she arrives. Tell her to deliver it to Mrs. Carrollton."

"And shall I make up a story about this young lady going off with her friend?"

Whitney heard better than he liked to pretend.

Devon threw back his head and laughed. "Of course, Whitney, of course!" He then took Leah's arm and steered her through the maze of bookshelves. "We shall go out the back."

Whitney made no reply. He'd probably gone back to sleep.

As they stepped into the back room, Leah hesitated. "This is madness." She made as if to turn around, but Devon held her fast.

"It's an adventure," he said.

"But someone will see us. And if they do I will be ruined."

Devon was feeling reckless enough that he didn't care—but he wasn't a complete fool. Hanging from a peg by the door was an oilskin cape. "Here, put this on." He handed it to her. It had been raining earlier, and the cape would not cause comment.

Outside in the alleyway, puddles of water dotted the rutted lane. He hurried ahead to signal a hackney cab before returning and guiding her shrouded figure to the vehicle. Within moments, they were on their way.

The cab's coach was confining. He pulled the shades down over the windows.

She dropped the cape. "Now will you tell me where we are going?"

"No."

She sighed, muttering something under her breath about foolishness. The sides of their legs brushed. Devon didn't move, but she practically jumped, as if given an electric jolt.

"I shouldn't be doing this," she said, her voice barely a whisper.

"Leah, if my intent was merely seduction, I could have done it a half dozen times right there in Whitney's."

Her eyebrows came together. "What makes you so certain?"

"Well, because of this," he replied matter-of-factly before leaning toward her. He slipped his hand around her waist. He didn't touch her anywhere else, but hot red color rose up her neck and into her cheeks. Her heart thumped against her chest. He could hear its rapid beat.

"What are you doing?"

"Nothing," he murmured, leaning closer until his breath brushed the sensitive point of her neck. She almost melted against him. It took all of Devon's willpower not to give her the kiss she desired.

He pulled back.

"Oh dear," she whispered, flustered.

Devon smiled, pleased with himself.

"But is it possible to believe you really do love me?"

For a long second, there was only the sound of the iron-rimmed wheels rolling across the cobbles. Then Devon said simply, "Yes. I love you. I will never let harm come to you."

A small frown line formed between her eyes. She looked away.

The hack came to a stop. Devon opened the door, hopped down, and offered his hand. "Don't worry about the oilskin. No will recognize you here. I'll have the hack wait for us."

Leah poked her head out the door and then drew in a sharp breath. "We're at the wharves."

"I'd wager you've never visited them."

"No."

"Too bad. They are the most fascinating place in London."

As he helped her down, she stared all around, taking in the excitement of a busy business day by the waterfront. It was a good day to visit. Huge white clouds, remnants of the earlier rain, floated across the sky, blown by a seafaring breeze. In between the clouds there was an occasional patch of blue.

Everyone was out and about enjoying the good weather. Journeymen and warehouse boys rolled kegs to be loaded on the ships. Businessmen argued, and quartermasters shouted out to any passerby to "hire on." Sailors with tarred pigtails strutted with a rolling gait, going about their business, while young clerks ran errands for their masters, weaving and dodging their way amongst those gathered to enjoy the day.

Devon tucked Leah's hand in the crook of his arm. There were other women here and there, but Leah, with her saucy chipped straw bonnet and cream muslin skirts, stopped all traffic. Grizzled seamen and gentrified merchants stared alike with open admiration until Devon frowned. Then they'd all hurried back to their business.

The fresh air brought a bloom of color to Leah's cheeks. "You like it here," he said.

"Yes. I'm truly a country girl. I like clean air. I don't even mind the smell of wet wood and fish when compared to the soot and stench in the city." She stopped, taking in the graceful lines of a sloop moored by the wharf. "I wish I could travel on one of these ships and see Spain, where my mother was born, or Italy. I would dearly like to visit Rome."

"Perhaps you will someday," Devon answered. "Here." He pulled her forward and pointed at the third ship down. "That is my ship."

Leah stared in surprise before walking toward it, obviously impressed by the four-masted merchant ship. She read the name on its bow. "*The Indigo.*"

"She isn't as large as most, but I sail her for spices and silk, and she's made me a fortune," Devon said.

Leah glanced back at him. "This is what you wanted me to see."

"I wanted you to see that I'm *not* a pauper. Other men can spend their money on valets and clothes. I bought a ship. Not to mention that I will someday be a marquess."

"If you inherit."

"Oh, I'll inherit," Devon said easily. "Grandfather can't disown me. But this is *mine*. The ship has been so successful, I'm buying a second."

"They say your grandfather pays more attention to your cousin Lord Vainhope than he does to you. Why is that, if you are the heir?"

So, she had heard that much. "I'm my own man," he said quietly. "I'm as complete and good as Rex in every way."

He had spoken without realizing how odd those words might sound. Fortunately, she, like everyone else, didn't know the complete story, so she didn't understand what he really meant. Instead she said, "Well of course you are as good as him. Even better. No one likes Lord Vainhope, and everyone likes you."

"Except Julian," he couldn't resist adding.

A reluctant smile tugged at the corner of her mouth. "Except Julian."

"Come this way." He pulled her in the direction of a warehouse. "You need to see this."

Inside the cool darkness was row after row of kegs and stacks of burlap sacks. She sniffed the air experimentally. "What is the smell?"

"It's a spice warehouse. I bring my cargo here. What was unloaded two days ago has already been sold." He rested a proprietarial hand on a bag. "This is pepper. Over there, cinnamon bark."

"It doesn't smell the same here as it does in the kitchen."

"Because you need to crush it to bring the flavors out."

Leah touched the bag of pepper, wrinkling her nose from the scent of raw spice and dust. "Julian says a gentleman does not deal in trade."

"Julian says a great many things," Devon murmured. He wondered what she would say if she knew his other investments and holdings.

She ran her hand back and forth across the rough cloth. "You don't agree with him."

"Obviously."

"Why not?"

He considered the danger of contradicting her precious brother—but, then, she had asked. "There is nothing wrong with Julian's opinions. They are shared by many. He's part of the old order, Leah, of a society that doesn't see the world is changing. On the other hand, I embrace change. I believe a man must make his place in the world. It's exciting times we live in. Revolutionary times. England rules the world, and with that rule comes opportunity, new ideas. Inventions! Why, Leah, I have seen designs for new mechanics that will change even the way we travel from one place to another. Roads won't be needed."

"Roads? We'll always need roads."

"And lights. We won't need candles."

"You must have candles!"

"Leah, there are already streets with gaslights, and someday, there will be gaslights in our own sitting room. Some homes already have them. I've dined in them."

"I've never dined in a house like that."

"You have to leave the Marriage Mart and the narrow thinking of the ton to find houses with gaslights." He shook his head. "A wise man is one who involves himself in what will be the future. I'm happy to let men like my cousin Rex and Julian worry about the past. I'm building an empire of my own."

Leah somberly considered his words. People milled around them, occupied with their own concerns, but Devon scarcely noticed them. He centered on her: Her opinion seemed important to him.

Her lips twisted thoughtfully. "I think I like your view of the world better than Julian's," she said at last. "He is always so angry. Perhaps each of us should search for our own happiness. To be bold and not afraid of change. But I don't like revolutions," she admitted candidly. "However, I think you are happier than my brother, who spends his time gaming and drinking."

If he hadn't already been in love with her, he would have tumbled head over heels in that moment.

She smiled at him, almost as if she could read his approval. A glint of anticipation appeared in her eyes. "Now, my lord merchant, where do you hide your silks?"

He laughed. "Spoken like a woman. The silks are next door up the stairs on the first floor. That way, if there is flooding, they are safe. Come, I'll show them to you."

Unfortunately, the door to the silks was locked. The warehouse manager had left on errands. Leah was obviously disappointed.

"I wanted to see the silks. Are they lovely?"

"Exquisite," he answered as they marched down the stairs.

"Will the warehouse manager be back?"

"Perhaps. But we can't linger. Not if I am going to return you home without rousing suspicion." He started walking toward the hack, but she didn't come. "Leah?"

She was looking up at the building. "Do those upper windows go all around?" She didn't wait for his answer but charged toward the corner of the warehouse.

"What are you thinking?" he asked, following.

She glanced right and left to see if they were alone. This side faced another warehouse with only a walkway in between. "I could peek in that window up there if you'd give me a leg up."

"A leg up? You're not serious."

She began taking off her shoes. "I have my secrets too, my lord. Why, I'm the best tree climber in all Nottinghamshire."

"You're joking."

"No, Julian and William could never keep up with me." Her eyes danced with excitement. "Come along, Huxhold, be adventurous."

He laughed to have his own words turned on him. "We have no trees here."

"Of course not. I'm going to climb you."

Now she had his attention. Intrigued, he made a step with his hands. She placed her stocking foot in it, knocked off his hat, and climbed up on his shoulders with the balance of a trained acrobat.

Devon pushed her skirts aside with his nose. He stood very still lest she fall. He faced the opposite warehouse; she faced the windows.

"Why, Miss Carrollton, you are a hoyden," he said with mock sincerity.

Her peal of joyful laughter rang loud and clear.

"Yes, I am, my dear Huxhold. A terrible hoyden. To be honest, I miss the freedom of being myself. It seems the only time I can be me is when I'm with you. Now move over two steps to the right. I can't see in the window."

Just to tease her, he took a step to the left. She had wonderful balance and laughingly coaxed him in the direction she wanted to go. It was fun. It was silly. But it was also spring, and they were young, and it seemed completely right and natural.

Leah directed him. "Closer to the window. Over a bit. Ah, yes. I can see!"

She attempted to rise up on her tiptoes. Devon held her slim ankles. It would do no good to anyone if she fell.

"This window is so dirty," she complained.

"It's the salt air."

"Yes," she agreed absently. She rubbed a spot clean before making a disappointed sound. "I can't see a thing. There are rolls of fabric, but they are covered in sackcloth."

"I know."

"You knew!" she echoed with a quiver of indignation. "Why didn't you tell me?"

"Well, I would have, but then you started climbing me and it was a temptation I couldn't resist."

"Temptation?" she asked suspiciously.

Devon nodded. "Very much of a temptation." To add meaning to his words, he lightly nipped her ankle.

She wiggled at his touch, giggling. "Stop that."

"Stop that or you'll what?" he demanded, looking up at her. He let his fingers stroke the silk of her stocking.

"Or I will be very angry," she said, trying not to laugh. "Let me down now."

"I can't. You'll have to climb down the way you came up," he quipped, anticipating the feel of her body skinnying its way down his—and the kiss he would claim at first opportunity.

They were so involved with each other that they didn't see the man turn into the narrow walkway between the buildings until his drawling voice said, "Huxhold, amazed to see you in these parts. Don't come here often myself." It was Sir Godfrey Rigston, a friend of his grandfather's.

Leah made a soft cry, and Devon felt her go rigid with the fear of discovery.

"Sir Godfrey," he said in greeting, attempting to act as if it were the most normal thing in the world for him to have a woman standing on his shoulders.

Sir Godfrey stared up with no little curiosity, but since Leah's back was to them, Devon hoped she was safe from recognition. "What brings you down to the wharves this time of day?" he asked.

"No purpose," Sir Godfrey answered. He was a portly man with a protruding lower lip and a nose like a parrot's beak. He enjoyed wearing a curly wig. "Had a friend preparing to sail with the tide and accompanied him for the ride. Seemed a good place to visit on such a fine day."

"That it is."

"I say, Huxhold."

"Yes?"

"Is that a woman standing on your shoulders?" the man asked with perfect English understatement.

Leah muffled a small sound with her hands as Devon answered with equal seriousness, "Yes, Sir Godfrey, it is."

"You lead a devilishly fine life, Huxhold," the older man confided.

"I believe I do, sir."

Sir Godfrey nodded his head. "Well, carry on. Give my best to your grandfather."

"I will when I see him, sir."

Swinging his walking stick, Sir Godfrey continued on his way.

Devon waited until the man turned a corner before sighing with relief. Then, with a heave of his shoulders, he lifted Leah off and caught her in his arms.

She burst out laughing, laughter he joined in.

"Do you think he recognized me?" she asked.

"I'm certain he didn't. Have you ever met him before?"

"Not ever."

"Then we have no worry. He won't be expecting a virtuous woman by the docks, let alone London's loveliest debutante."

She grinned. "I can't believe it. He acted as if it was nothing to see you with a woman standing on your shoulders."

"I have a certain reputation," Devon couldn't help saying, and they both laughed all the harder.

He helped her put on her shoes, and they hurried back to the hack, giggling like children. But once inside, and safely on their way, the laughter stopped.

For a second, they stared in each other's eyes. Then she said solemnly, "Hold out your hand."

He lifted his hand, palm out.

She placed hers an inch apart, and immediately, an irresistible force pulled their hands together. He clasped his fingers around hers.

And then their lips found each other.

Kissing Leah was as natural to him as breathing. Once started, he couldn't stop, not when she so eagerly responded. Their tongues touched, and he drank her in. His hand rested at her waist but he wanted to explore lower, to lift her skirts, to feel the soft skin of her thighs and to feel her heat, her moistness.

She broke the kiss. "Why is this happening to us, the two people in London who can never be happy together?"

"Don't ever say that. It's not true. I am going to marry you."

His bluntness caught her by surprise. She searched his face. "But how?"

"I will talk to your father—"

"No! Why, Julian would never let you close. He hates you, Devon."

"He doesn't know me except by reputation. We've never said two words to each other."

"He doesn't have to know you. He hates you for no other reason than your last name is Marshall."

"Are you refusing me?" The words came out stilted. He had never thought of asking a woman to marry him, let alone that she might reject him.

She hesitated.

"Say it," he demanded. "Just blurt out what you are thinking."

"I don't know."

It was not the answer he wanted.

Leah laid her hand on his arm. "Please, Devon. If I agree to marry you, then it may mean turning my back on my family forever. I don't know if I can do that. And think about yourself. Do you really believe your grandfather would accept our marriage?"

"I don't answer to my grandfather." Anger and disappointment colored his words. He broke the silence between them. "Do you at least return my love?"

She pulled her hand back and clasped both hands in her lap, squeezing her fingers before answering. "I don't know. I need time to consider it more. There is so much at stake. Can you give me just a bit more time before demanding an answer?"

Bitterness filled him. "I wait . . . but not forever."

"That's fair," she admitted, but there was sadness in her voice. They didn't say any more to each other after that. Silence seemed best.

Devon had the hack stop at the baroness's house, and he borrowed a maid to play the role of a Hamlin servant. He wasn't certain, but he thought he caught sight of tears on Leah's face as the hack pulled away.

"Something is amiss, *cher*," Charlotte said to him. "You are not your swaggering, cheerful self and Miss Carrollton seems unhappy."

"I'm in love," Devon confessed brutally.

"Ah," she said with understanding, and then, "love is never easy."

"Now you tell me." He tipped his hat, not wanting further conversation. He needed to be alone. He would have started on his way, but Charlotte stopped him.

"You did not ask me why love does not come easy, *cher*."

"What reason could that be?" he asked sarcastically, smarting from his own discoveries.

She smiled, the expression sober. "Because in order to love, you must be worthy of love."

Her words haunted him for the rest of the day, especially as he relived over and over his words with Leah. She had to love him. She must.

But in the end, what he wished or she wished didn't matter.

Unbeknownst to them Sir Godfrey had recognized Leah. She was the Season's Reigning Beauty and Sir Godfrey was not as oblivious to a pretty woman as Devon had suspected or as cloistered. He had seen her from afar at numerous parties. So Sir Godfrey mentioned her standing on Devon's shoulders to several members of his club, who repeated the words. Soon the gossip spread.

Scandal always traveled fast in London. Mc-Dermott was the one who told Devon of the gossip later that very same day.

Devon hurried to repair any damage that might be done to Leah's reputation. He made up some cock-and-bull story about not recognizing her and helping a damsel in distress. It all sounded silly, but there were enough gentlemen interested in pursuing her who were willing to forgive anything.

She had that sort of impact on men, he realized. It was a gift. Some women had it; some didn't.

He wondered if it was love he felt, or was he, too, a victim of her spell? He planned on finding out when next he saw her at Whitney's.

Of course, that never happened. That evening, when he returned home, he found Julian Carrollton waiting to call him out.

Part Two

Yorkshire, 1815

CHAPTER 4

Devon's long legs ate up the distance to the cottage. He had to find help. Halfway there Leah's body trembled, but not from the cold. A spasm gripped her. It took hold of her like a giant hand pulling the strings of a marionette.

The only birth Devon had ever witnessed had been that of a horse. He remembered the animal's struggle to push a life out into the world. Leah was so petite that he couldn't imagine her surviving such an effort.

Gallant nickered a greeting as he passed. Devon didn't pause but shoved the cottage door open with one shoulder. Entering, he spied a bed in a room off to the side. He headed for it.

He had just started to lay her down when she whispered, "No, I can't." She started to make as if to rise from the bed, but he gently pushed her down.

"Leah, rest. I have to get help."

Now panic set in. Her fingers dug into his coat. "Can't leave. Too late. Don't leave."

He covered her hands with his own, trying to calm her. Her hands were no longer lotion soft but callused by work. Hard work. "Where is your husband, Leah? He will want to be here."

"Oh, Devon." Her voice sounded sad. She released her hold, turned her head away from him. "I have no husband."

She said the words so softly that he almost hadn't heard them. *No husband.* He nodded, concern mixing with a strange, elated relief.

"I'll get help." He started to leave.

Her hand gripped his. "No! Stay."

"Leah—"

"Please—" Her protest was cut short by the next contraction. It doubled her up. Her knees bent, and she cried out in pain.

He couldn't panic, he warned himself. Women had been having babies for centuries. It was natural, a force of nature. It was also damn scary.

And in spite of his fear, he couldn't help but wonder who the father was.

A middle-aged woman with an ample bosom, dressed in black from head to toe, wandered in the front door. "Good heavens, why did she leave the door wide open?" Her apple cheeks flushed with indignation. "Where's Leah? Has she no sense?"

She was talking to a young man who shared her same fair coloring. "Mother, I wish you'd leave her alone—"

His words were interrupted by his mother's

sharp cry of surprise upon seeing Devon. She raised her prayer book protectively in front of her.

Her son stiffened at the sight of Devon, but then his gaze slid to Leah on the bed. He cried out her name and started to move for her.

His mother stopped him by grabbing his arm. "What are you doing in *my* bed, missy? And who are you?" she demanded of Devon.

Leah started to rise, but Devon placed his hand on her shoulder, holding her in place.

"You don't understand—" Leah protested to him, but he shushed her.

Facing the woman and her son, he announced, "I am the Viscount Huxhold."

The woman's blue eyes went wide, and she clasped her leather prayer book to her chest. "Huxhold!" She was obviously familiar with the name.

Devon couldn't resist sending Leah a rueful smile. There were advantages to having a shocking reputation. He rarely had to introduce himself twice.

"Please, Devon," Leah begged. "I must move from Mrs. Pitney's bed."

Devon ignored her. "She's having the baby," he informed Mrs. Pitney and son.

"Well, she can't have it there," Mrs. Pitney replied briskly. "That's my bed."

"Mother!"

"Oh, Adam, can't you see what is plain as the nose on your face? She's one of Huxhold's doxies. They say he has bastards from here to Cornwall. He's come to claim the child. And he can hie her off to another bed as far as I'm concerned!"

Adam jerked at her words as if they'd physically assaulted him. "Is that true?" he said to Devon. "Did you do this to Leah and abandon her?"

A denial was on the tip of Devon's tongue, but then he looked into the young pup's eyes and hesitated. Adam was in love. He would fight Devon for Leah. He was ready to champion her.

There was only one way to dismiss the lad's adoration. "Yes," he answered.

"No," Leah corrected, but Mrs. Pitney drowned her out.

"See?" she said to her son. "I warned you, but you wouldn't listen. All you could see was her pretty face."

Adam was in no mood to hear his mother crow—and Devon almost felt sorry for him. The lad had been planted a facer. Love hurt. Especially loving Leah. Devon knew that firsthand.

Leah might have challenged the claim, but another pain took hold of her body. She cried out.

"She must have help," Devon said. "Mrs. Pitney, do you know about childbirth?"

"Not a thing!"

"What about a midwife?"

"Wait a minute!" she snapped. "That's my bed. She can't have the child in my bed. It'll muss the sheets."

Her son rounded on her. "What do you expect, Mother? That she have the baby out in the stable?"

"I don't care. I wish you'd never brought her here, Adam. Then you'd already be married to the miller's daughter. As it is, your chances may be ruined!"

Devon reached into his coat pocket and pulled out his money purse. He tossed it at Mrs. Pitney's feet, where it landed with a heavy thunk. "There. You can purchase a wagonload of beds with it. Now go fetch the midwife."

"Well, I never—" she started to say even while she bent to retrieve the purse. She caught her son frowning at her. "I'm not wrong for wanting my bed. She's just the farm girl."

Adam frowned in silent disapproval. His mother made an impatient sound, clutching Devon's purse tightly. "I can see you won't listen to me. Well, then have it your way. I'll be over at your aunt Lisbeth's. Come fetch me when the brat is born and *she* is out of my house. I'll not have her here a day longer than necessary." She flounced out the door and was gone in a blink.

Adam stood in the middle of the room, staring at the door. Devon doubted if the lad had ever gainsaid his old goat of a mother.

Leah moaned, bringing Devon's attention back to her. He stepped back into the bedroom and rested his hand on her brow. Cold sweat covered her skin. Her breathing was shallow.

"Is she all right?" Adam asked.

"I don't know," Devon answered candidly. "Is there a midwife available?"

"Yes, Old Edith. Leah has talked to her several times."

"Is she close by?"

"Only through the woods and around the far hill. Maybe a fifteen-minute walk."

"Use the horse by the door. Bring her here."

Devon didn't have to say it twice. Adam started for the door.

Devon called after him, "Be careful. The animal has thrown a shoe. Don't push him."

Adam nodded, but at the door, he paused. "I love her." He stood waiting as if expecting Devon to challenge him.

When Devon didn't answer, the lad left.

Devon wasn't certain Leah had heard Adam's declaration. Her eyes were closed, her focus on the life inside her. Devon sat on the edge of the bed and, taking her hand in his own, rubbed the tender skin of her wrist with his thumb.

Her eyes opened. "Devon, I'm afraid. I don't want to lose my baby."

"It's going to be all right, Leah. I'll make it all right."

His words seemed to reassure her. She relaxed slightly, staring at some distant point in the room, anticipating the next wave of pain.

Even in the throes of labor, and after all that had happened between them, she still attracted him.

Devon wasn't surprised Adam had fallen under her spell. He, too, had been that foolish once, but that was the past.

He was wiser now.

The midwife, Old Edith, was a Scotswoman and one of the ugliest people Devon had ever met. Her pushed-in face looked as if someone had punched her and left the fist mark. She had more hair on her upper lip than she did on her head, but he could have kissed her when she entered the bedroom, dropped her canvas bag of supplies onto the floor, and, with calm authority, ordered him out.

He gave Leah's hand one last reassuring squeeze and then hurried into the other room, where Adam waited in white-faced silence.

Each man took an opposing corner of the sitting room. The bedroom didn't have a door. Only a curtain of off-white homespun separated the two rooms, so Leah's soft cry as the midwife examined her was all too clearly heard.

When Devon had been in there, he'd managed to calm her a bit. He'd reasoned that she had to ease into the pain. To try and relax. And it had seemed to work. But now she sounded as if once again she was lost in the tempest of pain and fear.

"Is the baby really yours?"

Adam's young voice intruded on Devon's thoughts. Almost as an afterthought, the young pup added "my lord?" in a less than respectful voice.

Devon considered his rival. Leah could do far worse. Adam was maybe twenty, stocky of build, with golden brown hair and eyes green with jealousy. Devon had no intention of answering him. One of the few perquisites to being a viscount was the fact that one didn't have to answer to inferiors. It wasn't a game Devon played often, but he could when he wished.

Adam's face flushed a bright red as the silence

stretched between them. His fists clenched.

Devon silently dared him to try it. He wouldn't mind a good mill to take the edge off this moment.

Suddenly, the curtain was flung back from the bedroom door. Old Edith stepped into the room. She instinctively noticed the animosity in the room. Her glance flicked to first one, and then to the other.

She spoke, her Scottish burr thick. "Adam, where is your mother?"

"She left."

"To your aunt's?"

Adam nodded.

"Good, you go there too," the woman ordered. "I will send word when the lass drops the babe."

"But, I don't—"

"Adam, I don't need you here." Her words were sharper than any admiral's command. "You are in the way. Begone."

He shot a frustrated look in Devon's direction. "What about him?"

In the other room, Leah moaned softly, a moan that ended with her whispering Devon's name. The sound of it hung in the air a moment. Adam had his answer. He abruptly turned on his heel, threw open the door, and left the cottage.

Devon crossed to the door and firmly shut it behind him, but not before he noticed the sky had grown darker, the clouds more ominous. The air let in through the open door chilled him to the bone.

Old Edith moved to the fire. Kneeling, she began to build it up. "We need boiling water."

"I'll fetch it."

"The bucket's over there." She nodded to the wooden pail by the door.

Glad to have something to do, Devon started to cross the room when Old Edith's voice stopped him.

"The lass's labor is not normal. Something happened to set it off." It was not a question but a statement, and yet Devon knew she was asking him what he had done.

He went very still. In his mind he could see the image of Leah falling, hear the sound of her body hitting the frozen earth. "Will she be all right?" His voice was almost that of a stranger.

Old Edith sat back on her haunches. "That's not for me to decide. It's in God's hands now, but it will not be easy for her. She may lose the bairn."

Coldness gripped his heart. "And her? Could we lose her?"

"Birthing is always dangerous."

If anything happened to Leah, Devon would never forgive himself. It wouldn't be possible.

"I'll get water," he said stiffly.

"Aye." She watched him open the door and then said, "Are you the father of her babe, my lord?"

Devon turned to her.

"Aye, I know who you are," she said. Her squinty eyes seemed to bore right though him. "A fine friend of our own Lord Ruskin you are. We've heard tales. Your name is well known."

At that moment, Leah called for him.

Old Edith's lips twisted into a grim smile. "*Auch,* she needs us. You'd best get that water and then wait out in the other room. It will be a long night."

Numbly, Devon went to do her bidding.

CHAPTER 5

The first hour did not pass quickly. Or the second.

Devon had tossed his jacket and neckcloth onto the table. He was not a patient man. Waiting did not suit him. He paced the perimeter of the outer room, listening to Leah's soft moans in the bedroom and worrying. And it did not sound as if Leah was coming closer to having the baby. The pains were not steady and regular.

This was his fault. He shouldn't have chased her. He didn't even understand why he'd done so.

When he thought he heard her call his name, he decided he had had enough. Impetuously, he flung back the curtain.

Old Edith sat on the far end of the bed. Leah lay on her side, her legs bent, her eyes shut. She was naked save for the sheet covering her body. Her arms hugged her belly protectively. She appeared oblivious to the world around her, concentrating completely on the child struggling for life.

"There must be something I can do," he said

almost desperately. "We can't just let her keep on like that hour after hour."

"Have you ever been in a birthing room, my lord?" Old Edith asked bluntly. "It takes time. The babe comes when it is ready. It knows no clock but its own. Your only choice is to leave us be and wait."

She might have had her way, except Leah opened her eyes. She reached out with one hand. "Devon."

He hooked back the curtain and knelt beside the bed to take her hand. "Dear God, Leah, I'm sorry. So very, very sorry."

Another pain started to build. She cried out, her body tensing reflexively to the pain.

Modesty be damned. Devon slipped his arm beneath her shoulders and began coaching as he had before the midwife had arrived. Leah had seemed to be doing better then. "Try and relax, Leah. Don't fight it."

"They are hard pains she's having," Old Edith said. "But nothing's coming of them."

Devon didn't want to ask the questions crowding his mind. He feared the answers. Instead, he began running the side of his thumb up and down along Leah's spine, pushing the sheet down. Her skin felt clammy and cold. It worried him. Leah's head rested against his arm, and he could feel the movement of the pain through her body. He massaged harder, wanting to ease those tight muscles.

Leah looked up at him with half slit eyes. "That

feels good. It helps. Thank you." After a few minutes, she relaxed.

Old Edith stood. "Well, it seems as if you might have an idea about how to go along after all, my fine lord. I'm going for a spell of fresh air. I'll be back in a moment." She left them alone, slipping outside to see to her private needs.

"This is my fault," Devon whispered to Leah. "All my fault."

"I shouldn't have run away," she answered in a voice slowed by fatigue.

"I surprised you. You weren't expecting to see me here."

She shook her head. "No, I didn't mean today. I meant in the beginning. From London."

Devon went still. "So your parents don't know you are here?"

"No one knows. I left by myself."

"Why, Leah? Why did you run away?"

She lifted her lashes, and her eyes flashed with irony and her old spirit. "Isn't it obvious?"

Why could she not have turned to the man who had done this? He didn't ask the question that burned in his mind. Now was not the time. Instead he said, "You could have come to me."

"I didn't think you would want me." Another spasm gripped her body.

Not want her? He'd begged her to leave with him.

She squeezed his hand as she rode the pain. He brushed his lips across her forehead, wishing he could bear the pain for her. He'd never felt so helpless in his life.

Outside, the gathering storm began. Drops of ice hit the window, softly at first, and then harder. Old Edith burst through the front door and slammed it shut. "I made it just in time." She hobbled into the bedroom. "How are you doing, lass? Do you feel the baby?"

"Just pain," Leah answered.

"Any movement?"

Leah shook her head, too tired to answer.

The midwife rested her hand on Leah's belly, her gaze focused on the far wall, her mind working. At last she said, "I must check the babe. I'll have to ask you to leave the room, my lord."

Leah's hands tightened their hold on his arm. "No, please let him stay."

"This is no place for a man," Old Edith said decisively, "excepting, of course, the father of this bairn."

"I'm not leaving," Devon replied.

Old Edith's sharp eyes met his. "So are you saying you are the father?"

"Yes," he answered. After all, what difference did it make? He'd already said as much to the Pitneys to scare off the lovesick Adam.

Leah made a sound of protest, but Devon silenced her. "Leave it be. Think about the baby. There will be time for explanations later."

Old Edith performed her examination with quick efficiency. Devon didn't watch. Instead, he cooed to Leah, knowing this was hard for her.

The midwife folded the sheet back down and stood up.

"Is my baby all right?" Leah asked drowsily.

"Oh, yes, he's going to do fine," Old Edith assured her, but her eyes and nose had turned suspiciously red. She walked into the next room.

"Let me get you some water to drink," Devon said. Leah nodded, and he followed Old Edith, dropping the curtain behind him as he left. Cornering the midwife by the fire, he demanded quietly, "What is happening?"

She refused to look at him as she poured hot water into a cup to brew tea. She replaced the kettle before answering, "I don't know. Sometimes things don't go easily for a first babe." She shrugged, her casual gesture belied by her need to swipe a tear from her cheek.

A beat passed, then Devon confessed, "She fell."

Old Edith considered this information. "Well, that could be the problem. She might have torn something inside. Or it could be something else."

Anger surged inside him, causing him to lash out, "Don't you know anything?"

"Aye! I know that girl can die in there and the babe with her," she whispered furiously. "Even if I knew why her pain isn't regular, I don't know there would be anything I could do to help her." She turned away.

Rex had lost his wife during the birth of his last son. Her death had barely registered with Devon at the time. Mary had been a colorless woman, and their paths had rarely crossed. Now in this room, with the ice relentlessly pelting the cottage and full witness to Leah's struggle, he thought of Mary. Poor Mary, dead and forgotten.

Devon stared at the cup of hot water, watching the tea slowly steep as he struggled with her meaning. Leah could die.

"No," he denied. "We can't let her. It's not possible."

"Oh, it's possible," Old Edith answered. She pulled a pottery flask from a skirt pocket and poured a generous drop in the cup. Liquid courage.

"Devon?" Leah called him, her voice weak.

"Go to her," Old Edith said. "She needs you right now more than she needs me. But don't tell her. If we are going to save her, we need her fighting. Go on."

His feet moved like lead weights. He pushed back the curtain.

"Are you and Old Edith fighting?" Leah asked.

He knelt, taking her smaller hand in his. Tears stung his eyes. Hardening his jaw, he forced them back and attempted a smile. "Old Edith doesn't mince words about my obligations as the father of the baby."

"But Devon, you aren't—"

Her voice broke off in a gasp as again a contraction took hold of her. Old Edith came to the doorway holding her teacup, her experienced gaze watching.

"Is it supposed to hurt like this?" Leah moaned. "I feel as if I'm being ripped in two."

"It can," was the midwife's terse reply.

Leah seemed to accept her words. Devon held her tight, her arm around his neck. "It will be all right," he said softly.

She didn't answer but arched as if searching for a more comfortable position. Devon tried to help her. His hand touched her belly—

He felt the baby move!

It was a miracle. He'd never imagined such a thing. It took him completely by surprise. He looked from one woman to another. "I felt it. I felt the baby." It moved again. Beneath his palm, he could make out a limb. The baby shifted. "There it is."

"Good! Good!" Old Edith declared, her renewed enthusiasm giving Devon hope. "This is a good sign. Maybe the baby has decided to wake up and help us." She gave Leah a toothy smile. "Do you think, Leah? Do you think this bairn is ready for the world?"

"I hope so," Leah answered weakly.

"Aye. We all do," Old Edith answered. "I pray we see his sweet little face soon." She left to finish her tea.

Outside, the ice changed to cold, unforgiving rain.

Leah was completely lost in the chaos of her body. The baby didn't move now, but the pains started coming closer together. Ruthless and hard, they drove her to exhaustion. But she didn't complain. She'd never been one to complain.

Devon held her in his arms. He was accustomed to feeling the baby now. Old Edith said it was a good-sized child.

Leah's moods changed rapidly. At one point, she started crying, a soft hiccuping sound.

"Leah?"

"I'm so sorry." She started sobbing, her tears wetting the skin of his neck.

"For what? You have nothing to be sorry for—" He stopped speaking. He knew. She was apologizing for having taken a lover.

Devon enveloped her in his arms—even as he wanted to push her away. "It doesn't matter, Leah," he heard himself say roughly. "It's the past. Don't think about the past."

A contraction took hold of her. Her muscles tensed. "Easy," he said gently.

In answer, she practically snarled at him, a reversal of her behavior only seconds before.

"Aye, don't fight it," Old Edith said from her post at the end of the bed.

"I don't want to fight," Leah ground out. "In fact, I don't want any of this. The baby can stay the way it is."

To Devon's surprise, she kicked out at Old Edith and made as if to rise from the bed.

"Hold her down," the midwife snapped. "It's a phase they all go through. It's a good sign."

It took a surprising amount of strength to keep Leah from climbing out of the bed. She arched her back, her hair flying loose and free around her.

Old Edith leaned forward. Her Scot accent gave

her voice authority as she said, "Now listen, missy, and listen well. If you want this baby, you stay right here."

Leah appeared stricken with remorse. She fell back against Devon. "I want the baby. You don't know how much I want my baby."

"I know, I know," Old Edith answered. "Now sit up best you can. Bend your legs."

Leah was crying again, the silent tears streaming down her face. She did as Old Edith said, bracing her back against Devon's chest.

"Be ready, lass. Be brave."

Leah nodded. Another contraction ripped through her. She dug her heels into the bed. Old Edith was whispering, "Come on, come on, you bairn," as if encouraging a racehorse to reach the line.

The pain subsided.

"Relax, lass. Save your strength. Your bairn is not ready yet . . . but it will be soon."

Leah collapsed. Old Edith stood, rubbing the back of her neck. "I need to reheat the water in this bucket. Soon," she promised Leah. "It'll be soon." She left the room.

"You're doing fine," Devon whispered.

Leah nodded, but her breathing was too fast, too shallow.

"Slow down," he warned. "Take deep breaths. Try and relax." He pressed his lips against the skin of her neck. She was going to make it. She could not die—

"I love you."

Devon went very still, not sure if she'd spoken, or if he'd imagined those words out of his deepest desires.

She looked up at him. "I've always loved you."

At one time, he'd ached to hear her say those words. Now his gladness mingled with jealousy, searing hot jealousy.

"I didn't mean it when I said I hated you," she whispered. "I was angry. Confused."

He didn't know if he wanted to talk about this. Not now. "We both were," he said curtly.

The next contraction started building again. She tried to talk in spite of it. "You weren't. I should have gone . . . with you."

Devon glanced into the other room, where Old Edith puttered with cloths and kettles. He wished she would get back into the bedroom.

This contraction didn't seem to grip her like the others. She drew a deep breath. "Mother wanted me to marry Lord Tiebauld, but I couldn't if I had a baby in me."

"Leah." It had been common knowledge that the Carrolltons had decided on Lord Tiebauld. When the news had reached Devon in Scotland, he'd gotten mind-numbing drunk for a week.

And it still hadn't relieved his sense of loss.

"Mother wanted to take my baby from me, Devon. She wanted to kill it before it could be born."

"Don't think about it," Devon said quickly. Her confessions roused too many contradictory emotions. "Think about the baby."

"Yes, the baby," she repeated dreamily. "And Whitney's. I always remember Whitney's when times are bad."

Suddenly, she stiffened. "I have to push."

Her words sent Devon shouting for Old Edith. For the next hour, Leah pushed until she was beyond the point of exhaustion.

At last, Old Edith said, "Save your strength, lass. Relax a bit." She walked into the other room.

Devon hated the midwife for her calmness. He followed. "Why did you tell her to stop pushing the baby out?"

"Because the baby is not coming out," Old Edith said. She took a sip of the tea she had continued to drink as the evening had worn on.

Devon wasn't certain he'd heard her correctly. He grabbed the cup from her and sampled a taste. "This tea has enough rum in it to intoxicate a sailor." He dashed the contents into the hearth. The flames hissed and flared.

"I need a bit," the midwife whined. "It's hard losing a mother. Hard to watch them die."

Her words tore through him. "She isn't dying. You saw her in there. She's making a valiant effort. We're not going to lose her!"

"We are," she assured him in a low voice. "I've seen it too often. For a while, you made me hope she'd make it, but she won't. The baby's not right."

"What do you mean, 'not right'? I felt it move."

Old Edith ignored his question, lost in her own thoughts. "Aye, but she was a bonny lass and was always kind to me. Some people aren't kind to those of us who aren't as lovely to look at, you ken?"

"We can't lose her," Devon repeated. He'd rather have a thousand shards of glass pushed into his body than accept what Old Edith was telling him.

"It happens, my lord," she whispered sloppily. "It happens."

In the other room, Leah called to him.

"Have a wee nip, my lord. I'm going to give the lass a bit. Help her relax. It's a slow death."

Devon couldn't think. He couldn't breathe. Suddenly he couldn't even stand being in the cottage. He threw open the front door and ran out into the rain, slamming the door behind him.

It was darker than Hades outside. The storm seemed to drive right through him. Raising his fists to the heavens, he shouted, "No!" Once was not enough. He yelled it over and over until the air rang with his denial.

He lowered his arms. Rivulets of water ran down his face, over his shoulders, along the line of his back. He couldn't let her die.

He wasn't going to lose her again.

Even if it meant fighting the devil himself.

Devon returned to the cottage. Old Edith was in with Leah. He overheard her trying to get Leah to drink from a cup. The two bedroom candles cast an eerie light around the room. Their flames danced as he closed the door.

He picked up a towel from the stack Old Edith

had brought with her and dried himself off.

"Devon?" Leah called to him. Deep circles underlined her eyes. Her face was pale and waxy.

He stood in the doorway, feeling very much like a madman. "We're going to have this baby, Leah. I'm going to help you. We'll do it together."

He nodded to the midwife. "Edith, put that cup down and take your position at the foot of the bed. I'll hold Leah up while she pushes, and if you have to reach inside of her like a farmer would a calf, then do it. You pull that baby out of her. Do you understand?"

"Yes, my lord," she answered, a slight tremor in her voice. "But I can't see. It's too dark."

"Then place a candle on the floor where you can see," he snapped.

Old Edith scurried to do his bidding. Devon gathered Leah up in his arms. "Do you understand what we are going to do? You must be brave, Leah. You must use all your courage."

"Devon," she whispered. "When you ran out, I grew so afraid."

"But I'm here now."

She nodded, almost too weak to respond.

"Are you ready, Edith?"

"Aye, my lord."

He leaned his mouth close to Leah's ear. "Come now. You can do it. You've already given up so much for this child. Let's bring him into the world."

His words were the impetus she needed. From a place he could only imagine, she found the strength to try again. Her body strained with the force of her pushing. Her face contorted.

Old Edith shouted encouragement. "Come on now. Bring that bairn out. You can do it, lass. You're strong, healthy. Push!"

And yet the baby would not come.

Leah collapsed, exhausted.

"It has to happen," Old Edith muttered. "She can't go on much longer."

"Let's shift her," Devon said, desperately. "Change her position." He'd seen it work with the horse.

"Aye. Lift her up higher."

Devon climbed up on the bed. He braced her back against his chest, placing his hands on her thighs, spreading them. He didn't think of her nakedness. Her body was for a different purpose now. He raised her up.

"Wait," Old Edith said and attempted to feel the baby. Her expression broke into a grin. "His head! I touched the bairn!" Her voice betrayed a hope that had been missing earlier. "The babe has a bonny head of hair!"

Leah was weary. She nodded, acknowledging Old Edith's encouragement, but her breathing was ragged. Wrapping her arms around the arm Devon used to brace her, she whispered, "Promise me, Devon, if anything happens to me, you'll take my baby. Promise you'll raise him."

She knew.

She was aware of how close to death she was.

He stared down into the face he'd loved, and he didn't know what to say.

Her grip tightened. "Promise."

"Don't give up yet." The words were hard to speak past the lump in his throat. They came out hoarse and guttural.

"Lift her again," came the bossy Scottish voice. "I'm losing the baby. We must do it now."

Leah leveraged herself up, using Devon's arm. He could almost hate this baby for threatening her.

"Shake her!" came the midwife's command.

"Shake her?" Devon had never heard of such a thing.

"Shake her."

He did as ordered, gently.

"Harder," Old Edith said.

Devon shook Leah's whole body harder.

"Push, lass, push. Yes, that's it!" Old Edith cried. "The babe is coming!"

Leah started trembling and laughing. "I can feel him! I can feel!"

"Push, push, push! Now's not the time to stop," Old Edith growled.

The superhuman strength Leah applied to the task humbled Devon. He was shouting with Old Edith now. He believed.

And then he saw the head emerge. Old Edith had been right. The baby had a full head of coal black hair.

The midwife's orders were garbled with excitement and joy. Then suddenly, she shouted, "Stop. Don't push!"

Leah froze. "I have to push. I need to."

"Don't."

Devon leaned forward and saw the problem. The umbilical cord was wrapped around the baby's neck like a noose. Old Edith unwrapped it. Once. Twice. Three times—and the baby slid out easily.

"It's a boy!" Old Edith crowed. She tied the cord and cut it.

A boy.

Devon fell back on the bed, bringing Leah down with him. She was laughing and crying at the same time as he rained kisses of joy all over her face. She was braver and stronger than any man he'd ever known. He hugged her with fierce pride.

Then, suddenly, Old Edith interrupted the celebration with a keening cry. "He's dead. The babe's dead."

CHAPTER 6

"De—" Leah couldn't finish the word. Her body stiffened as reality struck. "No!" she cried out, that one word echoing the shattering of her very soul.

Devon rose from the bed, attacked by an irrational fury. "It can't be!" He practically snatched the child from Old Edith's hands.

The baby was a marvel. Legs, arms, feet with ten toes . . . a perfectly formed boy—save for the fact that its face, head, and body were blue.

"Devon? Please, tell me it isn't so," Leah begged.

He could not speak.

"Not my baby!" The words were ripped from her heart. They rang in the rafters of the cottage.

"It's God's will, child. God's will," Old Edith was repeating over and over even as she reached for her teacup.

Damn God's will, Devon wanted to cry. It was his fault. He'd bartered with God: the baby's life for Leah's . . . and now that he'd gotten what he wanted, he discovered it wasn't enough.

How precious this baby was. How fragile.

Devon held the child with both hands. Behind him, the women sobbed. Leah was inconsolable. He'd failed her.

He fell to his knees, the guilt a weight he could not bear.

Dear God—

He stared down at the quiet form in his hands. Outside, the winter wind blew with a force that seemed to find every crack in the cottage. They'd struggled so hard to bring this boy into the world, and now he would never grow to be a man. He would never know how much Leah had loved him.

Damn you, God. Damndamndamn! Why did You allow this to happen?

Just as quickly, Devon regretted the words. He tasted his own tears, and they were bitter. He cradled the child to his chest, rubbing the length of the wee, strong back with the heel of his hand.

Why? The eternal question.

And in answer, the baby gave a small cough.

Devon turned the boy over. He coughed again, and a heartbeat later, the cough was followed by the angry cry of new life.

Leah heard the sound of her son's first breath, and her heart leapt in her chest. She began laughing through her tears.

"I knew you would save him," she told Devon. "I knew it. Here, let me have him. Let me have my baby."

But Old Edith whisked the child out of Devon's hands, cleaned him off, and wrapped him in a warm blanket that she had pulled from her bag. Then, with respectful deference, she offered the child to Leah.

Feeling the weight of her baby in her arms was reward enough for all the times Leah had persisted in spite of doubts, all the times she'd been afraid but had continued. "He's beautiful."

She didn't need confirmation from anyone else. She had only to look at his hands, balled into little fists. What precious fingers with their miniature nails! They were a miracle of creation, and his skin, still wrinkled and rosy red, was softer than goose down.

She had never imagined such joy as that which filled her. She looked up at Devon. "Thank you."

He grinned in response, more noble and handsome than she'd ever imagined him, even in her dreams. The months before seemed like the nightmare now. One she prayed to forget. Devon was here. Devon had made it right.

"Yes, we did it," Old Edith said, reaching up and slapping Devon on the back. "And a game one you were, my lord."

"I'm only grateful you were here," he replied, and then surprised the older woman by joyfully grabbing her around the waist and doing a whirling jig.

Old Edith laughed, giddy with excitement. The pounding of their feet on the hard dirt floor rivaled the howling of the wind outside the cottage, filling it with exuberance.

"Stop now! Stop!" Old Edith cried. "Or I'll be dizzy for a month of Sundays. Besides, I had a bit too much of my own rum. My stomach's still dancing." She paused beside the bed. Her pushed-in face beamed with pride. "I was afraid," she admitted. "But God was with us. Put that babe up to your nipple, Leah. It's nursing he needs. He's used all his strength and he needs to build it back up."

The Scotswoman's earthy language broke through Leah's haze of happiness. She was suddenly aware that she lay there naked, save for the quilted cover Old Edith had thrown over her once the baby was born, and that Devon had been with her during the most intimate moments of her life.

Devon must have read her mind, because he suddenly went still. He was like that, ever sensitive to the nuances of others. Their eyes met—and everything that had happened between them in the past suddenly reared its ugly head, destroying the moment.

Old Edith sensed the sudden chill. She looked from one to the other and then stepped between them. "Here now, I'll take care of her," she said to Devon. "Why don't you go into the other room and make yourself comfortable best you can?"

Devon nodded. He started to leave, but Leah suddenly didn't want him to go, not yet. Not until she'd done something to thank him for being there, for setting their differences aside, and for saving her baby's life.

"Devon."

He paused, his hazel green eyes unreadable.

She was suddenly aware of how wild she must look. The neat braid she'd worn earlier was long forgotten, and she had to appear as tired as she felt.

"Name him," she said softly.

"What?"

She swallowed. "I want you to name the baby."

His eyes narrowed. His beard, always heavy, shadowed his jaw. His dark hair hung over his brow, and he looked decidedly rakish. This was the Devon she remembered.

"Leah—"

"Please."

His gaze dropped to the child nursing in her arms. It embarrassed her, and yet she would not deny her son.

A flicker of emotion she did not recognize flashed in Devon's eyes. If she hadn't known him better, she would almost have called it longing.

He looked away. "What of the father? Shouldn't you name it after his family? Or yours?"

The happiness of the moment evaporated. Some of what she felt must have shown on her face. "Never mind," he said brusquely.

Before she could respond, he left, dropping the curtain between the two rooms.

Leah looked down at her son in her arms and felt the weight of a terrible weariness.

"So. Huxhold is not the father." Old Edith's voice reminded Leah that she wasn't alone.

Sadly, she shook her head.

"It is too bad," the midwife said simply. "Well, now, we can't be wishing for things that will never happen, so let us take care of what is before us. Let me have another look at that wee lad, and you try and get some sleep."

Devon stared into the dying flames of the fire. *She wanted him to name her son. The one she'd had with another man.* Jealousy roared through him. Once more, he was the outsider.

Of course, Leah Carrollton was the only woman walking the face of this earth who could tie him in knots and make him feel damn stupid while she did it. If he had any common sense, he'd walk out of this cottage right now, sleep with Gallant out in the open stable if he had to, and leave at first light. Walk all the way to London, if he had to. Anything to be as far away from her as he could.

He kicked a log with his booted toe and watched the burning embers flare and spark.

At that moment, the curtain drew back. Old Edith entered the room, carrying the baby in her arms. The birthing seemed to have sobered her. "Did you boil any water for tea, my lord?"

Devon frowned. He was a viscount. He didn't boil water, although black as his mood was, he could set a cauldron to boil just by sticking his finger in it. Nor did he play lackey to a village midwife and her pig girl!

The midwife obviously didn't have any idea what he was thinking, or else she wouldn't have made herself comfortable in his presence. She grunted as she sat heavily in a cushioned chair before the fire. "Poor wee thing," she cooed to the baby. "Not even a nappy for his bum. I will talk to Vicar Wright on the morrow. The women in the village should be able to help out the lass and her bairn."

Devon stiffened, wishing he could close his ears to the woman's prattle.

"Would you be so kind, my lord, to pull that drawer out of the cupboard over there and bring it to me?"

"What for?"

"Why, to make a bed for the baby."

Devon turned in surprise to look at the cupboard. It was a rough-hewn thing made of pine. Hack marks and the scrape of the plane were still visible on it. It even listed slightly. "You can't put a baby in a drawer."

"Where else shall we put him?" she asked with interest. "I don't like for them to sleep with their mothers, especially when it is all so new like this. Poor Leah, she's worn clean through. I'll make up a crib out of the drawer and scrap of material and let the baby sleep out here by the fire."

"Why don't you just hold it?"

She gifted him with a smile, the expression lopsided in her pushed-in face. "I wouldn't mind some sleep, too. But never mind, my lord, I'll fetch that drawer myself. I shouldn't ask such a high and mighty personage as yourself."

She was laughing at him. He knew it—her barb

struck home. But before he could move, she hobbled over and started pulling out the drawer.

Something was already in it, and it was obviously heavy. "Here," he said impatiently, stepping forward before the drawer crashed to the floor.

"Oh, don't mind the drawer, my lord. Hold the baby."

Before Devon knew what she was about, she thrust the child into his arms. The boy was asleep. He looked very much like a small rodent, Devon thought uncharitably—and then couldn't help but smile. Especially when he remembered the feeling of holding the baby in his hands as it drew that first breath.

Old Edith dropped the drawer in front of the hearth. She lined it with a cotton rag. It was a mean bed for a child.

"On the morrow, when the weather lets up a bit, I'll walk to the church," she said. "They have a clothes box for the poor. There should be something for such a small bit." She rubbed the babe's soft head as she said those words. "Poor wee thing. It will not be easy for him."

"Life isn't always easy," Devon said cautiously.

"I know that," she answered and pulled a straw-stuffed pallet from behind the cupboard. "The lass's bed," she explained. "I'll sleep here in front of the fire . . . if you don't mind."

"It's fine."

"You can put the bairn in the drawer when you are tired of holding him, my lord."

Devon nodded. She stretched out on the pallet.

"I'm more tired than if I hadn't slept for a month of Sundays. What is the rhyme? 'Sunday's child is fair of face.' The bairn is lucky. Another hour later, he'd have been Monday's child. The one who has to work hard for his living."

She crossed her arms and closed her eyes, but if Devon thought she was going to sleep, he was wrong. Instead, she started talking. "You should have seen Leah the day Adam Pitney hired her at the Limton fair. He's apprenticed to the miller, you know. His mother plans on him marrying the miller's daughter, but I don't know if it will come to naught. Adam is better at caring for living things than grinding seeds into flour. He was always bringing me birds with broken wings or a fox pup that had been orphaned. A good heart that boy has."

Devon wasn't certain he wanted to hear a list of Adam Pitney's virtues.

"He brought Leah directly to me," Old Edith continued. "She was half starved, her belly already overlarge, but her face was clean and she had pride."

Yes, Leah would always have her pride.

The midwife smiled sleepily. "I fed her and told Adam to bring her here. We both knew his mother had extra room even if the Widow Pitney hasn't heard one word the Lord says about charity throughout all her years of churchgoing. I reasoned it would be good for Adam to have the girl close to him. He never had a taste for the miller's daughter. That was all in his mother's head. For her part,

Leah worked hard . . . even though we all could see she wasn't accustomed to it." She sighed contentedly.

Devon waited for her to continue her story, interested in spite of himself. It wasn't until she started snoring that he realized she had nodded off.

He sat in the chair, the baby still tucked in his arm. He could put the baby down in the drawer . . . but he didn't want to. Instead, he studied the child, watching it breathe, marveling at its sweet perfection. Already the baby was changing. His color was better and his features more relaxed. Then, to Devon's wonder, the baby opened his eyes and yawned.

It was such a charming gesture. It made Devon want to laugh. But the child closed his eyes, seemingly content to be held close.

For the first time in a long while, Devon experienced a sense of peace. He ran his fingers gently back and forth along the child's arm.

Words stirred in his memory. Leah's words. *I will never forgive you. I will hate you as long as I live.*

With the words came memories of the dueling field, of Julian spewing hate, of Julian bleeding. Devon had promised Leah that no harm would come to her brother, but in the end he hadn't been able to keep that promise. Julian had lived, but he was crippled.

The memory shivered through Devon. He'd left

London the day of the duel and had not returned since.

He cradled the baby closer. The unnamed child slept, trusting him to make everything right—just as Leah had once trusted him to do the same.

CHAPTER 7

Leah woke. For several minutes, she lay still in the dark, completely disoriented. She believed herself safely in her bed in London, but she'd had the strangest dream. She'd dreamed she'd been pregnant and life had been unbearable, but then she'd had her baby and had experienced a moment of pure joy.

Old Edith's light snoring brought her back to reality. She had not been dreaming. She propped herself up on one arm, her hair falling back in a tangled mess. The air carried the smells she associated with the cottage, the lingering scents of baked bread and the sweet, pungent peat used to start fires.

Leah listened. Other than the snoring, it was quiet. Even the rain had stopped. The fire in the hearth cast shadows against the curtain separating the two rooms.

Was Devon still here?

He'd appeared out of nowhere, a demon prince

conjured from her dreams and her deepest regrets to save her son.

Her baby. She sensed immediately her son was not in the room with her. She would have felt his presence.

She searched the bed, looking for him. Where was her son? Her body ached in places she hadn't known existed. Old Edith had helped her put on her petticoat and chemise after the baby was born.

Leah combed her hair with her fingers and loosely braided it so it would be out of the way. Feeling her way in the dark, she reached up for the peg by the door where Old Edith had hung her wool dress.

She had to stand to retrieve it. The world spun giddily for a moment and her legs were shaky, but she had to find her baby. She needed to see him, to hold him. To assure herself he was all right.

Not bothering to lace the back of her dress, she took her first tentative steps. It felt funny to have her body back, to look down and see her toes on the cold floor.

She pulled back the curtain and heaved a sigh of relief at the sight of the drawer in front of the fire. Old Edith had told her that a drawer was fine enough for a baby. They'd had this conversation only a few days ago. It had come when Leah had been feeling particularly guilty. She feared for her son's future. He would never know his station in life or have access to the most basic privileges.

Old Edith had laughed. "Love is what a baby needs," she'd replied with firm Scottish conviction.

And a drawer, she had added. Babies could safely sleep in a drawer.

Each step stiff, Leah moved closer to that drawer. Old Edith slept on Leah's pallet. She'd placed it far enough away from the fire so that she was still warm but the glowing light wouldn't disturb her sleep.

Suddenly, Leah realized that Devon was there. He slept in the chair with its high wood back to her, so that she couldn't see his face. His long legs were stretched toward the fire, one booted foot crossed over the other.

For a second, she couldn't breathe. How often, when she'd been alone and afraid, had she wished for his strength, his teasing humor, his presence?

The recriminations and anger that had driven them apart seemed insignificant now.

On silent feet, she inched toward the drawer. Snippets of conversation, the moments of her labor—what he'd said, she'd said, how she'd responded—were confused and jumbled in her mind. She would be able to sort it all out after she'd taken her baby and retreated to the bedroom.

She reached for the drawer, using both hands to lift it—and discovered it empty.

Alarmed, she looked up . . . right into Devon's eyes.

In the golden firelight, his expression appeared grim. The neck of his shirt was open, the sleeves rolled up. Her baby was nestled protectively in the crook of his arm.

With a soft gasp of mother love, she reached for

her child, but Devon's deep, silky voice stopped her. "Who is the baby's father?"

She froze. Her mouth went dry. Her heart pounded in her chest.

He waited.

A part of Leah wanted to run. But she'd never been a coward. Through sheer strength of will, she raised her chin in defiance, her gaze not leaving his.

She could have challenged him, told him she didn't owe him explanations, but in truth she did. Devon's hand rested on the baby's blanket-covered feet as if he were keeping them warm. Her son, and perhaps herself, would not have lived if it hadn't been for Devon. So she answered, "David Draycutt."

He repeated the name softly before saying, "I do not know him. Is he in London?"

"No."

"Do you—" He paused, then continued, "Do you love him?"

Love.

What a fool she'd been to let this man slip away. "I pretended I did."

"Where is he now?"

There was an edge to his voice. One she'd not heard before. One she didn't trust. "I want my baby."

"And you shall have him, *when* my question is answered."

His eyes reflected the flames of the fire. It gave him a dangerous air. She decided not to test him.

"He's dead," she said, her voice faint.

Silence.

"You wouldn't lie to me, would you, Leah?"

His question caught her by surprise.

"Devon, if he was alive, I'd kill him myself."

Her words surprised a sharp bark of laughter out of Devon, his teeth flashing white. "Well said, Leah."

"May I have my baby?"

"Here he is." But he made no move to offer him.

Heat rose in her cheeks. Devon was daring her to come close. Could it be that he knew how awkward she felt?

Her hastily made braid was coming undone. She flipped it over her shoulder and then wished she hadn't. Her breasts tingled with a need to nurse. They overfilled the bodice of her chemise and dress she should have taken the time to lace.

But it was too late for that. All she had left was her pride, and her pride wouldn't let her hesitate in front of him. Conscious of his every breath, she stepped forward. She turned her head as she reached for her son so that she wouldn't be looking directly into Devon's face and those all too knowing eyes. To her relief, he easily relinquished the baby.

Leah raised her sleeping baby up to her lips, overwhelmed by the perfect grace of her child. His skin was velvety soft. It smelled of newness and endless possibilities. His weight felt good to her. Here was something solid. Something, someone she could love.

"Thank you," she whispered.

She turned and would have escaped to the bedroom, except his arm blocked her way. He pulled her down to sit in his lap. She attempted to jump up, but his arm stiffened, holding her prisoner. She glanced at Old Edith. If she cried out, she could wake the midwife.

And then what?

She knew Devon wouldn't hurt her. Ever. And she was all too aware of his superior height and strength.

"How did Draycutt die?" he asked.

"Devon—"

"Tell me, Leah."

"Why are you doing this?"

For a second, he frowned, as if he didn't have an easy answer. At last he said, "I must know."

Leah lightly ran the pad of her thumb back and forth against her baby's cheek. "What you really want to know is why I chose him?"

"God, yes!" The words almost exploded out of him.

Leah shot a warning glance in Old Edith's direction, but Devon didn't seem to care. For her part, the midwife slept on, oblivious to the differences of the two people only feet away from her.

He did, however, lower his voice. "Why him? Why would you run away with him but not me?"

"I didn't run away with him. I left on my own."

"But you said he was dead. I thought that was why—?" He broke off, puzzled.

Leah pressed her lips together. The story was

inside her, one she hadn't told to anyone before. One that still filled her with pain.

"What happened, Leah? Tell me," he asked softly.

If he had demanded or threatened, she would not have spoken. But this was Devon, the man who had saved her son. She owed him this.

"Do you remember the day on the wharves? When you told me you loved me?"

"Yes," he replied warily.

"I heard what you said, but I didn't believe." She shifted the baby in her arms to a more comfortable position. "Later, I couldn't run away with you, not after you shot my brother."

"I had no choice."

"You promised, Devon. You told me that no harm would come to him."

"And I tried to keep my promise."

"Julian said you shot to kill."

Hearing the words out loud in Devon's presence, Leah suddenly realized how stupid they were. Especially when he answered, "If I had aimed to kill, Julian would be in the grave."

He paused, shaking his head. "Leah, he challenged me. I did all I could to reason with him."

"I know that . . . now."

"But then? What did you know then?"

"I knew I felt so guilty. It was my fault. All of it."

"That's not true. Julian could have accepted my apology. I wanted to marry you."

He would have married her. Her suspicions and

doubts had been mistaken. "Devon, what happened that morning?"

"You mean you don't know?" he said tersely. "You sent me away without knowing?"

Tears came to her eyes. She blinked them back. "I was wrong."

An angry muscle worked in his jaw. Leah slid off his lap. He did not stop her.

She looked down at him. "All I know is that my brother returned home with his hand shattered. He'll never be able to use it again, and he's more bitter than ever. I blame myself. I knew better than to start with you."

Devon rose from the chair, turning from her. For a second, she feared he was going to walk away, but he didn't. Instead, he spoke, his voice tight. "I did try to see he didn't come to harm. But he refused my apology. Your brother was a madman that morning. He was furious when I deloped by shooting into the air and claiming all responsibility. He insisted I reload or he'd shoot me where I stood. You can ask McDermott or any of the seconds. They'll tell you. I did the best I could under the circumstances."

"Julian would not have done anything dishonorable," she said with less conviction than she ought.

"No, he'd just blow my brains out."

Leah didn't like hearing this, especially when she recognized the ring of truth. "You are a crack shot. You aimed for his hand."

"I did."

"The nerves are severed. He can't bend it or use it. Your bullet has destroyed his pride."

"And you feel guilty." It was a statement, not a question.

"I couldn't leave with you after that. They would have cut me off. And they needed me. I had to marry rich to save them."

He looked around the room and then replied, "Well, you've done a damn fine job of it."

His harsh words went right to her heart.

She sat in the chair, her legs suddenly unable to support her. She'd thought as much to herself a hundred times . . . oh, but why did it hurt so much now?

Because now, she was even more aware of what she'd lost when she'd chosen her obligation to her family over Devon's love.

Quietly she said, "I have done many things I regret, but I do not regret my son. I will never apologize for him."

"What happened? How did he come about? You barely let me kiss you back then." The anger was gone from his tone, and in its stead was a sense of disillusionment.

Leah drew a shaky breath and said, "After you left London, I told myself I didn't care. But I did. I missed you. My parents, of course, were unhappy with me. Julian takes laudanum constantly for the pain—he barely acts like himself anymore—and poor William still gambles and drinks. He doesn't know where he belongs or what he wants to do. Devon, I tried to be what they wanted me to be. I tried to forget you. But everything was so horribly wrong. I turned hard. Selfish. Arrogant even. Dear Lord, it feels like a lifetime ago, and I seem so old now compared to then. I was incredibly naïve. Redgrave was interested, and I think I could have brought him up to scratch, but then Mother decided he didn't have enough blunt."

She couldn't face him as she spoke. She stared at the fire instead. "Draycutt was a cavalry officer. He was blonde with a huge mustache. An opposite of you. Nor did we need to sneak and hide the way you and I did. I could dance with him in the open. Mother had gotten pushier. She was desperate for money. She started urging me to be more encouraging to the gentleman."

She stopped and looked up at Devon. "Do you know you were the first man I'd ever kissed?"

He shrugged, unwilling to comment.

"Well, that changed," she said simply. "I was going to the highest bidder, and there were those who wanted to sample the wares. Then David arrived in my life, and he didn't have money or connections or anything my parents wanted, and I was a foolish, rebellious young girl."

"So you became—" He paused, then forced himself to say the word. "Lovers."

"No." She focused back on the fire. "Not until Lord Tiebauld's family approached my parents with a marriage offer." Lord Tiebauld was a Scottish lord who lived at the very ends of civilization and was rumored to be quite mad. His wealthy family needed someone to breed an heir off of him.

Leah said, "The stories they tell of him are frightening."

Devon made no comment, neither confirming nor denying her fears. But they sounded silly to her now. Immature, self-indulgent. She'd learned a great deal over the last months.

She continued. "Lord Tiebauld's sister expressly said she wanted a virgin. She even hired her own physician to examine me. Something about rights of succession. She is a stickler for protocol. I found it humiliating. I was very upset, and I told Mother I did not want to marry Tiebauld. What if my children were born mad? I couldn't bear the thought." She leaned over and kissed her son's head before adding softly, "I couldn't stand the thought of him touching me."

"But she didn't agree."

"She laughed at my fears." Leah looked up at him. "I took it into my head that if I wasn't a virgin, then I would not be forced to marry Tiebauld." She frowned sadly. "And I wanted someone to love me. I wanted to believe I hadn't made a terrible error when I sent you away."

After a moment, he said, "So you gave yourself to Draycutt."

"Yes." She didn't look at him when she made the admission. She couldn't. What had once been between them was over, but it still wasn't easy to be in his presence and confess her sins.

"I hadn't ever dreamed I'd become ... with child. Nor was I the only woman in Draycutt's life. In my desire to find someone to love me, I'd believed all his lies. But the truth was he had other lovers, married ones. He was wounded in a duel with an irate husband. He died of the wound only days later."

"Did you mourn for him?"

The question surprised her, and she hated Devon a bit for making her admit, "I was sorry he was gone, but my heart wasn't attached. I did tell Mother that I was no longer a virgin. She was furious. Still, I managed to cajole her into a few more weeks before they accepted that madman's offer. Perhaps I could have caught the eye of a duke."

"Or a marquess," he said softly, a reminder that he would be the very wealthy marquess of Kirkeby.

A flash of temper surged through her. "You would never have been acceptable to my parents. Ever."

"Yes, of course," he admitted, his tone surly. "When did they discover you were pregnant?"

"My maid Mae was the first to realize. I had morning sickness almost immediately. She told Mother. Mother decided that since I had already been examined by the physician and officially declared a virgin, then I could marry Tiebauld without anyone being the wiser if we got rid of the baby."

A wave of pain washed through her. She hugged her sleeping baby close. "Oh, Devon. How could she not have loved me enough to see that I couldn't marry Tiebauld? And I couldn't let them harm the baby. He was innocent. He deserved to live. I feared having the sin of his death on my family."

His fists clenched. At one time, he would have gathered her in his arms. Now he stepped back as if afraid to be close to her, his expression unreadable.

"I ran away," she said almost defiantly. "I wouldn't let them have my baby. You once said that it was good to be bold and to be willing to change. I didn't know where I was going or what I would do, but I wanted this child. One night, my brother William came in drunk and happy. He'd won at gambling—a first! I waited until he'd gone to sleep and stole his purse. I left London on the first stage."

"What happened then?"

"I learned about life," she said simply, but there was a wealth of meaning behind each word. "I was tricked out of my money, forced to sell the clothing I'd brought with me in order to eat, and learned that the world has no sympathy for petted debutantes."

"You could have come to me." The words were stiff.

"Could I?" she wondered sadly. "I wanted to . . . but we both know it would not have been wise. It would not have been like it was before."

The truth in her words filled her with indescribable sadness. She was scarred. And yet, for her son, she must be strong.

He was waking. His body gave a small jerk, and

his eyes came open almost as if he still wasn't certain where he was and why. He was so beautiful that her heart wept for him.

"He's worth it," she said to herself. "Worth more than any sacrifice."

"He's hungry," Devon said flatly.

"Yes, and he needs me." Tears blurred her vision. "Old Edith has been schooling me about babies. Of late, she's been a better mother to me than my own. And what's so sad is that at one time, Mother and I were very close." She looked up to him. Devon had stepped back, deeper into the shadows. She wanted to reach out to him. To ask his forgiveness. But she couldn't. She wouldn't.

She waited.

The silence was deafening.

It was the baby who broke it. He began crying, his body shifting restlessly. He wanted to eat.

Devon spoke. "Feed your child."

Before she realized what he was about, he reached for his coat and jacket heaped on the table and opened the door. A blast of cold air blew through the room. Devon stepped out into the night, shutting the door tightly behind him.

Leah felt as if someone had squeezed her heart into pieces.

But then, what had she expected? She'd been the one to send him away.

"But you came back," she whispered, staring at the closed door. "You came back."

Old Edith spoke. "You'd best pay attention to what is at hand."

Leah turned to her. "You heard?"

"Enough. Do you think he'll return?"

"I don't know." He hadn't returned when she'd sent him away after the duel.

Old Edith sighed, the sound filled with the weariness of the world. "The past is gone. You must look to the future now, missy. Do as he said, feed your son."

Leah did as she was told, but as her son suckled at her breast, tears rolled down her cheeks.

Old Edith patted her head as she walked by. It was a motherly gesture, meant to console. "If it wasn't meant to be, lass, then you must let it go."

Leah cried harder.

The next morning, Adam charged into the cottage with youthful goodwill and little warning. "Did she have the baby?" he shouted at no one in particular.

Old Edith growled at him. "Where's your manners? It was a long night. Stay in this room," she added, in case Adam had visions of bouncing in to see Leah.

A second later, the curtain flapped open as Old Edith joined Leah, who was having an impossible time of changing a newborn's nappy. "Here, you need to make the knot looser in the future or you'll have to cut them off," she advised Leah. "I'll be off to the parish this morning and get some more for you from the poor box."

The poor box. Leah tried not to let it bother her. Accept change, she reminded herself. Be bold.

Forget Devon. He's forgotten you.

On the other side of the curtain, the ever cheerful Adam was building the fire back up. "It's wet and cold and a bit muddy outside but no rain," he informed them.

Old Edith grunted. "Winter." She shuffled toward the sitting room. "I could use a cup of tea."

Leah nursed her son. Both she and the baby were getting better at this. Then she dressed.

Adam pushed back the curtain just as she'd started combing her hair with her fingers. He'd been doing that a lot lately, invading her personal privacy. She tried to be good-natured about it. He looked at the baby lying in the middle of the bed. "Boy or girl?"

"A boy," she said softly. She began quickly braiding her hair, tying it off at the end with a piece of lace she'd saved from a blouse she'd sold.

Adam shifted from one foot to the other. "I'm glad he's all right."

"Thank you. I am too."

"Leah?"

"Hmmm?" She picked up her son.

"Will you marry me?" Adam's words came out in a rush. For a moment, she thought she hadn't heard him correctly. She hadn't *wanted* to hear him correctly.

"Please, Leah."

In the other room, Old Edith stared with wide eyes. Her gaze met Leah's. There was a hint of laughter there. She had to know that Leah was panicking.

And yet, Adam was offering her a solution. He was a good man. He probably would have trouble earning a living after the miller threw him out for rejecting his daughter, but there were other things he could do—except one. He didn't inspire in her passion or love.

She knew she would never be able to give him that, and it would ruin his life.

She smiled sadly. "Adam, you honor me with your request."

"Then you'll say yes?" he asked eagerly.

"I can't."

His eyebrows came together. "Why not?"

"Adam," she started, but how could she explain without hurting him more? He had been kind to her. A champion when she'd had need of one.

The front door burst open. Mrs. Pitney made a dramatic entrance. She was followed by her sister Lisbeth and her sister's husband, a dull man named Hugh.

"I hope I'm not too late," Mrs. Pitney declared. "You haven't asked her to marry you, have you, Adam? You haven't thrown aside all your chances for a decent marriage because of *this* woman?"

Adam's face turned a beety color of red, and even Leah felt heat spread across her cheeks. Old Edith grinned.

Manfully, Adam said, "I asked her, Mother. I'd be *proud* to have her as my wife."

"It would kill me," Mrs. Pitney responded. "Kill me!" she repeated, turning to her sister and her husband, who made commiserating noises.

"I love her, Mother."

Leah cringed at Adam's declaration. She sent a helpless glance toward Old Edith, who shrugged. She could not save her.

"It is *your* fault!" Mrs. Pitney accused Leah in ring-ing tones. "He was always biddable until he met you."

That description did not please Adam. He stepped forward to defend himself. His aunt Lisbeth jumped in with a few choice words of her own about "foolish young men." Meanwhile, the baby decided the world was way too noisy. He began to cry.

Leah wanted nothing to do with any of it, especially as Adam attempted to shout both the women down. She picked up the baby blanket lining the cupboard drawer and covered her child to protect him from the cold air sweeping in through the still open front door.

She should leave. Mrs. Pitney wouldn't let her stay anyway. Perhaps the vicar and his wife would help her find a new situation.

Suddenly, Mrs. Pitney gasped so loudly that she quieted everyone. She motioned to her son and relatives. "Hush! Hush! Look who has arrived! Why it's the earl, right here at my doorstep."

Leah peeked around the others, who stood crowding around the doorway. Sure enough, the earl of Ruskin's finest coach rolled into the small barnyard. The bold red and green of the Ruskin colors stood out against the burled wood. A red-

and-green liveried coachman drove the matched set of high-stepping bays.

Leah had met the earl several times in London. She'd been living with Mrs. Pitney for a month before she'd realized who owned the land. A confirmed bachelor, Rusky, as his friends called him, wasn't one to mix with debutantes. He and Devon were fast friends and chummed around together at sporting events and the like.

The coach door opened. Mrs. Pitney was already making a curtsey, the ribbons on her black bonnet quivering with excitement. But instead of the amiable Rusky alighting, Devon climbed out. He wasn't wearing a hat, since he'd left it in the cottage last night along with his wool greatcoat. Climbing down from the coach after him were the vicar and his wife.

Mrs. Pitney and the others stepped back from the doorway. Leah discovered herself in the forefront of the small crowd, holding her baby protectively in her arms.

She wished she could run and hide too.

Devon looked as if he'd spent the entire night up. His hair was disheveled. He hadn't shaved. His sharp gaze honed in on her.

Leah's heart beat an anxious tattoo as he took one step and then another toward her. He stopped when there was less than a hand's width of distance between them.

"Benjamin," he said, his deep masculine voice rolling the syllables.

The name was unfamiliar to her. "I'm sorry."

"You told me I could name the baby. I've decided to name him Benjamin Marshall, after my grandfather."

Marshall. Devon was giving his surname to her son. He was claiming him as his own. She was speechless, but Old Edith wasn't. She gave an unreserved Scottish whoop for joy.

CHAPTER 8

"Exactly as I suspected," Mrs. Pitney declared. She turned on her son. "*Now* will you believe me? That baby is nothing more than a Huxhold by-blow."

Leah would have corrected her, but Old Edith grabbed her arm, warning her to silence.

Instead, Devon said, "The vicar has a special license."

"To marry us?" Leah asked inanely.

"Yes," he replied with all the sangfroid of one who has just been asked whether the cheese pleased him.

Vicar Wright was more kindly. "Lord Ruskin insists we keep one at all times at the vicarage. As a bachelor, he claims life is uncertain and wishes all options available to him. I'm sure he will be more than happy to let his good friend Lord Huxhold use it."

Leah faced Devon. She saw no emotion in his hazel green eyes. "You don't want to marry me."

A flicker of irritation crossed his features. "On the contrary, I have returned to marry you."

At one time, such a proposal would have been her fondest dream. Now, it filled her with uneasiness.

Vicar Wright intervened in his soothing parson demeanor. "Lord Huxhold has explained everything. My wife will serve as a witness, and perhaps you will witness, too, Mrs. Pitney?"

"Yes!" she replied enthusiastically even as her son stepped forward with fists clenched.

"Tell him you don't want to marry him, Leah," Adam said. "Tell him I love you."

"You don't know what love is," his mother snapped.

"I know I don't feel anything for the miller's daughter," he answered, a comment that sparked a response from both Lisbeth and her husband. Everyone in his family wanted him to forget Leah. Vicar Wright and his wife attempted to make peace while Old Edith cackled in glee at the nonsense.

It was Devon who restored order. Calmly he checked his pocket watch. Closing the case, he tucked it in his watch pocket and said in a commanding voice, "I must be on the road in fifteen minutes. Leah, do you wish to marry this puppy?"

Adam took offense at the description. "I love her," he declared nobly.

"Yes," Devon answered, "but you can't support her. And I will not let Ben lead the life of a yeoman. Good God, man, can't you see she was bred for better things?"

"It's her decision," Adam insisted stubbornly. "I won't let you bully her."

Devon didn't like that comment. His jaw tightened even as Mrs. Pitney grabbed her son's arm and attempted to pull him back. "Adam, watch what you say. This is Huxhold."

Leah stepped between the two men, her sleeping baby still in her arms. "Stop it before one of you says something that can't be taken back."

"Tell him you wish to marry me," Adam begged. "He can't just sweep you away."

"Adam," the vicar said, "this is Miss Carrollton's decision."

"But he will take her from me," Adam said. "I won't let him without a fight."

Gently, Leah said, "I can't marry you, Adam. You deserve more than what I can give you."

"Yes!" Mrs. Pitney agreed. "That is what I have been trying to tell him."

"It's because he's a lord," Adam accused her bitterly.

"It is because he's the father of her *bastard*," his mother countered.

Anger shot through Leah. How dare the woman attack her son! She stepped forward, but Devon took charge. "I advise you to leave immediately, Mrs. Pitney." His eyes snapped with a fury Leah had never seen in him before.

"But it is my house," the woman said.

"Then I'll run your son through and we'll call ourselves even."

He said the words so pleasantly that it took everyone a moment for the implication to sink in. Vicar Wright began making placating noises while Mrs. Pitney and her relatives pushed Adam toward the door. But Adam wasn't ready.

"Leah, I love you."

"But Adam, I don't love you."

Those blunt words were hard to say because she knew they would hurt him. He had saved her life, and she would have given anything to spare him pain—but she had to be honest.

Everyone froze, uncertain what to do or say.

Adam acted genuinely surprised. He stood a moment, stiff and awkward, before suddenly turning and running out of the cottage. His relatives followed, his mother calling his name and making promises about the miller's daughter.

"Well," the vicar's wife said in the silence that followed, "that matter is settled."

"Yes, it is," Old Edith agreed without remorse.

Vicar Wright nodded absently and then said, "Um, I believe we can get on with the marriage ceremony then."

"No," Leah answered. "Devon, I must talk to you."

"*After* we are married," came his firm reply.

"No, now. In private." She could be as obstinate as him.

"There are few private places in this cottage," he responded reasonably.

"In the bedroom," she answered and walked in there, expecting him to follow, which he did.

She waited until he'd dropped the homespun curtain in place. Through the room's only window, winter sun flooded the room with gray light. It suited Leah's mood. She was conscious of movement on the other side of the curtain door. She knew Old Edith would eavesdrop and probably the vicar and his wife, too. Well, there was naught she could do for that.

However, Devon had the same idea. He ripped back the curtain and caught the eavesdroppers, who scurried to the other side of the room with red faces. He dropped the curtain back in place.

"You can't marry me," she said in a quiet voice, coming directly to the point.

"You didn't like the name I chose?"

"The name?" she repeated, puzzled, and then frowned. "Benjamin is a fine name. But I don't think your grandfather will be pleased."

"My grandfather is dying, Leah."

His words sucked the air out of the room. She sat on the bed. "Dying?"

"The family has contacted me. I was supposed to be in London last night, if possible. I was taking a shortcut when Gallant threw a shoe. That's how I ended up here."

"Dying?" No one close to her had ever died. Of course, the marquess of Kirkeby wasn't in her immediate circle, but his personality had loomed large in her life. He was the "dreaded enemy." His presence had tainted every decision her family had ever made.

As if reading her mind, Devon said, "It's hard to imagine, isn't it? I thought he would live forever. And now I'm not going to him without you and Ben. Now let us marry."

Blunt and businesslike. It was hard to believe that this man had been the same one who'd laughed with her a year ago. "Devon, you don't want to marry me."

"I'm not leaving you behind, Leah. You heard Mrs. Pitney. Do you really wish to expose Ben to the bastard's life?"

"But why should you care?" she asked quietly.

Devon's gaze fell on the child. He reached out almost timidly and placed his hand on the baby's back. "I gave him life." He met Leah's eyes. "I felt him draw his first breath. I don't care who fathered him. I have more claim to him than any other man."

A chill of disappointment swept through Leah. She realized she had been anticipating another answer. A more personal one. Once, he had begged her to run away with him because he loved her.

He had not spoken of love since they'd seen each other again.

At her continued silence, he said, "Nor do I worry what country folk or even the ton think of me. I'm Huxhold. I make my own rules."

She nodded, her heart heavy. "What of your other children?"

"What other children?"

Leah looked away from him. "It's well known that you have fathered children off at least a half dozen of your mistresses."

"*Only* half a dozen mistresses? What did I do with the rest?"

He mocked her. Her temper flared. She stood. "I'm happy I amuse you, my lord."

"Leah, don't pout. I'm just amazed you listen to the gossips. At one time, we knew each other better than that."

"There are times I believed I barely knew you at all."

That mark hit home. "Then we are equal," he answered. "You've more than surprised me too."

"That wasn't my purpose," she replied stiffly.

"Nor mine." He raked his fingers through his hair. She remembered that he'd had very little sleep the night before. He'd been busy on her behalf . . . and she'd not yet said thank you.

But the words died in her throat when he said, "Leah, I have no children."

"What?" Her regrets over her churlish behavior vanished. "But everyone says that you have a host or more. You're famous."

"*In*famous is more like it," he said, his eyes glittering with self-mockery. "I know what they say, Leah, but I also know who I am. I've had the keeping of three mistresses, *one at a time*. I pay my bills. Honor on my word. And have never sired a child out of wedlock. Not one. Disappointed?" he asked cynically.

His jab stirred her conscience, but not enough

to prevent her from pointing out, "That doesn't mean you are good material for a husband."

"Well let me call Adam back," he snapped.

"I wasn't comparing the two of you," she answered curtly. She began swaying, gently rocking her son while standing in place. "Regardless of who I marry, I lose all my freedom. That is a sobering thought."

He raised one eyebrow and glanced around the room, his actions saying louder than words that he didn't think much of her present freedom.

"It isn't a great deal," she agreed. "But it was mine. I was attempting change, Devon, to change for the sake of my child."

"Then continue on the bold course, Leah. I promise Ben will not lack for anything."

Leah stopped rocking. *What about us, Devon?* she wanted to ask. *What will happen to us?* But those were questions she couldn't ask. She feared the answers. Instead, she pushed aside her personal thoughts and considered the situation for Ben.

Devon was right. Her romantic nature wanted to believe she could pursue her own path; her common sense warned her she and Ben would starve. "Will you claim Ben as your own?"

"I will."

"But he cannot inherit the title."

He shifted. He'd obviously thought that far. "No. The family would never allow that. Rex or one of his sons will inherit from me."

"Or one of *our* children." There, she'd said it.

It was the closest she dared go toward discussing intimacy between them.

Suddenly the air vibrated with memories of the passionate hunger that had once existed between them. Leah didn't flinch. She was a woman now. A woman with a child for whom she would do what she had to do.

Instead, it was Devon who took several uneasy steps toward the window and placed distance between them. A frown had formed on his forehead. "Or ours," he repeated, his voice so low she could barely hear him. "Let us worry about that when it happens."

She sensed there was something he wasn't telling her and then decided it was her own hypersensitivity to the subject. "What of the feud between our families?"

"It ends with Ben," came his hard reply.

"You and I can agree to that, but will your grandfather?"

"Or Julian?" He sounded exasperated. "Leah, I can't promise you that everything will be rosy in the future. I don't know what the future holds. I do know that I won't have Ben living hand-to-mouth. For once, think of someone other than yourself. Think of your son."

"That isn't fair! I am thinking of Ben. There will be much gossip. I have been missing for months. And when I show up married to a Marshall, our ancestors will spin in their graves and tongues will wag."

"Tongues will always wag. However, you will

return to London a viscountess. You won't have to answer to anyone. And if you play your cards right, you may soon be a marchioness." There was no disguising the bitterness in his voice.

"If it was money and a title I wished, I could have married Ticbauld," she responded proudly. "Take your offer to the devil. I won't marry you." She would have charged out of the room, but he stepped in her path.

"You would refuse me? For nothing more than your own pride?"

His words pinned her to the spot. She had no answer.

Suddenly, the tension left him. He reached out and ran the back of his hand over the baby's downy head. "May I hold him—or am I not allowed to do that either?"

She should tell him no, but she couldn't. Silently, she gave Ben up.

Devon held the child as if it were the most precious gift in the world. He put the baby to his shoulder and almost immediately started rocking gently back and forth the way she had rocked Ben only moments ago.

Few men would be a better father than Devon, with his joy of life and good humor.

He smiled at her, a hint of self-consciousness in his expression. "Ben proved he's a fighter last night, didn't he? He'll grow up to be a fine man."

Leah felt herself relent. "If we do marry, what will we tell people about his birth?"

"A bit of the truth and a bit of a lie. How many

people would suspect Draycutt is the father?"

"I don't know. I only confided in one friend, Tess Hamlin, and she is in Wales. But people knew he was courting me."

"There's been a herd of men courting you, Leah."

"Yes," she agreed tightly. "Your point?"

Devon shrugged. He focused on something in his own mind before saying, "How many people knew Draycutt or would have registered his death in their minds?"

"Few. He was in Essex when it happened."

"Then we tell the truth. Ben is Draycutt's son, and you ran away with him."

"But I didn't."

"It doesn't matter. We will put out that you and Draycutt were married clandestinely—"

"And he had an affair with another man's wife and was shot by the husband," she finished sarcastically. "That doesn't flatter me, does it?"

"No. But it is the truth."

And, she realized, few people would question it. "But you've already told the villagers that Ben's last name is Marshall."

"I said it for convenience."

"Then why not say he is yours? Why bring up Draycutt at all?"

"Because the dates aren't right, Leah," he said flatly, but she sensed there was something else. Ben wasn't his . . . and intuition warned her that Devon was sensitive to that fact.

"Everyone in London knows about the duel and

that I left the city immediately. They have only to figure the date and count nine months. It won't fly."

"All right," Leah agreed. "But I still don't feel comfortable about this. I don't like secrets."

"Everyone has them," Devon answered dismissively.

"That doesn't mean they are easy to live with."

"No," he agreed, "but then, our marriage won't be easy either. We will not be a love match, Leah. There's too much between us. You are free to go your way. I ask that you are discreet."

His words shocked her. She'd never expected such from Devon. "Why?"

He didn't answer, his features set.

"You don't say anything, but I think I know. You wish to punish me."

"It's nothing like that," he quickly denied.

"Then is it Draycutt? That I chose another?"

"It's many things. I loved you once. But time changes one's affections. If we marry, it will be for Ben and Ben alone."

His blunt words rocked her back. "I see." She added grimly, "Now I understand why you are not worried about *our* children inheriting."

He shrugged, his expression guarded.

His indifference told her more than words that the love he'd once felt for her, the love she had rejected, no longer existed. Last night, when she had feared she was going to die, she'd desperately confessed her feelings.

He had not responded in kind.

She knew why now. He did not love her any-more.

But he loved her son.

Tears clouded her vision. She crossed her arms and looked away.

He was right. She should think with her head and not her heart. Devon would take care of them. Any other man would have abandoned her yesterday. Devon had stayed. If not for him, both she and Ben would have died.

She glanced back and noticed the way his fingertips gently stroked the back of the baby's head. What right did she have to deny Ben such a father?

"I will marry you."

If he was happy or had doubts, she couldn't tell. His expression did not change. He nodded. "Fine. Let us see the deed done and be on our way."

That was it. No glad declarations, no giddy promises.

With an efficiency that would have made a field officer proud, he threw open the curtain, Ben still in his arms. Old Edith had made tea, and the vicar and his wife joined her around the table.

"Miss Carrollton does me the honor of giving me her hand in marriage," Devon said formally. "Let us start the ceremony before she changes her mind."

His quip irritated her, but Old Edith and Mrs. Wright were so pleased that no one noticed her feelings—or cared.

Devon held the baby. Mrs. Wright and Old Edith stood as their witnesses.

The room grew suddenly close. Leah found it difficult to breathe. She reminded herself that she was doing this for Ben. Ben. It was a good name, but she feared her family's reaction.

And yet, they weren't here. They had not supported her when she'd needed them most.

From this marriage, she would gain respectability and security for herself and her son . . . but what was Devon receiving?

The question tormented her as the vicar read the marriage ceremony from a small black book. Every debutante had dreamed of hearing these words and knew them almost by heart. Leah was no different.

Devon repeated his vows in a clear, strong voice. He did not look at Leah the whole time he said them.

Her tongue stumbled and tripped over the simplest of the vows. Her knees shook, and she knew it wasn't from fatigue.

She and Devon never touched.

Vicar Wright paused. He looked over his gold frames to Devon. "It is here I customarily bless the rings if there are any."

"Use this." Devon handed Ben to Old Edith before removing his signet from his left ring finger. Carved in the face of the heavy gold was a leaping stag and the Marshall family motto, *Je reviens.* "Let her wear this until I can have something made in London."

The vicar passed his hand over the ring, blessing it. "You may now place it on the bride's hand."

At last, they were forced to face each other. Leah held out her hand. It trembled.

If Devon noticed, he gave no indication.

As he held her hand in his and repeated Vicar Wright's words, she remembered the night of the masquerade. "Hold out your hand," he had said, and what had flowed between them had been something real, something magic.

She didn't feel the magic now.

Devon fitted the ring on her finger. It was too large. She made a fist to hold it in place, the cold weight of it as heavy as her heart.

What was she doing?

And then, before she realized it, the vicar said the final blessing that bound them together as man and wife for an eternity.

It had taken minutes.

Her head bowed, she stole a look in Devon's direction. He seemed to concentrate on a point beyond the vicar's shoulder. She wanted to weep, but she was done with crying. She'd made her decision.

At that moment, Ben woke and started crying.

Leah's breasts immediately tightened uncomfortably. Her milk was in.

"Just the right timing," Vicar Wright said with satisfaction as he closed the book.

"The baby's hungry," Old Edith announced. "Go along, Leah. You should feed him before you leave."

Leah welcomed the opportunity to escape to the

bedroom. She overheard Devon say, "We'll leave the moment she is done."

"Aye, my lord," Old Edith answered. "And you be careful with the lass. I don't want her coming down with childbed fever. It's not wise for her to travel."

"I have no choice."

"You take care of her," Old Edith reiterated, and Leah could have kissed the woman.

Her son nursed eagerly. She watched him, this simple act giving her a sense of satisfaction, of completion. And an understanding that she was doing the right thing for Ben.

Old Edith pulled back the curtain and stepped into the room. She carried a huge basket. "Mrs. Wright had this out in the coach. It is filled with clothes and nappies, and there's a nice thick blanket made of fine fleece to keep that wee one warm. Lord Huxhold also managed to find a wool cape for yourself. He has another hamper this size full of food. Mind me, you eat well. Drink ale. It will keep your milk coming. And don't move unless you must."

"That's one piece of advice that won't be hard to follow," Leah said, still sore from her labor. She burped Ben on her shoulder, already handling her baby with confidence, before rising. "Thank you, Old Edith. Thank you for everything."

The Scotswoman's eyes grew misty. "Don't thank me. It was him that did it. I could have lost both of you. He wouldn't let me." She pushed a stray lock of Leah's hair back from her face. It was a motherly gesture. "Listen, missy, one piece of advice and then I will say no more. Sometimes, the marriages that start off the worst are the best. Just remember, marriage is work. Every day, it is work."

"Well, I know how to work," Leah admitted ruefully. And she had the calluses to prove it. She began changing her son and wrapping him in the fleece.

"Aye, you do," the midwife agreed softly. "And don't be afraid of it."

Leah nodded, unwilling to betray her doubts.

"He cares for you, lass," the midwife said as if reading her mind.

Leah didn't answer. Instead, she pressed a kiss against the older woman's cheek. "It is time for me to go."

Out in the main room, the vicar and his wife had already left. Old Edith made Leah drink a cup of tea and eat some bread and cheese. The cheese was buttery smooth and like nothing Leah had eaten since she'd run away. It must have come from Lord Ruskin's pantry.

Devon paced restlessly outside the door. She had to go.

"Don't forget the drawer," Old Edith said.

"But the cupboard—?" Leah started to protest.

Old Edith waved her on. "Adam can make another for his mother. Your son needs it."

Old Edith placed the red cape around Leah's shoulders. Made of the finest material, it enveloped her and her son. "You are a true lady, lass," the midwife reminded her.

A lady. The words made her light-headed. Leah wasn't certain what it all would mean. She'd have to sort it out in her mind before they reached London.

Devon called from the door. "Leah, we must leave." He took the drawer from Old Edith and put it on the floor of the coach, placing warming bricks around it. He offered his hand to Leah. Instead of letting him help her up, she took off the signet ring and placed it in his palm, explaining, "I will lose it."

His hand closed around it, and then he placed it back on his hand. "Let us go."

She climbed into the coach.

To her surprise, he turned and thanked the midwife for her services. "I wish I hadn't thrown my purse at Mrs. Pitney to buy a bed, but you will be compensated as soon as I reach London."

"Take care of Leah, and that will be compensation enough," Old Edith answered.

Devon nodded his reply. He stepped up into the coach, signaling the driver for them to be on their way before he'd even shut the door.

Inside, Devon sat back in the green velvet seats and ran his hand over his jaw. "I should have shaved."

She didn't answer or look at him. Her baby in her lap, she stared out the window until they'd rounded a curve and the small farm that had been her haven vanished from sight.

She was on her way to London. The road was deeply rutted with frozen mud, and the coach rocked back and forth in spite of its good springs.

The reality of what she'd done in marrying Devon struck her full force. Her father and brothers would be furious. And what would she say when she saw her mother, the woman who had threatened to destroy her baby?

At last, she roused herself from her dark thoughts to face Devon. She turned—and discovered he'd fallen fast asleep. He was slumped down in his seat, his arms crossed, his long legs bent in an uncomfortable position in the close confines of the coach.

He looked like anything but a hero.

Once again, some inner voice whispered he had an ulterior motive in mind for marrying her. For all his seeming nonchalance, he was a proud man. She just couldn't divine what his true reasons were.

Of course, even if she could, would it make a difference?

He wanted her child but not her—and suddenly it made Leah angry. Her own parents had experienced more than their share of disappointment and disillusionment, but through all their trials, their love and commitment to each other had remained firm.

Now viewing the world with a woman's eyes, Leah realized she wanted that kind of love. Her hand rested on the seat, her fingertips so close to Devon that she could touch the buff-colored

leather of his breeches. Devil-may-care Devon. At
one time, there had been magic between them.
Would she really let it go without a fight?

No.

As a debutante, Leah Carrollton had charmed a
host of men. Now, as a woman, it was time to win
the heart of her husband.

CHAPTER 9

The baby's crying woke Leah. She hadn't realized she'd been dozing.

The world around her rumbled and moved. Slowly, she came to her senses. She was in a coach on her way to London, her body ached, and her breasts were full. Ben.

She started to sit up but stopped when she realized her feet rested on Devon's lap. He was holding Ben, his thumb up to the baby's lip. Ben suckled eagerly.

"He's hungry," Devon said to her. He looked down and answered the unspoken question about how her feet ended up in his lap. "You looked uncomfortable. I thought you would sleep better stretched out."

She nodded. He'd even thought to remove her shoes. She was very aware of the hard muscles of the thigh beneath her stockinged foot. He had a horseman's thighs, each muscle strong and elongated.

Her stocking had a hole in it, right over the big toe. She curled her foot reflexively to hide it. The action pushed her heel even harder against him. His muscles tensed.

So, he wasn't completely immune to her.

Some perverse whim tempted her to leave her foot there, but that was a bolder action than she wished to take. She wasn't ready to dare him into the intimacy of a marriage. Even if her body had been healed enough for it, which it wasn't, she had discovered from her liaison with Draycutt that the act of love itself, the coupling, was much overrated. After the flush of infatuation wore off, being pawed by Draycutt was both boring and messy. They'd been intimate three times, but it had been two times too many for her.

Sitting up, she pulled her feet back until her skirt covered the hole in her stocking. She held her hands out for her baby. "Let me feed him."

If Devon noticed her retreat, he made no comment . . . and it made her sad. She remembered standing on his shoulders, his hands around her ankles holding her so fast that she was in no danger of falling.

"I changed him," he replied matter-of-factly. "I put the soiled nappies under the drawer."

"*You* changed him?" Leah asked, surprised. She'd heard from the village women that men wanted to have very little to do with babies and even less with a baby's nappies.

"He fascinates me," Devon replied. He handed

the baby to her. "I swear he knows me, Leah. He responds to the sound of my voice."

Right now, Ben was responding to his hunger, but Leah hesitated over nursing the baby in front of Devon. Women nursed in public all the time. It was a fact of life, and yet she wasn't certain she wanted it to be a fact of *her* life.

Nor was she ready to expose a breast to Devon. She'd done so last night—but that had been life and death. Now, she pulled the red cape up over her shoulders.

"Are you cold?"

"No, I'm going to feed the baby." She turned her back to him and awkwardly undid the back laces of her dress before slipping one shoulder down.

"I've seen breasts before, Leah."

She didn't answer. What could she say to such a comment, especially when it made her cheeks flame with color? Then Ben clamped onto her with gusto. The strength of his mouth surprised a small gasp out of her.

"Is anything wrong?" Devon asked, immediately concerned.

"No, he's just more aggressive than he has been," she managed to squeak out, even as she felt another wave of hot color rise in her face.

Devon settled back into the far corner, ungracefully shoving his hands in his pockets. He stared out the window. It was a dismal day, with threatening clouds hanging low in the sky, just like the day before. The silence stretched out between them. Leah switched Ben to her other breast, just as Old Edith had instructed her. In spite of traveling, everything seemed to be going fine. She had plenty of milk.

Ben finished. She brought him out from under the cape and placed him on her shoulder. The awkward silence made her feel ill at ease.

She cleared her throat. Devon didn't waver from his concentration on the passing scenery.

"I'm glad we aren't going to have a normal marriage," she said.

That captured his attention. "In what way?"

Leah took her time answering. Let him have a taste of the silent treatment. Ben had already fallen back to sleep. She checked to make sure the bricks were still warm, and then she placed the baby in his drawer, tucking the fleece in all around him.

Devon watched her, his foot tapping impatiently, and she had to hide a smile.

"It's just nice to know," she said at last when she knew he wouldn't wait any longer. She was proud that she'd kept her voice carefully steady.

Devon's eyes narrowed suspiciously. Beneath the red cape, she slipped her arms back into her dress. His gaze dropped to her arm movements, and then he seemed to hold his breath.

Experimentally, she let the red cape drop while she reached behind her to tighten the lacings of her gown. The action thrust her chest forward, her breasts already generously overfilling the bodice of the gown.

Devon shifted restlessly now. His toe stopped

tapping. He stared at an imaginary point in front of him.

Her husband may be angry with her, but he was completely male, and he thought as all males. There was hope. She could secure his affections. She knew she could. The thought made her smile.

"Why are you smiling all the time? Little smiles, like you hide a secret," he demanded, sounding outright surly.

Leah couldn't help tweaking his nose. "I was imagining what type of cicisbeo I would take on once we get to town."

"Cicisbeo!"

She nodded, her expression serious, or as serious a one as she could muster. "I think it best to be—as you put it—discreet. After all, isn't a cicisbeo the type of man that a woman pays, and therefore he has a reason not to rattle on about his lady friend's affairs?"

Suddenly, Devon lunged across the seat. Leah found herself pressed up against the side of the coach, the weight of her husband's body holding her prisoner. He captured her arms by the wrists and held them against the wall close to her head.

"What game are you playing?" His face was so close to hers that she could see the textured shades of green mixed with the brown of his eyes.

"I play no game," she said bravely.

"Oh, yes you do." He leaned closer, the roughness of his whiskered jaw barely touching her skin, his breath hot against her cheek. "There was a time

when you played a merry tune and I danced because I believed we had something special, Leah.
Then you sent me away. I will not trust you again."

"Then you shouldn't care what I do," she whispered defiantly, forcing herself to meet his gaze.
Her heart beat in her throat, but she'd rather have
this than his indifference.

He moved his body against hers suggestively,
and she felt his erection. His lips twisted in a self-
mocking smile. "Oh, I care. I care too damn
much." He bent his head and traced the line up the
curve of her neck to a sensitive point just below
her ear with his lips.

"Devon." She shivered, a combination of fear
and anticipation.

Then as unexpectedly as he had attacked, he left
her, throwing himself back to his side of the coach.

His eyes burned with anger. His breathing was
labored, as if it had taken a great force of will to
separate himself from her. "Is that the reaction you
wanted from me?"

She flinched at the disdain in his voice. "Devon,
please—"

"Not right now, Leah." He bit out each word.
"It's still too raw within me."

"What is? My liaison with David? Or that I rejected you?"

"I don't know," he said honestly. "It's all jumbled in my mind. I loved you. Out of all the
women in the world, I loved you."

"Perhaps our marriage was a mistake."

"Perhaps."

"Or you can give me another chance to earn your love."

"I can be damned too." His jaw hardened. "You're a witch, Leah. A spell-spinning witch. There was a time that I thought you were different from the others."

"I never lied to you, Devon. You know my family needed me to marry for money."

"Well," he said brutally, "you didn't disappoint them, did you?"

If he had struck her, he could not have inflicted more damage. She sat back and hugged her arms against her waist. Guilt abided deep within her. She had hoped that perhaps Devon still cared for her . . . even a little.

"Leah?"

She refused to acknowledge him.

"Damn it all, Leah, what is it you want? Why can't we be in each other's presence without being at each other's throats?"

"*I* am not at your throat," she corrected. "*You* are the one who is angry."

"I am not angry."

" 'What are you smiling about, Leah?' " she mimicked him in a gruff voice. " 'What game are you playing?' " She frowned. "The only time you have expressed any emotion besides anger is when you are talking about the baby. I made a mistake, Devon. All right," she amended, "I've made *several* mistakes. But I'm my own woman, just like you are your own man. Did you not make mistakes in your life?"

"The rules of the game are different for women, Leah," he returned hotly.

"Yes, and I imagine you change them at will, too!" It felt good to be angry. It had been so long since she'd been capable of standing up for herself.

"Great!" Devon snarled. "I've married a shrew."

The name sent her sputtering. She could barely find her voice, she was so furious. "I-am-not-a-shrew," she ground through clenched teeth. "But if I was, I'd toast you with my tongue right now!"

For one second, her outburst was met with surprised silence, and then Devon started laughing. He roared with laughter, practically doubling up with it.

Indignation reared its ugly head inside of her. This time, she was the one who launched herself across the coach at him, her fists doubled, ready to pound sense into him.

But Devon was quicker than she was. He caught her wrists and twisted her around until she lay across his lap.

Frustrated, she jerked and tugged to break free. He held her until she saw she was not going to overcome him, that she was only adding to his amusement. "I'm furious with you," she said. "How dare you laugh at me!"

He had the audacity to grin at her. "Mayhap this marriage might work after all," he murmured before bending his head down and kissing her.

Leah wanted to hiss and spit like a cat. Anything to push him away, and yet, once their lips touched, it was as if she were in a different time, a different place.

Her resistance evaporated. No one kissed like Devon. Her toes curled with satisfaction as his mouth opened and he deepened the kiss. His hands released hers, the better to pull her closer. Her hands slid around his neck. His tongue stroked hers, and suddenly she was sitting up in his lap and it was hard to tell who was kissing whom.

The magic was there.

He couldn't deny it now. She dared him to.

What was there about Devon that she had not found with any other man? What force drew her to him?

His hand covered her breast. She gasped at the sensitivity of it, breaking the kiss.

Devon pressed his lips against her neck, nibbling the skin. "I could eat you right now."

Leah struggled for sanity. Her body protested. It was too soon. "But we can't," she said, breathless.

"I know." He pulled back, his hands dropping to her waist. But she could feel his arousal pressed against her. He knew it too. Almost drolly, he said, "You will drive me to madness, you know."

"That's true for both of us."

He drew a shuddering breath, his expression bleak. "What do you want, Leah? Do you want a marriage that is something other than in name only? Because if you don't, you are in a precarious position right now."

I want you to love me. "I don't know what I want. But I—" She hesitated.

"Go on."

She searched his face. "But I don't think I want us to be married in name only. I don't think we can be."

His face split into a wide smile. She hastened to add, "But I'm not certain I like the carnal side of marriage."

The smile flattened. "The carnal side?"

She nodded.

He digested her meaning for a moment and then said, "Well, maybe you shouldn't be sitting on my lap if that is the truth."

She slid off immediately, sliding over to the far side of the coach.

Devon crossed his arms and leaned back. "Oh, you don't need to worry I will ravish you on the spot," he said dryly. "That Scottish midwife threatened if I even thought of touching you before your body had a chance to heal, she'd have my bullocks."

"She didn't!" Leah said, startled but not surprised by Old Edith's blunt language.

"She did, and she had every right to do so. She didn't know me. There are men who wouldn't hesitate to force themselves on their wives." He pinned Leah with his gaze. "But I'm not one of them. I can control my emotions. You tell me when the time is right."

Leah studied her hands in her lap. If she had her way, they would never be intimate in spite of the way his kisses could drink her soul, but she sensed she couldn't tell him that. It would be better if she kept it her secret. And when the time came for them to consummate the marriage, she would do as she'd learned to do with Draycutt—close her mind to what was happening and think of other things.

Devon noticed her silence. "Leah, did I say something wrong?"

"No," she replied, forcing a smile.

At that moment, the coach slowed and started turning. "We can't be in London yet," Leah said.

"We are spending the night at an inn."

"I didn't know we planned to stop. I thought you needed to drive straight through."

Devon stretched and started to retie his neckcloth. "You and Ben need a good rest for the night."

"But what of your grandfather?"

"Leah, I'm not going to jeopardize yours and the baby's health in trying to reach him before he dies. I sent a messenger from Rusky's. My aunt and cousin should have it by now. Besides, the weather is too miserable to drive all night."

When he opened the door, she realized he was right. Low fog drifted along the ground. It would be dangerous to travel.

"You could ride on ahead," she suggested.

"Absolutely not," he said, jumping to the ground. "I wouldn't think of letting my wife and child travel alone."

There was a proprietarial air when he said those words. An air that thrilled a bit.

He buttoned his greatcoat while looking around

the busy innyard. Coaches of all shapes and sizes were crowded together.

"I can't drive her closer than this, my lord," the coachman said. "Must have been some event in the area to draw a crowd like this."

"We're close enough," Devon answered. He reached for the baby. "Come now, cover up," he told Leah. "The skies could open on us at any moment."

"Where are we?" she asked, thankful for the red cape that protected her from the damp.

"The Golden Ring."

Leah froze. "You're joking." The Golden Ring was one of the most expensive and exclusive inns on the main road. "Devon, we can't stay here."

"Whyever not?"

"Money." She mouthed the word, not wanting to be overheard by the coachman. One of the lessons she'd learned over the past months was exactly how precious money was.

He took her arm. "You are my responsibility now, Leah. You needn't worry about it."

"But you gave Mrs. Pitney your coin purse."

"I have credit, Leah."

"Don't talk to me like I don't know what credit is. I know all too well. How else do you think my family lives but on credit? Credit they'll never repay."

"And I am not your family." He made an impatient noise before scratching his chin, the gesture endearingly masculine. "I've got to shave. And I want a decent meal."

She hung back. "But, Devon—"

"Here, hold the baby." He plopped Ben into her arms, and before she knew what he was about, he swung her up in his arms, just as the skies opened and rain poured down.

"Cover yourself," Devon shouted.

She pulled the hood of the cape over herself and Ben as Devon's long legs ran toward the door. He'd left his hat in the coach, and his hair was quickly plastered to his head.

Dodging around a coach, he said, "You need to eat better. I've dogs that weigh more than you."

"What a lovely compliment, Lord Huxhold. Where do you get your conversation?"

He grunted his response.

The innkeeper held the door open for them. "Lord Huxhold, what a pleasure!"

"Francis," Devon said, acknowledging the man as he charged out of the rain and into a very busy tap room. "We need your best room and a bottle of claret."

"Yes, of course, my lord."

Devon was just about to set her down when a man's voice with a definite lisp hailed him. "Huxhold! There, see, Whelan, now we have enough people for a game."

The lisp sounded familiar, and there was no mistaking the sudden tension in Devon's hold or the muttered "Damn" under his breath.

Leah peeked out from under the hood of her cape and feared her heart would stop. The man speaking was Lord Carruthers, a braying noble

who always put the worst possible spin on any
story. A tall, thin man, he stood in front of the
roaring hearth surrounded by every Corinthian and
society buck in London.

They all hailed Devon by name with raised tankards, urging him to come over and join them. Leah
ducked back under the hood and snuggled closer
to Devon, one protective hand on her still sleeping
baby's back.

"What are you all doing here?" Devon asked
with less enthusiasm than they had greeted him.

"We came for a race between Armistice and
Wind Cloud that never materialized," Lord Carruthers said. "It was all just a rumor. But what of
you, Huxhold? Where have you been? No one has
seen you around town in months. And what have
we here?" A hand grabbed one of Leah's exposed
ankles.

His question was met by a chorus of catcalls.
"Leave it to Huxhold to find a woman where there
is none!" one man shouted out.

"Well, then he should share!" Carruthers
shouted gleefully and began pulling on Leah's
foot.

She tried to kick him away. Her actions served
only to encourage the man's boldness until
Devon's voice cut through the shouting and nonsense. "Let go of her."

Carruthers released his hold immediately. "I say,
Huxhold, we were just having a bit of sport. No
offense. 'Course I don't see why you would mind

unless," he paused dramatically, "we have caught you *in scandal*."

His pronouncement was greeted with a clattering of tankards on tables and giggling laughter. Having grown up with brothers, Leah was not surprised. Men were childish.

Flush with the others' enthusiasm, Lord Carruthers crowed, "So what is it, Huxhold? Is this another man's wife? Sweeping her off for a secret tryst?" He waved his arms with so much force that he almost lost his balance and tumbled to the floor.

His friends hooted wildly.

Then Devon spoke. Everyone shushed to silence the better to hear him. "As a matter of fact, Carruthers, you have caught me with a wife."

Lord Carruthers laughed with the joy of discovery. Here was gossip he could take back to London and feast on for a week. Leah knew how he thought. "So tell me, who is she?" he asked eagerly.

"My own."

The gentlemen's laughter and catcalls abruptly turned to gasps of astonishment. Lord Carruthers actually dropped his tankard in surprise. "You? Married?"

Devon stepped around him and carried Leah up the stairs.

CHAPTER 10

Safely out of hearing, Francis the innkeeper apologized repeatedly. "They've been drinking since noon, my lord. I shall be fortunate if they don't disturb all my guests."

"I know those men, Francis. I've rarely seen them sober. You'd be best to drug their wine."

"If only I could," the innkeeper lamented.

Leah popped her head out from under the cape, practically overcome with panic. "Are they following us?"

"Not yet," Devon replied with a calmness she was far from feeling.

"I cannot abide Lord Carruthers." She could still feel his grip around her ankle. "Of course, I was never comfortable around his wife either. She is even more nosy."

"But does she drink like he does?" Devon demurred.

Leah gave him a sharp glance, uncertain if he teased. But before she could say anything, Francis opened the door to a spacious bedroom. "Here we are, safe and sound." He lit candles and hurried to personally set a fire in the hearth.

Devon put Leah down and helped her off with her cape. Ben was awake. He blinked in the sudden light. "Poor baby." Leah gave his serious little forehead a kiss. "Lord Carruthers should be horsewhipped—" She paused, looking around. "Why, this room is lovely."

"Aye, my lady," Francis said over his shoulder. "Best room in the house. We call it the Blue Room. The Prince of Wales stays here and, of course, our favorite guests, like Lord Huxhold."

Holding Ben with one arm, Leah ran an appreciative hand over the cherrywood table. The polish reflected the flames of the newly lit fire. She now appreciated the amount of work it took to raise a shine like this.

The canopied bed was also of cherry, with dark blue bed curtains. They matched the French print of the bedcover. Even her parents' home wasn't this luxurious.

The coachman knocked on the still open door. He carried Devon's pack of personal items and Ben's basket from the church. "Thank you, Timothy," Devon said. "That should be all for the night." Two maids carried in hot water and scurried out again.

Timothy hovered by the door. "I should warn you, my lord, there is a rowdy party of lads foxed beyond sense downstairs. They are planning a visit."

"Thank you, Timothy."

"They wouldn't," Leah declared, protectively holding Ben.

"They won't," Devon assured her. "Francis, I want a round of drinks for my friends downstairs. Something heavy like mead or several bottles of good port."

Francis chuckled. "Of course, my lord."

"And how about one of your pheasant dinners for my wife and myself?"

"As you wish."

Timothy left. As Devon stood another moment in the doorway talking in a low voice to Francis, Leah wandered over to the fire, swaying gently to keep Ben happy.

"Why don't you sit down?" Devon suggested to her. He took his shaving kit out of the leather pack Timothy had brought and crossed to the wash-stand.

Leah shook her head. "It feels good to stand." She surveyed the room again. "You have become very rich, then?"

Devon tossed his jacket onto a chair. "I am wealthy." Almost as an afterthought, he said, "I have two ships now and I am planning on purchasing a third." He splashed water in the bowl and prepared to shave. The scent of his citrus shaving soap filled the air. "I can't wait to get rid of this beard."

Leah barely heard him. Three ships. Devon was very wealthy for a man who received no support from his father. If Julian had applied himself the way Devon had, her family would have no worries.

She stared at the scuffed toes of Devon's boots. Her father and brothers were all meticulous about their boots and traded recipes for blacking. They spent hours discussing the merits of champagne versus spit. But Devon didn't care about such things. He'd never given a fig what the world thought of him.

Or did he? Was he truly as independent as he behaved?

She turned her hand over and studied the calluses. When she had run away, she'd thought she could be independent like Devon, that she could make her way in the world. She quickly learned that she'd been wrong. And yet, she'd learned a great deal, too. Lessons she would have never known in the petted hothouse atmosphere of the ton.

One of the first had been that things were rarely as they seemed.

"What are you thinking, Leah?"

She frowned, unwilling to share her thoughts, and found herself looking at a half naked man. Devon had taken off his shirt. Muscles rippled across his chest, and she couldn't help but stare. The one time she'd seen Draycutt unclothed, he'd not looked like that.

"Are you all right, Leah?"

"What?" She came to her senses. "Oh. Yes. Fine."

"You appear dizzy. You should sit down."

Leah moved toward the bed, where she could

only see Devon's back. She sat down. "Yes, I was a little dizzy." Even his back was a marvel to behold. Then she caught a glance at her own image in the mirror. "I'm glad Lord Carruthers didn't discover my identity. I look like a hag."

"You look like anything but a hag." He began scraping the lather from his face, his gaze meeting hers in the mirror. "You've had a child. You appear tired . . . but lovely."

Lovely. The compliment made her suddenly shy—and all too aware of him.

She changed the subject from herself. "My brothers would never shave themselves."

Devon's eyebrows shot up. "What do they do when they are somewhere without a valet?"

"They are never in those circumstances."

He laughed, and even she had to smile. That life seemed so far away. But downstairs were remnants of it.

She turned serious. "Devon, I'm afraid."

"Afraid of what?" He wiped his face, setting the towel down.

Her gaze dropped to her son. Ben looked around the room, his blue eyes still slightly unfocused, but he was very aware. "Of returning," she said softly. "Of what people will say."

Devon crossed to the bed and knelt before her. "Leah, you have nothing to fear. You are returning to London a viscountess. There is power in that title, if you will but use it." He lightly ran his hand over Ben's head. The baby turned in his direction. "You must stare everyone down with the haughtiest of expressions. Do that, and no one will say anything, except to exclaim over what a lucky woman you are to have landed a catch like me."

His words startled a laugh out of her.

But before she could reply, the door practically bounced with a banging from someone on the other side. Devon rose with a sigh. "What is it, Carruthers?"

"How did you know it was me?" he shouted through the door.

Looking at Leah, Devon rolled his eyes and answered, "Who else would it be?"

"Come downstairs for a drink," Carruthers called. "Whelan and Scarleton are here. We all want you to join us. Ask your wife to join us."

Devon frowned, disgusted. "I'd best go down. They won't give us a moment's peace until I do, and you and the baby need rest."

"You need rest, too."

"I'm fine." He reached for the leather pack and pulled out a clean shirt. He pulled it on over his head as he walked to the door. "I'll be down in a moment, you rascal. Uncork a bottle of claret for me."

"And your wife?" the nosy Carruthers quizzed.

"My wife is not to be disturbed," Devon answered in a voice that brooked no argument.

Carruthers accepted defeat gracefully and took himself off.

Devon tied his neckcloth with his customary inattention. Leah placed Ben in the middle of the bed and went to her husband. Gently, she pushed his hands aside and retied the knot decently.

"It needs starch," she said.

"Starch makes my neck itch."

She smiled. "Yes, I imagine so. There." She stepped back to admire her handiwork just as there was another knock on the door. This time it wasn't Lord Carruthers. It was their dinner.

The maids set the meal on the table. Devon grabbed a pheasant leg and took a hurried bite. "Delicious," he pronounced it. "Don't wait up for me. It may take some doing to outdrink Carruthers." He paused long enough to give Leah a very husbandly kiss on the forehead. It had been perfunctory, and yet it filled her with a sense of wellbeing she'd never had before.

It made her feel like a wife.

"Pardon, my lady," Bess, the head maid, said after Devon left. "But where do you want the crib to go?" As she spoke, a stable lad carried one carved out of oak through the door. It was obviously quite old.

"A crib?" Leah said, pleased. "Place it here, beside the bed." This must have been what Devon was discussing with the innkeeper. She scooped Ben up into her arms. "Do you not see?" she whispered. "Your *father* is taking care of us."

Ben didn't act impressed with the title, but Leah felt that she and Devon had crossed a threshold over the course of the afternoon. The magic was there. She'd seen a glimmer of it. But there was something new here, too, something she'd never trusted before. Devon would take care of her. Always. She would have a security in her life that she'd never known before. And in return, she would make him love her again. She would see that he did.

She wanted to laugh and dance and stomp her feet like a crazy woman, she was so giddy with joy.

Another maid appeared at the door, carrying a dress of midnight blue velvet and crisp white lace. "I found this one, Bess. Will it please Lord Hux-hold?"

Bess looked to Leah. "My lady, your husband asked Mr. Francis if he had any dresses." She dropped her voice. "Women leave them for payment from time to time. Do you like it? Lord Hux-hold was most anxious we find something suitable. It may need a stitch or two. Oh, and there are these." She reached into the overlarge pocket of her apron and pulled out a silver-handled brush and some soaps. "Lord Huxhold also asked Mr. Francis for these, but the innkeeper would like to give them to you as a bit of a wedding gift, my lady." She confided, "Lord Huxhold is a great favorite of all the staff here."

The soaps smelled of wild honeysuckle and spring. Leah took the two smooth, round balls in her hands and promptly burst into tears. "I'm sorry," she managed. "I'm just, I mean, it is such a lovely gift. It was so thoughtful, and the dress, too." Ben decided he was hungry and cried along with her.

The two other maids exchanged glances, but

Bess laughed. "It's all right, my lady. I've had three children myself. It's the birthing that makes us so emotional. You cry it out. You'll feel better, and in a day or two you won't be so weepy."

She collected the dirty nappies, promising to return them clean in the morning, and the maids left.

"Oh, Ben, this is better than I ever imagined," she whispered as the door shut. Her son didn't agree. He wanted to eat.

She nursed while sipping a glass of very fine claret and nibbling on pheasant. Devon had been right. The bird was delicious. There was also a pottage of winter vegetables and crusty bread, fresh from the oven. The creamy butter melted on it, and Leah groaned aloud at the sweet taste. Her bread had never been this light or her butter so smooth. In fact, she appreciated the whole meal much more than before because she knew how much work went into the making of it.

Her baby fell asleep, and she snuggled him down in the crib. Mellowed by a second glass of wine, she filled the basin with fresh warm water and bathed.

She'd forgotten what it was like to have all she wanted of the simple things like soap with a rich lather and a heavenly scent or using all the water she wished without worrying about fetching more. Still, when she rinsed her hair over the basin, she poured the discard back into a pitcher and reused it. A year ago, she would not have done so.

She dried her hair in front of the fire before trying on the dress. The bodice was too snug. However, it did allow her to display a generous amount of cleavage, and, she mused, perhaps that wouldn't be such a bad thing. Perhaps Devon would like that.

The hem was another matter. It dragged the ground, but even so it would see her to London, and she would not feel so foolish presenting herself to her new in-laws.

Thoughtfully, Leah undressed, then hung the gown on a peg in the wardrobe. She wasn't certain how the marquess or the other members of Devon's family would accept the marriage. It could be annulled.

She rejected the idea immediately. Devon was an honest man. He'd never misled her except for the time over the duel, but he had explained that, and the explanation had been reasonable. Julian did have a hot temper. She didn't doubt that he hadn't forced Devon to duel.

Now, a year later, she had a radical thought. Perhaps Julian *had* received what he'd begged for. And was that Devon's fault?

She climbed into bed. The feather mattress was like sleeping on a cloud after so many months on a straw pallet. Hugging the pillow, she realized that whether Devon loved her or not, she had done what was right for her child. Yes, everything would work out.

The bottle of wine was empty by the time Devon joined Carruthers in a private room set up for cards. Sitting with Carruthers were Scarleton and Whelan. They were good-natured men who knew each other too well to gamble seriously.

The gentlemen hailed Devon heartily and made a space for him at the table. More wine was poured. Needing his wits, Devon asked for ale. Cards were dealt.

Devon waited. His purpose now was to protect Leah and Ben. He and Leah had discussed the timing of the duel and her pregnancy . . . but now he wondered how much the ton really knew about events of a year ago? After all, it was common knowledge he and Julian had dueled over Leah, but he did not want to initiate the topic.

They played one hand. Then a second. No one said very much, and Devon caught himself smiling. Men loved gossip, but they hated working for it.

Then Carruthers said, "I say, Huxhold, didn't know you had tied the parson's knot. 'Course, we haven't seen you around and about town for ages either."

Devon didn't look up from his cards. "Yes, well." He shrugged.

"Sorry I grabbed her earlier," Carruthers said with boozy bonhomie.

"It is forgotten," Devon answered.

Whelan said, "Carruthers should probably offer an apology to her himself . . . of course, he hasn't been introduced," he hinted.

"That's true," Devon murmured.

His answer obviously frustrated them. Scarleton

cut to the chase. "Well, when did you get married, and who is the lovely bride?"

It was then Devon remembered Scarleton was a good friend of his cousin Rex. Perhaps if one of the others had phrased the question, Devon would have answered it differently. He realized suddenly that anything he said would be repeated to Rex. Not just to society. *Rex.*

Rex and his mother Venetia had long been a thorn in Devon's side. His aunt had never been a nurturing woman. She had no use for the orphaned Devon, who had stood in the way of her precious son's inheriting the title. Over the years, her spiteful little digs about his unworthiness to be the marquess of Kirkeby had gnawed at Devon's self-worth.

With a flash of insight, he realized his marriage would needle her to no end. Especially since she didn't know about it first.

And so, because he knew it would bother his aunt and because few knew of his whereabouts or business for the last months, Devon answered, "Why do you think I left London?"

"To get married?" Scarleton quizzed him in disbelief. "I thought you left London over that duel with Julian Carrollton. What was that about anyway? Oh, yes, his sister. Good-looking filly. Had Redgrave dancing in circles around her."

Tension vibrated through Devon.

"What do you believe happened to her?" Whelan asked with a burp as he poured more wine. He handed the bottle to Carruthers.

"Who can say?" Scarleton answered. "With a Carrollton you never know. Ain't that right, Huxhold? I'd wager glad you put a bullet in Julian. Justice served at last."

Here it was—the moment when Devon could say *I married Leah Carrollton.*

But he didn't. He hesitated. Their marriage would be a shock . . . and not one that people would soon forget. It would forever hover on the edge of people's minds.

Leah had warned him, and he had dismissed her concerns. He did what he wanted to do, when he wished to do it, and he decided now that he wasn't quite ready to tell all.

He'd won the two hands they'd played and the less said, the better. Now it was time to leave for the night. "If you gentleman will excuse me?" He rose, tossing his cards on the table, just as the duke of Weybridge entered the room. "Here, Weybridge, you can take my place."

"But you must let us win our money back," Carruthers protested.

"I have a better idea," Devon answered. "My winnings will go to the wine. I'll send Francis in."

There had been a time when he would have played cards with them until dawn. But as Devon made his way up the stairs to his room, he realized such pursuits had ceased to entertain him roughly around the time he'd first met Leah.

She was asleep when he entered the room. He started to undress. The fire cast a cozy glow, and, in sleep, she appeared as serene as an angel. And as innocent.

Leah. His wife. She could tear his heart out if he let her. She'd done it once already.

He thought about the answer he'd given Scarleton. Perhaps it was not a bad thing for people to believe Leah had run away to join him. It would make sense and add a touch of romance to their story. The ton loved romance.

It would also lead some people to assume Ben was his child.

He wandered over to the crib. To his surprise, Ben was awake. He lay quietly, as if still not certain where he was or his purpose for being here.

Carefully, Devon lifted Ben up into his arms. The baby startled at his touch and then nestled in against his chest. Love and a strong sense of contentment welled inside Devon for this defenseless child.

This was fatherhood.

He'd never thought he'd have the opportunity to experience it.

For a moment, Devon let himself do the unthinkable: he rocked the baby in his arms and pretended Ben was his, all his.

Leah wasn't certain what woke her. The hour was late, probably time for a feeding, but Ben hadn't cried.

The fire in the hearth cast shadows around the room. Leah pushed back her hair and squinted in that direction until she realized she wasn't alone.

The silhouette of a man stood in front of the hearth.

Devon.

He wore nothing but his leather riding breeches. It took a moment before she realized he held Ben in his arms.

She leaned back on both elbows, mesmerized. Devon hadn't realized she was awake. He talked and cooed to the baby in a very low voice, as if they were alone in the world. His hand supported Ben's neck and back so he could see his face. He swayed back and forth in the gentle way she did when she rocked her son.

In that moment, Leah fell in love.

True, she had believed she'd loved Devon before. But those feelings were nothing compared to how her heart expanded and overflowed with love for him now.

Love turned out to be something deeper, finer, and more satisfying than the "magic" she'd felt when they'd first kissed. Love was a private joy that sprang just from being in the presence of the ones she loved.

Devon and Ben.

Happiness erased earlier doubts and fears. It was enough to love . . . and with love came trust.

She spoke his name.

Devon turned to her. "I didn't mean to wake you."

She had not bothered to braid her hair before bed. She shook it back. "You didn't. You seem surprisingly sober."

"Carruthers and the others were already too far gone when I joined them. I drank ale and let them sink under the table."

Ben heard the sound of her voice. He started fussing.

"He's hungry," Devon said. He carried the baby over to her and laid him beside her. Leah rolled on her side. Ben automatically started rooting, and they both laughed.

"He's healthy," Devon said with satisfaction. "Last night, I worried." He started to rise from the bed to give her privacy, but Leah stopped him.

"Don't go."

Devon paused, his expression uncertain.

"Come to bed," she said. "Lay beside us."

She didn't have to ask twice. She heard him slip his breeches down his legs and fold them. He lifted the covers on the other side of the bed. The mattress gave under his weight.

Conscious of his presence, Leah slid the shoulder of her chemise down her arm. Her nipple puckered in the night air until Ben found it and began nursing.

Devon leaned with his chest against her back. His legs aligned with hers as he propped himself up on one elbow to watch Ben.

It was a very private moment. A moment of joining them as a family.

Devon pushed her hair away from her shoulder. "I always dreamed of taking your hair down, one pin at a time."

Leah loved the image.

He rested his head on her shoulder, bringing his arm across her to cradle both her and the baby. "He's a gift, Leah. You will never know what he means to me."

"He's your son," she said softly.

Devon pressed a kiss against her shoulder. "My son."

Happiness filled her. Beneath the covers, his body radiated heat, a heat that warmed her soul. "He is the first of many," she promised.

She'd expected him to agree. When he didn't reply, she glanced over her shoulder, and froze.

The expression in his eyes had turned so bleak that it frightened her. "Is something wrong?"

He startled, as if being recalled to the present. "No, nothing." But his smile seemed forced.

"Devon—?" she started but he cut her off.

"I must sleep, Leah. Tomorrow will be an important day. Tomorrow, I introduce you to my family." He lay on his side and did exactly that, but his arm still held her close.

Ben finished and fell asleep at her breast, and it felt so good to snuggle him that she did not move him to the crib. Instead, she lay awake, sandwiched between her son and her husband, troubled by Devon's sudden withdrawal.

Devon rose first. The sound of his bathing woke Leah. Her eyes had trouble opening. Then Ben started crying, and she had no choice.

"I don't know if I will ever catch up on my sleep," she muttered.

He'd moved the privacy screen in front of the fire, but in the mirror over the vanity Leah could see his large body scrunched up in the tub. Lather from the citrus soap he favored covered his neck and chest. Its scent drifted through the air to her.

If she could see him, he could see her. Their gazes met, then his lowered to where her bodice still hung open, exposing the generous curve of her breasts.

A lazy smile appeared on his lips a second before he drew a breath and sunk down in the tub to wash off the bubbles. His legs came out over the edge. Water sloshed on the floor, and he looked so comical that she couldn't help but laugh. The doubts and misgivings that had plagued her sleep now seemed as nothing in the light of day.

Ben didn't want to wait any longer. She tended to him while Devon rose from the tub and dried himself.

Leah was very aware that on the other side of the screen he was naked. His body had felt good against hers last night. Comforting.

Devon dressed with economical movements. He wasn't given to vanity. He combed his wet hair back with his fingers. "I'll have Francis pack another hamper with bread, cheese, and ale for the road today. If we push it, we can make London by late afternoon. Can you be ready in half an hour?"

"Yes."

"Good." He paused long enough to rub Ben's cheek with his thumb before he opened the door.

"I'll send Bess up to help you. I'll be waiting for you downstairs."

He left. A moment later, there was a knock, and at Leah's call, Bess entered. With Bess's help, Leah was dressed in no time. Bess twisted her hair up and pinned it in place. Leah was pleased with how good the style looked. She didn't have gloves, or jewels, or even a reticule, and she still wore her half boots, more scruffy than Devon's and worse for wear, but she felt good about herself.

She'd dressed Ben in a soft wool dress donated from the church, and she swaddled his body in a blanket before wrapping him again in the fleece. She was ready to go, her red cape over her shoulders.

Downstairs, the tap room was surprisingly busy. Good-natured conversation filled the air, along with the shouting of orders. Ostlers rubbed elbows with lords, farmers with coachmen. She had assumed the drinkers would still be asleep this early in the morning.

Leah paused in the doorway, a step higher than everyone else, and searched the room for Devon. She didn't see him . . . but a curious thing did happen.

The two men conversing closest to her suddenly broke off their conversation. They stepped back, one of them tipping his hat. Then another group noticed her and fell silent, as did another and another and another until the general hubbub died completely and the room was filled with slack-jawed men.

No entrance Leah had ever made during her heyday as a debutante had created this sort of reaction. She shifted uneasily, her baby in her arms.

Then Lord Carruthers, whose bloodshot eyes indicated that he suffered from the disagreeable effects of too much wine, broke the silence. "Damn me, but it is Leah Carrollton."

She had been discovered.

CHAPTER 11

Leah wanted to retreat back to the safety of the room, but Devon came in the front door at the exact moment her name was repeated by Carruthers's cronies.

His keen gaze quickly assessed the situation. He pushed his way through the crowd to her side, coming up on the step beside her. "Here, let me take the baby."

Mutely, Leah handed Ben to him. "Courage," he said beneath his breath.

She nodded. He took her arm at the elbow and escorted her down into their midst. Her legs wobbled like wire springs, but she held her head high.

The gentlemen took a step back, clearing a path for them. Several doffed their hats as she passed.

She whispered to Devon, "Why must they stare?"

"You don't know?" he asked, bemused.

Before she could answer, they came abreast of Lord Carruthers. Leah decided that it was now or never. After all, the man had been the first to recognize her. There was no sense in further pretense.

"Lord Carruthers," she said in formal greeting.

"Miss Carrollton," he scrambled to acknowledge, as if he'd been shocked that she'd spoken to him.

"No, not Carrollton," Devon corrected him. "This is my wife, Lady Huxhold."

If Lord Carruthers had been holding another tankard of ale, he would have dropped it, just as he had the night before. He turned to Lord Weybridge and Lord Scarleton as if to see if they confirmed that his ears didn't lie. They were as stunned as he was.

"Come, Leah, we must make haste for London," Devon said.

"Please give my best to your wife," she said quietly before her husband hurried her toward the door.

Outside, Devon said, "I've never seen Carruthers speechless, and now I have witnessed it twice." He helped Leah into the coach and handed her the baby before climbing in. "Last night he and the others quizzed me about your identity." He knocked on the wall, a signal for the driver to go.

"Well, the secret is out," she said ruefully as she settled Ben in her arms.

"It couldn't be kept forever."

"No," she agreed. "It was so strange, though, the way they stared at me even before they realized who I was."

"You've changed, Leah. You don't resemble the girl you were a year ago."

His words challenged her. "Changed in what way?" She saw no difference other than the fact that she felt a lifetime older, not much wiser, and far too aware of the world's machinations and her limited place in it.

"It's in your face. You've lost the girlishness."

She sighed. "Yes, I've lost that freshness."

"No, you've lost the doe-eyed gaze of a debutante. There is a maturity about you now. A serenity even. Seeing you on that step, your child in your arms, reminded every man in that room of an Italian Madonna. I knew you were frightened, but no one else did. If anything, your vulnerability made every man's heart in that room beat a little faster."

What about you? Leah wanted to ask. *Did your heart beat faster?* But she didn't. She would have posed such a question to the man who had been in bed beside her last night, the man who had cradled her with his body while she nursed their son.

But she sensed Devon was not that man this morning. His earlier reserve had returned. He seemed preoccupied. His hand rested palm down on the seat between them, but he made no move to touch her.

He said, "Carruthers will hit town before nightfall. I'd wager by the morrow, everyone will have learned of our marriage."

Leah thought of her parents, her brothers. "I

wonder if Lord Carruthers is the right person to spread the news."

"No, you wonder what will happen when Julian learns of our marriage."

"Yes," she admitted. "What will happen?"

"That depends on him."

They made good time, considering the poor condition of the road. The team was fresh, and Devon had given orders for the coachman to push them as hard as he could, changing teams as often as necessary.

The closer they drove to London, the more quiet Devon became. He held Ben most of the way. The growing bond between them helped settle Leah's anxieties about the future. She'd decided to hold all questions until after Devon saw his grandfather.

Still, she couldn't help asking, "Has it been a long time since you've seen your grandfather?"

"Maybe a year." A year. Since he'd left London over the duel.

There was an edge to his voice that didn't invite confidences. She settled back onto the seat, burdened by her own doubts.

Gradually, the scenery became more populated, the road busier. Leah had traveled this road to London several times in her life, but on this trip she noticed things she'd never seen before. Now she identified with the faces along the street as the coach entered the city. She was no longer blind to the poverty or to the number of motherless children running loose on the streets.

As they drove by a woman sitting right on the edge of the road nursing her baby and drinking gin, Leah had to reach for Ben and hold him close.

"Leah, are you feeling ill?" Devon asked. "Your face has gone white."

"I just saw something that distressed me."

"What?"

She started to answer, and then paused. Devon wouldn't understand. No one who hadn't experienced it could understand the fear and the uncertainty of a woman alone. "It was nothing," she murmured.

He looked as if he might challenge her, but they were moving into a smarter section of town and toward Montclef, the marquess of Kirkeby's home in Pall Mall.

Her family claimed that Montclef was one of those treasures the Marshalls had stolen from the Carrolltons. She had never thought to walk through its doors and now, she could someday be its mistress.

The coach rolled to a stop, and Leah caught her breath. The gray stone porticos seemed to reach to the sky. Windows stretched across the house, lit by what seemed to be a thousand candles in the gloom of the overcast day. This wasn't a house. It was a palace.

Devon spoke. "There's no black wreath hanging on the door. We've made it in time."

The lacquered door opened. A butler and several footmen came out on the steps.

Devon didn't wait for the coachman to open the

carriage door but did so himself. He jumped down. Leah lifted Ben out of the drawer where he'd been sleeping. She drew a steadying breath. In minutes, she would be meeting her new in-laws.

She wished she could hide in the coach.

"Wills," Devon said, acknowledging the butler. "How is my grandfather?"

"Holding on, my lord. We are most relieved to see you. You are not a moment too soon." Wills was of middle age, with a receding hairline. He was dressed in starched black, while the footmen wore the Kirkeby colors of green and gold.

"See that this coach is returned to Lord Ruskin with my apologies," Devon told him. "I will settle with him later."

"Very good, my lord. The rest of the family is with the marquess now."

"Thank you, Wills." Devon reached to take Leah's arm and help her from the coach, telling the butler almost as an afterthought, "And prepare rooms for my wife and me. We will be staying indefinitely."

If Devon had announced that Napoleon was now king of England, Wills and the footmen would not have been more surprised. Wills was the first to shut his gaping mouth. He bowed to Leah, standing on the walk beside the coach. "Welcome to Montclef, my lady."

"Thank you," she murmured, deciding the less said, the better.

"And we'll need a crib in the room," Devon added absently, seemingly unaware of the impact his words were having on the servants. Instead, his focus was on his grandfather. "This way," he said to Leah, guiding her through the front door.

His steps echoed on the black and white marble tiles of the front hall. A cantilevered staircase of carved walnut swept down into the hall from the floors above.

A footman stepped forward for Devon's coat and hat and Leah's cape. She was doubly thankful for the dress. Her presence was having a more dramatic reaction than she had anticipated, and she hadn't even met Lady Vainhope or her son yet.

They started up the stairs. Portraits of Marshall ancestors frowned down upon them as they made their way. Everything she saw, from the crystal wall sconces, the shining mirrors, to the thick carpet covering the stairs spoke of wealth. Immense wealth.

The hall at the top of the stairs had rooms off to either side and a set of double doors at the end guarded by a footman. Devon started walking determinedly toward those doors. Leah trailed behind. She caught sight of herself in a brass mirror and shifted Ben in her arms to tuck in a stray tendril of hair.

In moments, she would meet her new family. She prayed she didn't faint dead away.

The footman bowed and opened the doors. On the other side was a small sitting room and another set of double doors. Four people were gathered there, including Rex, Devon's cousin, and Rex's mother, Venetia Trelayne, Lady Vainhope. She turned as the door opened. Arrogant, top lofty, disdainful, she prided herself on being one of society's sticklers.

Leah had always avoided her and even now attempted to hide behind Devon. She made sure that her son's sleeping head was safely covered. Fortunately, Lady Vainhope had other things on her mind and did not recognize Leah.

Instead, her hazel green eyes, so much like Devon's own, skewered him. "So, you decided to make an appearance."

Devon didn't respond to the chill in her voice. Instead he said easily, "Good afternoon, Aunt Venetia," as if they had just parted company the day before. He nodded to his cousin. "Rex."

Rex Trelayne was Venetia's only son and the current Lord Vainhope. Slimmer than Devon, he had the Marshall good looks, although his mouth had his mother's tight-lipped set of disapproval.

Devon acknowledged a short man with fuzzy red hair. "I've made it, Brewster," he said to his grandfather's man of business.

"Thank the Lord," Mr. Brewster said earnestly. "This is Dr. Partridge." He waved a gray-haired gentleman forward. "You remember him. He has been the marquess's physician for years."

"Decades actually," Dr. Partridge said easily. "It's good to see you again, Lord Huxhold, in spite of the circumstances."

"Thank you for all you have done," Devon said, holding out his hand.

"I wish I could do more," Dr. Partridge confided gravely.

"What exactly is wrong with him?" Devon asked.

Dr. Partridge frowned. "I can find nothing medically. I thought perhaps it was advanced age. But at seventy-three he is in excellent physical health."

"You must suspect something," Devon said.

Brewster answered. "Dr. Partridge speculates that the marquess is willing himself to die."

"My grandfather? Giving up?" Devon shook his head. "He vowed to outlive us all."

"That was until Mrs. Oswald died," Lady Vainhope said stiffly.

"Mrs. Oswald?" Devon repeated her name as if it were unfamiliar.

"His mistress," she explained in a telling tone.

"Grandfather?" Devon almost laughed.

"It's no joke, coz," Rex said. "Grandfather met her less than a year ago. They became fast friends, and when she passed away unexpectedly three weeks ago, he went into a decline. We thought he'd recover, but he's only grown worse."

"It's ridiculous for Father to be so goose-eyed over a woman at his age," Lady Vainhope said.

"Men are goose-eyed at every age," Mr. Brewster answered.

"Yes, Mother, especially when the woman is lovely," Rex agreed, bowing to Leah and making her presence known to everyone in the room.

The compliment caught her off guard. This didn't seem the time or place, but that didn't bother Lord Vainhope. He held out his hand. "I am Dev's cousin, Rex Trelayne, and you are—?"

"My wife," Devon answered.

The servants' earlier reactions were mild compared to Rex's frozen smile or Lady Vainhope's almost apoplectic fit. "You must be joking!" she managed to sputter out.

"No," Devon said, apparently taking pleasure in the concise reply. He turned to Dr. Partridge. "I wish to see my grandfather now."

"Absolutely not," Lady Vainhope declared. "Not until you explain yourself."

"Aunt, I haven't explained myself for twenty years. I'm not starting now. Be so good as to come with us, Dr. Partridge. Brewster, you wait here, and Rex, mind your mother."

Lady Vainhope stepped in front of the door. "No, I will not allow it. Not until you tell me who this woman is, her family, her background."

Devon's eyes took on an unholy light, and Leah feared the worst. She was right. "My wife is the former Leah Carrollton. You know the Carrolltons, don't you, Aunt? I believe Leah's grandmother gave you the cut direct once when you had your first season and you haven't stopped talking of it."

"Carrollton?" Lady Vainhope choked on the word.

Devon used his aunt's moment of shock to open the door. "Come, Leah. You, also, Dr. Partridge."

Lady Vainhope found her voice as Leah slid through the door followed by the bespectacled physician. "Wait! You can't take *her* in there!

What was that bundle she carried in her arms?" she asked to the room in general.

Devon shut the door, blocking her protests. They stood in the bedroom. It was curtained dark. Several wall sconces and a coal fire in the hearth provided the only light. The air smelled of medicinals and incense.

The maid sitting in a chair by the bed came to her feet and curtsied.

"Did he eat, Elsie?" Dr. Partridge asked.

She picked up a bowl from a tray on the bedside table and lifted the spoon to show that the bowl's contents were still there. "I couldn't cajole a spoonful past his lips. Mrs. Oswald could have, but I don't seem to have the gift."

Dr. Partridge frowned. In a low voice, he confided to Devon, "He hasn't eaten well since her death. This is what I mean about willing himself to die." He raised his voice. "Thank you, Elsie. Take the tray and leave us a moment, please."

The maid left the room. As the door opened and closed, Leah could still hear Lady Vainhope fussing.

Dr. Partridge crossed to the opposite side of the bed. "Kirkeby, you have visitors."

The man lying in the middle of the bed did not respond.

Leah had only seen Lord Kirkeby once in her life, but she remembered him as a robust man, almost as tall as Devon, with a headful of silver hair and Lady Vainhope's pugnacious attitude.

The man in the bed was nothing like that. His

skin was now so white that it appeared almost translucent. His eyes were closed; his hands were folded on top of the bedclothes.

Devon had gone very still. Leah touched his arm, conveying her sympathies.

Ben was starting to wake. His head moved against her shoulder, but then he settled back down.

Dr. Partridge raised his voice. "Kirkeby? Your grandson is here. Don't you wish to see him?"

Lord Kirkeby moved. First, he lifted a finger, and then he frowned before drawing in a harsh breath. He didn't open his eyes.

Devon approached the bed. "Grandfather, you sent for me. I am here."

His grandfather responded to his voice. He stiffened and then ever so slowly opened his eyes.

They were the same hazel green as Devon's. They weren't even faded by age, but there were tired lines around them and a deep sadness in their depths. He turned toward the sound of Devon's voice, and then his eyes lit with interest.

"Robin, my beloved son."

The air suddenly seemed sucked from the room. Robin had been Devon's father.

Dr. Partridge frowned. Devon appeared stricken. "Not Robin, Grandfather. It's Devon, his son."

"Aye, Devon." The smile faded from Lord Kirkeby's face. "You have changed. You look the very image of your father."

"I am about his age when he died."

"Yes, Robin is dead," Lord Kirkeby repeated as if remembering.

Suddenly, Devon reached across the bedspread to clasp his grandfather's hand. "I'm sorry, Grandfather. I'm sorry I wasn't more of what you wanted me to be."

The raw pain and emotion in her husband's voice alarmed Leah. She had not realized this was inside her confident, carefree Devon. She stepped forward, needing to touch him, to reassure him.

Lord Kirkeby shook his head. "Not . . . your . . . fault," he said wearily. "I . . . shouldn't . . . have . . . kept . . . secrets."

Devon lowered his head. "I was too full of pride."

Again, there was a flash of intelligence, of a will to live in his grandfather's eyes. "I was too." He paused and then said, "I missed you."

"I would have come at any time. You had only to send for me."

"Couldn't."

"Couldn't?" Devon asked.

"Wouldn't," his grandfather answered. He squeezed Devon's hand. "Arrie told me I was a fool." He spoke with difficulty, his voice raspy, weak. "She said I should have called you back years ago, but I didn't listen to her. She said I'd be sorry." He drew a deep, labored breath. "The truth . . . I didn't think you'd come."

"I would have. I should have. In fact, I should have been the one to breach the gap between us."

Lord Kirkeby shushed him with a wave of his hand. "It doesn't matter now."

"But it does," Devon said. A tear escaped from the corner of his eye.

That single tear moved Leah. It explained more than words what Devon was feeling. A sense of protectiveness rose inside her. Shifting Ben's weight to one arm, she placed her hand on Devon's shoulder.

Her movement brought her to Lord Kirkeby's attention. "Who is this?" he asked.

"My wife." This time when Devon said those words, they were softer, kinder than when he'd made the same announcement to his aunt.

"You've married?" Lord Kirkeby turned his head to take a full, good look at Leah.

"Yes," Devon responded almost defensively.

His grandfather weakly waved a finger. "I did not mean it that way, Huxhold. I am surprised. I had thought you incapable of settling on just one."

He'd said the words in jest and, again, there was a glimmer of the man he had once been. "Come closer, girl. Let me see you."

Leah handed the baby to Devon and dutifully leaned over the bed.

"Lovely," Lord Kirkeby said admiringly. "What is your name, girl?"

"Leah." She deliberately left off the Carrollton.

"Huxhold favors blondes. What spell did you weave to capture his notice? I've had women ask me that question for years."

She smiled at his humor and, alluding to their

meeting by the pigpen, said, "My lord, the truth is that Devon knocked me off my feet."

Her words surprised a chuckle out of Devon. "I have something else to show you, Grandfather." He laid Ben down on the bed and unfolded the fleece blanket.

"What is it?" Lord Kirkeby asked tiredly, staring up at the bed canopy.

"A baby." Devon said the words as if he were revealing the miracle of the ages.

"A baby?" Lord Kirkeby rolled his head in Devon's direction. "You, Devon? Boy or girl?" He sounded almost desperate for the answer.

"Boy."

With an energy Leah had not thought he possessed, Lord Kirkeby's face broke into a wreath of smiles. "A boy," he whispered. Devon nodded.

Something was being communicated between the grandfather and his grandson. Something Leah did not understand.

Lord Kirkeby tried to sit up, the better to see Ben. Both Devon and Dr. Partridge came to his aid, the doctor plumping pillows behind him. "Did you hear that, Partridge?" Lord Kirkeby asked, his voice growing more animated and strong. "Is it possible? Could it be?"

"Anything is possible," Dr. Partridge said. "We thought at the time that we didn't know for sure."

"Let me see the baby," Lord Kirkeby ordered gruffly. "Hold him up."

Leah's every instinct warned her to snatch her baby back, but Devon sat on the bed, blocking her access to Ben. Gently, he raised Ben up for his grandfather to see, holding him under his arms.

Ben was awake. He looked around with a newborn's distracted air. His bare feet dangled helplessly beneath the hem of his baby dress.

Lord Kirkeby raised his head. He reached out and carefully placed his aged hand on top of Ben's head. "He has a full head of hair, just like you did. In fact, he is the very image of you."

Devon replied, "His name is Benjamin. Benjamin Marshall."

Lord Kirkeby smiled with fierce pride. "Benjamin." He dropped his hand to the mattress. His gaze met Devon's. "They were wrong. They were *all* wrong."

"Yes." Devon cradled Ben in his arms.

Lord Kirkeby chuckled. It appeared to Leah that he was growing stronger by the minute even as she was feeling more and more uneasy.

"Rex will not be happy," Lord Kirkeby said.

"Aunt Venetia will be even more upset," Devon responded.

"Yes, she will." Lord Kirkeby relaxed his head back on the pillow. Tears came to his eyes. "But I am pleased. Well pleased. All this time wasted," he added sadly.

"No, not wasted," Devon countered, cradling Ben in his arms. "I had to become a man and I have, Grandfather. You will never be disappointed in me again. I promise."

"I can't be disappointed. You have brought me your son. It is the best gift I could have ever received." His voice was starting to fade now. Dr. Partridge hovered over him, but he shooed the physician back. "My Arrie said, in the end, our pride shouldn't matter when it comes to family." Suddenly, his face collapsed into lines of pain. He turned his gaze to Leah. "Do you love your wife, Devon?" He didn't wait for an answer but confided, "I didn't love mine. I didn't know what love was until I loved Arrie, and now she is gone. It hurts here." He touched his heart with a weak fist.

Leah was humbled by the man's pain. Her parents loved each other that much. She understood what the depths of that type of love were.

Ben broke the moment by crying. It was almost time for his dinner, and he'd been patient long enough.

Lord Kirkcby raised his eyebrows. "He has a healthy set of lungs."

"He's very strong," Devon assured him as Ben's hunger cries gained momentum.

His grandfather chuckled, pleased with the information.

The door to the bedroom burst open.

Lady Vainhope charged in, Rex and Mr. Brewster following.

"What is that crying? Father!" she declared dramatically. "What has he done to you?"

Devon stood, Ben screaming with newborn anger in his arms. "Everything is fine, Venetia."

His aunt skidded to a stop. She frowned at Ben as if he were the devil incarnate. "Whose baby is this?"

"Devon's son," Lord Kirkeby said decisively.

"Son?" The color drained from Lady Vainhope's face. "It can't be."

"Not here, Aunt Venetia," Devon said tightly.

"Why not here?" she demanded, her voice shrill. She whirled to face her father. "Do you know whom he has married?" she demanded in ringing tones. "I didn't recognize the face at first, but once I heard the name—"

"Aunt Venetia," Devon warned.

"Yes, Lady Vainhope," Dr. Partridge hurried to add. "This is not the time. Lord Kirkeby needs his rest."

But the marquess was having none of that. He actually sat up. "I don't care who she is—" he started, his eyes brightening with anger.

"She's a *Carrollton*!" Venetia practically spit Leah's family name into the air.

"*She* doesn't matter," Lord Kirkeby said. "This child is my grandson. He is a direct descendent of myself and Robin."

"But, Father, it is impossible! Devon can't have children. You know he can't."

Leah turned to Devon. His face could have been carved from stone. She reached for Ben with the same fierceness of a she-wolf protecting her cub. Devon readily gave him up, his attention on his grandfather.

"Why do you believe he can't?" Lord Kirkeby challenged his daughter. "Because you don't wish him to? Well, he has." He pointed a gnarled finger in Ben's direction. "I know my blood. That child is Robin's grandson."

Lady Vainhope immediately denied the possibility. Dr. Partridge started in about how no one knew for sure that Devon couldn't sire children. It had all been speculation, according to him. Rex appeared stunned, and Leah realized that Devon's claim that Ben was his natural child had changed Rex's prospects.

Slowly, she turned to face Devon. Their gazes met. He had not told her. He had known he couldn't have children but had deliberately neglected to tell her everything.

She ran from the room, holding her child close.

CHAPTER 12

Leah was out into the hallway and past the footman before Devon caught her.

His hand hooked her arm. "Don't say anything. Not one word," he ordered quietly.

They had an audience. Rex and Mr. Brewster had followed Devon out. They and the footman stared with obvious interest. Leah could hear Lady Vainhope haranguing her father, her concerns over her son's lost inheritance evident. Dr. Partridge repeatedly asked her to consider her father's welfare and to leave. She ignored him.

Adding to the confusion was Ben's demanding cry.

At that moment, a robust woman dressed in the Kirkeby green and gold stepped out of a room down the hallway. "Lord Huxhold," she greeted him merrily. "I have your rooms prepared."

"You are wonderful, Mrs. Knowles," Devon responded, moving his hand to the small of Leah's back and pushing her in the woman's direction.

"My son claims to be starved to death."

My son. Before when he'd said it, Leah had been thrilled. Now, it sounded ominous.

Mrs. Knowles chuckled. "Aye, my lord, those little ones can't wait. Come in here, my lady, and have the chance to wipe the dust of travel from your feet."

As Devon directed Leah into the bedroom, away from too observant eyes, he introduced Mrs. Knowles as the housekeeper.

"Anything you wish, my lady, you have only to ask. The staff is pleased beyond measure that Lord Huxhold has taken himself a wife." If she thought it odd the wife should appear without any fanfare, she didn't relay her concerns in words or deed.

Leah slipped gratefully through the door and into a lovely room, decorated in shades of gold and cream. A cheery fire burned in the hearth, and several oil lamps had been lit to dispel the late afternoon gloom. Vases of hothouse flowers graced side tables and the mantel.

"The nursery is through here," Mrs. Knowles said, opening the door on a charmingly peaceful room with white curtains and sky blue walls.

"Let me see to Ben," Leah murmured and hurried into the nursery without waiting for a response from Devon. She shut the door, thankful for the privacy. She needed a chance to frame her thoughts. Devon's claim had caught her completely by surprise. One part of her was furious, and another, confused.

On the other side of the door, she could hear

him talking to Mrs. Knowles. They spoke of pleasantries until she asked after his luggage. Leah listened as he spun a tale of their both being in Scotland when the summons had arrived to return to London. His story sounded so plausible that Leah could almost believe it.

Just as she'd believed Draycutt had cared for her. Or that Devon would not let harm come to her brother.

She closed her eyes. Had she once again been taken in by another charming rogue? Even after Ben finished and nodded off, she sat still, reeling from how easily Devon had told his lies.

The door had closed behind Mrs. Knowles some time ago. Leah knew she could not hide forever.

Carefully, she laid Ben in the elaborately carved crib. Animals created out of inlaid wood danced around its base. It must have been in the family for generations. She took a moment to steady the angry beat of her heart and then opened the door.

Devon waited on the bed, one booted leg dangling over the footboard.

She stood in the doorway, unable to take another step closer. "Why did you marry me?"

His expression grew guarded. "You know why."

"Remind me."

He considered her for a moment before saying, "To take care of Ben."

A jab of disillusionment knifed through her. Last night, she had begun to hope there was something more, that what had once been between them could be again. She'd been played a fool. "Or to claim him as your own?" she accused coolly.

Devon's jaw hardened. "You heard Dr. Partridge. No one knows for certain that I can't sire children."

"I heard Dr. Partridge say what he said because he believes Ben *is* yours. And you want them to believe that, don't you?"

"How could I not?" he demanded, swinging his leg around so that he could stand. "My grandfather is dying, Leah. He's only wanted one thing in life from me. I gave it to him."

"But why didn't you tell me you couldn't have children? Why did you make a point of saying that Ben could not inherit—and then claim him as your own blood in front of your family?"

"He can't inherit. When the bloodlines are searched in Parliament, it would be challenged." He raked his hand through his hair in frustration. "Don't you understand, Leah? I didn't know those words were going to come from my mouth until I said them. But in the end, it doesn't matter. I'll confess the truth, but not until Grandfather—" He stopped, unable to voice the word *dies*. He looked away from her, his expression solemn.

"Your aunt is so angry. She frightens me."

"Don't worry about her."

"Don't worry?" She took a step into the room. "Devon, she is *known* for her spiteful temper. She has ruined people."

"Then think how delighted she will be when she learns the truth."

Leah gave him a sharp glance. "You would tell her?"

"Eventually." He frowned, suddenly restless, his gaze shifting from her. A liquor cabinet sat next to the fireplace. He walked over to it and pulled out a decanter of wine. "I'm going to have a glass of this. Would you like one?"

"No," she answered impatiently as he poured wine into a crystal glass. "When are you going to tell her?"

The look he shot her spoke louder than words. He didn't like to be pushed. She didn't care. Her son's well-being was at stake.

"I'll tell her when I can safely assume Grandfather won't discover the truth." He drained the glass and started to pour himself another. "She'll be overjoyed. There's only one thing Venetia has wanted in life and that is the title."

"But she's a woman. She could never have the title."

"Venetia doesn't see herself as a mere woman," Devon answered. "In fact, she resented my father because he could have it. She felt him unworthy, and if the truth were known, she probably was more responsible than he was. I remind her too much of my father and my flighty mother. That's how she always refers to her—'flighty.' It's one of the many grudges my aunt holds against me. That and the fact that I stand in the way of her son's opportunity to claim the title. Her one consolation is that her son and her grandsons will be the future marquess of Kirkeby."

"Except now she believes Ben stands in her way," Leah reminded him softly.

"Don't worry about it, Leah. You are now a Marshall. You are free to join our favorite pastime of deceiving each other through trick or roguery. The prize is the Kirkeby fortune. Or whatever you can milk out of Grandfather by catering to his whims."

"Or by telling him what he wants to hear," she added quietly.

"No," Devon said soberly. "I wouldn't use Ben in that manner."

"How do I know?"

He swore softly. "Leah, I was the one in the family who always refused to play the games."

"And yet you wish a reconciliation."

"I do." His eyes snapped with anger. "I swear, you could interrogate a saint and find him lacking, and I'm no saint. My grandfather is my only family who matters to me. He's the living representation of my father. Do you think Grandfather is the only one who misses my parents?"

He turned from her as if needing a moment. When he spoke, his voice was hoarse with emotion. "I've been alone since their accident. I don't blame my grandfather. He's no different than other men of his age. He was trained to think of title and family duty first. You heard him. He admits freely he never knew what love was. Certainly he's never shown me any. But my parents did. I was seven when they died, old enough to remember. Is it wrong to want for Ben all the security a boy needs in life?"

His question tore into her soul. All her life, she'd lived with the tragic results of that fateful accident. It had destroyed her father . . . but she had never thought of what it had meant to Devon.

He set the empty wine glass on the mantel. "After my parents died, he doted on me. He took me everywhere with him. Then I came down with the fever, and I almost lost my life. Dr. Partridge brought in a specialist who examined me. They knew at that time that I would recover, but the fear was that the fever would have lasting effects. When my grandfather heard that I might not be able to sire children he said I might as well be dead."

"No," Leah murmured softly.

"He said it right in front of me." Devon shook his head. "I understand why Venetia is the way she is. Grandfather dismissed her talent and her intelligence. She was a non-person, good for only one thing, breeding children. Then overnight, I became a non-person, too. I was no longer the favored heir. Rex was. Rex was the Marshalls' future, and Grandfather set about preparing him for the role. He arranged Rex's marriage, and the day Rex's son was born, Grandfather was visibly relieved."

"And now you have a son," Leah observed sadly.

Annoyance flashed across Devon's face. "It is not the only reason I married you."

Hope rose in Leah. "What is the other reason?"

"You needed someone to take care of you."

But not because he loved her. Not because of the magic. "Oh, yes. Of course." She ran her hand along the polished wood of the bedpost, swallowing bitter disappointment.

"Well," she said, mustering her pride, "I thank you for telling me. It explains a great deal."

His gaze narrowed suspiciously. "About my family?"

"About you."

"What about me?"

Leah smiled tightly. "It explains why you were the heir and your family never pushed you to marry. The mamas on the Marriage Market always wondered, you know."

"No, I didn't know."

"You did." She was certain of it. When he didn't contradict her, she added, "Plus, it explains your reputation for womanizing."

Now she had his complete attention. "I don't understand what you mean," he hedged.

"Yes, you do," she replied lightly. "Don't you remember the day on the wharves? You said something strange. I questioned you on it because it seemed an odd statement. You said you were as complete a man as Rex in every way."

"I wasn't talking about my ability to have children," he returned levelly, but his eyes were bright with suppressed fury.

"You weren't? My mistake then. But there is no

mistaking that you are known as a lover. An infamous lover."

"How interesting of you to say that, the one woman to refuse me."

She crossed her arms against her stomach protectively. "How could I refuse what was never asked?"

"Oh, I asked, Leah. I offered you everything."

"Or were you just rebelling against your family by chasing the Carrollton chit?"

Her barb struck home. His hands clenched into fists. "Astute, Leah, very astute. Do you have any other theories you wish to convey?"

"Yes," she said. Tears of anger stung her eyes. She battled them back. It was important that she appear in control in front of him. "I believe you wanted a child more than anything. That's why you knew none of your former lovers had become pregnant. Because it mattered to you. Nor did you mind the rumors circulating that you had fathered children."

That last had been a blind stab. She was surprised when he drew back as if she'd physically assaulted him.

He straightened. "Ben is mine, Leah. I felt him draw his first breath, here in my hands. If it hadn't been for me, he would not be alive. I have more right to him than any other man alive. Or Draycutt, for that matter."

He was right.

The ugliness of her doubts assailed her. She sat on the edge of the bed, her legs weak, like two straws that could no longer hold her weight.

Devon crossed to stand in front of her. "Grandfather is dying, Leah. He's always missed his son, but right now, he feels it more keenly than before. You heard him call me Robin. Perhaps I am wrong, but the man I saw today is a shadow of the man I once knew. He's carrying deep regrets, and I don't want him to die that way. If it gives him peace during the last moments of his life, why can't we pretend? It will only be for a matter of days."

"But it's not the truth, Devon."

"To the devil with the truth! The truth never got anyone anywhere. Look at you. Has the truth served you well?"

"What you are doing is wrong. I fear the consequences."

Devon knelt in front of her. "I took a vow to protect you. I won't let anything happen. It is only for a short time, Leah. You saw him. Can you deny him this last happiness?"

The tears did come now. She couldn't hold them back. She swiped them away with one hand. "But can I trust you?"

It was a rhetorical question, asked of the world in general, but her husband's answer was very personal. "I'm not the one who took a lover, Leah. I'm not the one who betrayed the other."

There it was. The anger. She'd sensed it in him from the beginning, and now it spiraled around her, threatening her. "Is that what this is about?" she whispered. "Are you punishing me?"

He came to his feet with a growl of outrage. When Leah held up her hand as if to ward him off, it made him even angrier. He crossed the room, putting distance between them. The air vibrated with tension.

Just then, someone knocked at the door. Leah jumped, while Devon whirled to face the intruder.

"Come in," he barked.

The door opened, and a maid timidly stuck her head around it. "I beg pardon, my lord. But Mrs. Knowles sent me up to see to Lady Huxhold's needs."

Leah averted her face, afraid the maid would notice her crying. She anticipated that Devon would send her away. Instead, he gruffly said, "Then do it. Whatever she wishes, do it."

"Yes, my lord." The maid hesitated.

"What?" Devon snapped.

"I beg pardon, my lord, but Dr. Partridge told me that Lord Kirkeby is asking for you. He wondered if you could come across the hall."

Her words had a sobering effect on Devon's anger. "I will go to him now." He paused. Leah could feel him look at her, debating whether or not to say anything.

To her relief, he left without saying a word. In the wake of his departure, she felt exposed, confused.

"My name is Meggie, my lady. May I get you anything? A tray of supper perhaps? I don't believe anyone from the family is dining downstairs this evening. We'll all be waiting and praying for Lord Kirkeby."

Hunger was the last thing on Leah's mind. She almost said it to the maid, and then she remembered Ben. "Yes, a tray would be nice."

"Anything in particular?"

"It doesn't matter," Leah answered. "I'm not a finicky eater. But wait," she said as the maid started to leave. She could almost hear Old Edith's approval as she added, "Include a glass of ale."

"Yes, my lady." The maid left.

Leah lay back on the bed, exhausted.

The words she and Devon had thrown at each other chased themselves in her head. He was wrong, so wrong to use Ben. How could she trust a man who would do that? Especially when what she wanted from him was something he refused to give—his trust.

She must have fallen asleep, because when she opened her eyes, the room was dark save for the brightly burning lamps. She sat up. The pins had fallen from her hair, and it hung halfway down her back. On a desk in front of the room's double window was a pitcher and several covered dishes on a tray.

Leah rose slowly, assuming that Ben had woken her. Then a knock rattled the door. Ben still slept.

She had just started for the door when it opened. Lady Vainhope stood before her. Hanks of her usually perfectly coifed hair stuck out in different directions. Her eyes were red-rimmed and angry.

In the flickering of the lamps, she appeared as a thing possessed.

"I knew you were here," she said accusingly to Leah. "You can't hide from me."

"I was asleep. I didn't realize anyone was at the door."

"There are many things you don't realize. But mark my words and mark them well—you will never be the marchioness of Kirkeby. Never!"

With that promise, she slammed the door shut.

The noise startled Ben. He cried. Leah ran to him. She swept him up in her arms. Poor, poor baby. So young to be played for such a pawn.

"Nothing will happen to you," she whispered. "Nothing." She was shaking. She caught a glimpse of herself in the mirror over the washbasin. Her face was pale, her eyes dark and hollow, and suddenly something inside of her snapped.

Lady Vainhope would not harm her child. She would sell her soul to the devil before that happened.

And maybe she had already. After all, she'd married Devon.

Was it only yesterday that she had naïvely hoped he would fall in love with her? Again, she looked at her reflection in the mirror. He'd said this morning that she had a new maturity—but what had she done with it?

Seven months ago, she had taken charge of her fate only to find herself back where she'd started—living her life according to the whims of others.

Her baby watched her, his solemn gaze slightly

out of focus. He depended on her. She was his world.

Fierce pride filled Leah. She'd made her mistakes, but Ben wasn't one of them. And if she couldn't have Devon's love, she would have his respect—even if she had to leave him.

She would have thrown her and Ben's meager possessions into a basket and charged from the house . . . except for something that Devon had said earlier. The words tickled her memory. She concentrated and then realized Devon had admitted that he had not taken a lover since their parting. At the time, she'd been too wrapped up in guilt to realize what his words meant.

Suddenly, Leah realized she had been on the verge of making a mistake. She wanted a family for her son, a home, happiness. It would not come without a price . . . and perhaps her liaison with Draycutt had been necessary. It had given her Ben. In a roundabout way, it had also brought her and Devon together.

Leah had always believed in God because such a belief was expected of her. But now, she saw a pattern in her life that she had not anticipated. Those frightened prayers she had repeated over and over when she had feared herself lost and alone had been answered. Not in the way she had expected, but they had borne fruit.

The realization renewed her courage.

She pushed the crib from the nursery into the bedroom. She'd take no chances with Venetia's threats, but she would not run.

Sitting at the writing desk, she found a heavy cream-colored velum and writing quills in a drawer. Carefully, she dipped a quill in ink and penned a note to her parents. *I have arrived in London*, it began.

She signed it, sanded it, and waxed the envelope. The hour was half past nine. She rang for Meggie and said, "See this is delivered to Carrollton house on Cheswick Street."

"Yes, my lady." The maid left.

My lady. The title gave her a sense of her place in the world. What had Devon said? A viscountess didn't need to answer to anyone. She wondered if that meant she could create another scandal or two as she learned to exert her own independence?

The idea made her grin. Her debutante days were over. Instead, she began to relish a newfound sense of purpose. Whether Devon realized it or not, they were destined to be together. She and Devon and Ben.

With that thought, she set off to find her husband.

CHAPTER 13

Devon kept lonely vigil by his grandfather's bedside. A single candle on the table close at hand provided a small circle of light. The room was too hot. Or was it the tension humming inside him that made him so uncomfortable?

Dr. Partridge reported that his grandfather had fallen into a deep, uncomplicated sleep shortly after his argument with Venetia.

"I gave him a bit of laudanum, too, of course," Dr. Partridge had added. "Although she seemed more upset than he did."

Rex had left for haunts of his own. Dr. Partridge had confided that Rex didn't usually linger around the sickroom. It was just as well with Devon. He wasn't in the mood for his cousin's false heartiness.

No, he wanted time to be alone. Leah's words still rankled.

For a year he'd been telling himself her misplaced loyalty to her brother was the reason she'd refused to run away with him. Now, he knew differently.

"She doesn't love me," he said to his unconscious grandfather. "She never loved me." He didn't like hearing the sound of those words in the air.

What kind of a buffoon was he to tie himself to a woman who dared to accuse him of the basest motives? Of course, what bothered him was that she was right. He *was* lying to his grandfather.

And maybe to himself.

A clock ticked from one of the dark corners of the room. Devon listened to it, counting out the minutes, the seconds.

Ever since his parents' deaths, he'd felt like an outsider. Therefore, he'd behaved like an outsider. He'd rebelled because it was the antithesis of what his grandfather had wanted . . . or so he had thought.

What if Leah was right in other ways, too? What if he'd assumed the role of footloose rake not to irritate his family but to prove his manhood?

Last night, lying in bed watching his wife nurse their son, he'd felt part of a family. Those moments had seemed almost sacred and more intimate than any sexual encounter he'd ever had.

He wanted children. Hordes of them. Legions of them. Only a man who feared he'd never see his seed grow to fruition could understand the depth of Devon's need.

Ben erased that fear. Ben could be his future, his legacy.

"And I want Leah."

There. He'd said it . . . and he hated himself for his weakness.

The door behind him opened. Devon didn't turn. He assumed it was Dr. Partridge until a tingling awareness and the scent of honeysuckle warned him differently. He half rose from his chair. "Leah?"

She stood just outside the ring of light, Ben in her arms. Her dress's dark blue velvet blended into the shadows and made her seem a creature of the night. Her eyes reflected the candle flame. Her hair curled down around her shoulders, a curtain of shiny, ebony silk, just as he'd dreamed of it.

This morning, at the inn, she had appeared an uncertain Madonna, a woman lost before a sea of men. Now, she reminded him of a warrior queen. Her bearing hinted of an iron will and confidence.

She came forward. He straightened, waiting for her to state her purpose, to throw more recriminations at him. She shocked him when she raised herself up on tiptoe and kissed him.

I must be dreaming, Devon decided even as he instinctively placed his hand on Leah's waist and kissed her back.

This was no apparition. This was his wife. His *willing* wife. She broke the kiss. Ben, still cradled in her arms, wiggled.

"Hold him," she whispered. "He is yours. A bond between us."

Devon took his son into his arms. "Why are you doing this? What changed since earlier, when you accused me of every crime you could think of?"

"Your aunt." She told him then of Venetia's threatening her.

"And so you have come to me," he stated, the cynicism in his nature urging him to be wary.

"I'm not afraid of her, Devon. Or anyone else. But I have reached a decision. You are my husband. I am willing to trust that you will let no harm come to Ben."

"You couldn't have doubted that?"

She sat down in the chair. He sat on the edge of the bed across from her. Their knees touched. She looked over to his grandfather. "Are we disturbing him?"

"No, he can't hear us."

Leah still lowered her voice. "I feel as if I have been lost for a very long time and am just realizing that there was purpose to my journey." She placed a hand on Ben's head. "This baby is *ours*. Out of all the men I have known, you are the one I wish to raise him. I want you to teach him to be the man you are."

"What kind of man is that?" he asked from a hollowness in his own soul.

Leah smiled. "A man who embraces life." She placed a hand on Devon's arm. "This evening, I saw something of myself in your aunt. She has wasted her life yearning for something she cannot have—the title, if not for herself, then for her son. You, on the other hand, created your own destiny. You didn't wait. I didn't realize it then, but when you told me of your plans that wonderful afternoon at the wharf, you changed my life. I followed your example. I was afraid, and yet I tried." Silent tears welled up in her eyes and started rolling down her cheeks. "Ben is alive because of you. Now, I want you to save him from becoming like Lady Vainhope, or my brothers, who waste their time over what can't be changed. Or my parents, who are disappointed by the past and see no future. You must teach Ben to determine his own fate. He needs you more than he needs me."

Devon brushed a tear from her cheek with the pad of his thumb. "I don't believe that is true. A son also needs a mother who loves him."

"Yes." She fell silent.

"And what of us?" he asked.

She lightly brushed Ben's downy hair with her fingertips. "I have three requests." Slowly, she raised her gaze to his. "Meet them and I will do whatever you wish of me."

Devon had known it was coming—the moment when she promised him everything and then took it away. "What do you want?"

Her voice dropped until it was a mere whisper. "First, I must have your promise that you will tell everyone the truth about Ben once it is safe."

"I intended to."

"I know, but I am asking for your word."

"You have it."

"Second, this feud is madness. My father said that once. He was right. I expect the feud to end with Ben just as you promised. Our door must always be open to my family wherever we live."

"Even Julian?" Devon couldn't resist the jab. He'd never been fond of the braggart.

"Especially Julian. He is filled with hate, Devon, just like your aunt. Ben will never be safe until that hate is diffused."

"And what of your mother, Leah? She wanted to take your baby from you. Is she still a threat?"

Resentment flickered in her eyes. He didn't know if it was directed at himself for asking the question or at the memories. "Mother did what she thought best at the time," Leah answered stiffly.

"Yes," he agreed softly, "but can you forgive her? Should you forgive her?"

"I will do what I must for Ben. I've already written my parents. I told them I was in London and where. Now I will let them make the next move. I will have to wait and see what they do." She swallowed. "Then I will know how to react to my mother."

"If you can forgive her, then so can I."

She shook her head. "It is not enough just to forgive. When the time is right, I will host a ball as the new viscountess. My parents will be the guests of honor, and the ton will see that my father's claims of innocence are accepted by your family."

"Leah, he was the only person to benefit."

"He didn't take the money he won from the wager."

"Someone did."

She sat back, startled. "I didn't know that. But it wasn't my father. Devon, I know him. He would not do that. And you must believe me, because if you don't, there can never be peace between our families."

"You may be asking too much."

"I am asking you to accept his word as a gentleman. I don't know what your grandfather and your aunt have told you about the race, but Father said that he and your father had become friends at school. They thought the feud ridiculously old-fashioned. They were having fun."

"There was money involved, Leah. Money makes people do things they wouldn't normally do." He sighed in exasperation and shifted Ben's weight in his arms. "I'm not saying that he tampered with that lynchpin in an attempt to murder my mother and father. But I am saying that he may have done something innocent with tragic consequences."

"He didn't do it," she repeated. "But he has paid the price. Oh, Devon, he has faults. He's a terrible gambler, but he's not a murderer."

Devon squelched the urge to deny that statement. Meeting her requests was not going to be as easy as he'd first supposed. He could put the past aside for his son, but could he believe Carrollton innocent?

He ran his hand along Ben's arm, feeling the baby's muscles stretch and respond to his touch. His son pouted his lips. Devon had not seen him do that before.

What did Carrollton's innocence matter? Devon could pretend he thought Carrollton a saint if it made Leah happy. Anything for the privilege of raising this child.

Still, he couldn't help feeling he was betraying his grandfather. He shot a glance at the sleeping figure in the middle of the huge bed.

Leah was his wife . . . and he knew it wasn't just for Ben that he was making this agreement.

He spoke. "If your father said that he had nothing to do with the accident, then I believe him."

She released the breath she'd been holding. Her eyes shone with thankful relief. "You have not misplaced your loyalty."

"What is your third request?" he asked, changing the subject.

"I want an allowance."

This request seemed ridiculously easy after the other two. "Of course. You are my wife. I will cover all your expenditures."

"No, Devon," she admonished him gently. "I want my *own* money. Money I can spend without answering to you or anyone."

"Why?"

"If I told you why, then there would be no reason for my request."

It seemed such a small matter, and yet he couldn't help a niggling doubt of jealousy. "Leah," he started.

"Devon," she countered, the set of her chin stubborn . . . and he capitulated. Money wasn't worth a battle.

"I will settle funds into an account for you. I'll

give you five hundred pounds. That should be enough for anything you desire."

"Thank you." Her pleasure radiated from her. She stood and very sweetly, very sedately, kissed him again. "I promise that I am going to be a willing wife to you in every way, Devon. You will have no cause to doubt me."

He hoped not. He'd just agreed to give her enough money to travel the world three times over.

Nor did she linger over her gratitude. She scooped Ben up, and with a hasty "Good night" would have whisked herself and her son out of the room except that something had hold of her dress and pulled her back. She turned, a hand already reaching to release her skirt from whatever it was that prevented her exit. She discovered Devon's fist holding a good-sized portion of her velvet skirt.

She paused. "Did you want something else?"

Devon nodded. He twisted the material in his hand until she had no choice but to shuffle backward to him. "You thought that was a kiss?"

Her lashes lowered as her gaze shifted with longing toward the door. He coiled the material around his hand another time, forcing her back to stand between his legs. He released the material and came to his feet. "This is a kiss to seal a bargain like the one we've just made," he said, his hands on her shoulders, turning her to face him.

Yesterday, in the coach, he had kissed her in anger. Her kisses had always been somewhat chaste.

This time, he kissed as the man who would claim her.

His embrace included Ben. He was careful not to crush the baby, but he would give no quarter to Leah. At first, she tried to turn her head, but he had anticipated the move. His lips caught hers.

Vibrant, headstrong Leah. It was time she learned he could master her.

She resisted. She fought for control. But Devon was patient. He knew kissing, the nuances and secrets of a woman's mouth. He slid his tongue along her lower lip, tickling her so that she gasped and he could take fuller advantage. Slowly, her eyes fluttered closed, and she gave herself up to his kiss.

Mine, he wanted to tell her, *you are mine*. He found her tongue, sucking it gently and then with more force—and then she was kissing him back. It was a lightning moment. One second she resisted; in the next, she consented.

He taught her how it was between a man and a woman. Her breath mingled with his. His thumb rested on the pulse point at her neck, and he could measure the race of her heart.

It matched the excited beat of his own.

Sweet, willful Leah. She was his mate, his desire, his passion.

Reluctantly, he ended the kiss. Her lashes lifted, and he found himself staring into two gloriously astounded eyes. His own breathing was ragged.

"That is how you settle a bargain," he said.

She nodded mutely.

He lifted his hands from her shoulders. "I'll see you in the morning."

She nodded again and started for the door, walking in a dazed, beeline pattern.

Devon grinned, well pleased with himself. At the door, she paused with one last look backward. "Good night," he said.

She didn't answer but opened the door with a soft sigh, and slipped through . . . but before the door closed, he overheard her shuddering, "Oh dear."

He could have done a jig for joy.

Needing to crow, he whirled on his grandfather. "She knows she belongs with me now, doesn't she? All this time, I've been treating her with kid gloves when what she really needed was to be completely and thoroughly kissed."

He sat in the chair and leaned forward, his elbows on his thighs. "I have great plans, Grandfather," he said, energized with happiness and with no one else to confide in. "I'm going to build an empire the likes of which has never existed before. My ships will trade in every port and my warehouses will be full to overflowing. I'm going to do it all for her. And for Ben," he added quietly. "All of it will someday be Ben's."

Was it his imagination, or did his grandfather's mouth curve into the faintest hint of a smile?

Devon shook his head. He was becoming fanciful, but that was fine. The world was suddenly a very good place to be. Maybe Leah didn't love him yet, but she wasn't unaffected by him.

He'd just have to keep kissing her.

"Huxhold."

Devon heard someone calling his name. It was Grandfather's voice, faint and weak as if he were far away.

"Huxhold."

Slowly, Devon realized he was dreaming. Against his best intentions, he had fallen asleep. He sat up abruptly, disoriented.

"Huxhold." The voice was rusty from sleep, but the eyes were sharp and alert.

Devon leaned across the bed. "What is it, Grandfather?"

"What time is it?"

"Time?" Devon questioned, still groggy. He rubbed his eyes and searched for the clock he'd heard ticking. "Why, it is half past seven."

"I want Partridge. Send him in. Tell him I want my breakfast. Something substantial."

"Breakfast?" At last Devon came awake. "Do you mean you are hungry?"

"Famished." He struggled to sit. Devon helped by placing a pillow behind his back. "Where's that son of yours? I'd like to see him too. And I need some wine. Something to thicken my blood. Partridge will know what I mean."

Bemused, Devon couldn't help but see in the man's interminable will a reflection of himself. "Does this mean you've decided not to die?"

His grandfather's lips twisted into a faint smile.

"Not today." He held out a shaky hand. "Look at me. It was almost too late, but your coming has given me life."

Devon grasped his grandfather's hand. "I want our past differences behind us."

"And I want to see my great-grandson grow. I've done it wrong once, but Arrie was right. We do get another chance if we are lucky enough to recognize them. I'll be a better grandfather to Ben."

"This Arrie must have been a remarkable woman."

The marquess's eyes grew shiny. "She was the only person who ever challenged me. Other than you."

"I never thought to hear you claim that as a good thing."

"It's not!" he answered and then gave a sharp bark of laughter. Devon realized he'd rarely heard his grandfather laugh. Then the man sobered. "All these years I thought I knew best. I ruled, but I never loved. Don't make my mistake, Huxhold." He frowned. "What's the matter with you?"

"I'm just having a hard time believing you," Devon answered honestly. "You've always been so certain, so autocratic. It is almost as if some other man has taken possession of your body."

"I loved her, Devon. She made me see myself. Women have a habit of doing that."

Devon thought of Leah. "Yes, they do."

"Now, go on," his grandfather said. "Get Partridge and you go see to your wife and son. I'll not be meeting my Maker anytime soon."

Nodding, Devon went to do his bidding. The footman guarding the sickroom said Dr. Partridge had sent word upstairs that he'd arrived but was enjoying a bit of breakfast in the Morning Room. Devon decided to fetch the doctor himself.

The Morning Room was much smaller than the formal dining room and overlooked the back garden. It was a pleasant place even on the darkest of days. Devon found the doctor helping himself to a hearty breakfast. He explained what had happened and his grandfather's demand for breakfast.

Dr. Partridge chuckled. "Kirkeby may make it after all." He addressed the butler, "Wills, prepare a tray for Lord Kirkeby. Thin porridge as usual, but let us add a bit of butter to it and some of those fresh buns Cook prepared this morning."

"Yes, sir," Wills said and motioned for a footman to carry out the order.

"I'd like a bath sent up to my room," Devon said.

"Yes, my lord. I'll see to it."

"This house is old-fashioned," Devon said to the doctor. "I sometimes wonder if the family shouldn't sell it and purchase something more modern."

"You won't get Kirkeby to agree to that. I've been egging him for years to modernize." Dr. Partridge wiped his mouth and set his napkin beside his plate. "Well, I'd best attend to my patient."

"I'll go back up with you," Devon said. He followed Dr. Partridge out into the hall. "You said there was nothing physically wrong with him. You are still convinced this is so?"

"Absolutely. I'm also certain that your presence has been better than any tonic."

Climbing the stairs behind the doctor, Devon feared it wasn't his presence that mattered but Ben's. "Tell me more about Arrie," he said.

Dr. Partridge stopped at the top of the stairs. "She was a nurse I'd advised your grandfather to hire. He has trouble moving now. The steps are hard for his joints, and he needed someone to bully him or he'd have the servants carrying him here and there and catering to his every whim. Plus, if I may make an observation based upon my long association with your family—?"

"Please do."

"Lady Vainhope thinks she has her father's best interests at heart but her constant coddling makes him feel older than he is. Her constant complaining about you and the behavior of others also wears on him. Kirkeby is a man of rigid principles. I used to tell him it was not healthy to want to control everything. Only God is perfect, and even He had difficulties at time, but Kirkeby refused to listen to me."

"Do you believe she did it on purpose?"

The doctor shrugged. "I like to believe her heart is in the right place, but I was relieved when Kirkeby agreed to hire Mrs. Oswald. She was an apothecary's widow and knew a thing or two not only about sickness but also about the little tricks the mind can play on each of us. I'd worked with her husband and respected him. Of course, when he died, he left her penniless."

"So, you were helping her out, too."

"It seemed a good match," Dr. Partridge conceded. "But I didn't expect her to have the impact on Kirkeby that she did. Arrie wasn't ever a great beauty, but she was a handsome woman and a comfortable one. I know you can't imagine it now, young buck that you are, but when a man reaches a certain age, beauty no longer holds appeal. Comfort, on the other hand, is priceless."

"Apparently Mrs. Oswald was more than just a comfort to Grandfather."

The doctor agreed. "I have known him for over forty years. He became a new man within a week of being around Arrie. It was a miraculous transformation." He took off his glasses and cleaned them with a piece of flannel he pulled from his pocket. "If a man like Kirkeby can fall in love at his age, any of us can."

"He really fell in love?"

"Head over heels like any green youth. They were even lovers. If you have inherited your grandfather's stamina, then your reputation is well deserved. Arrie confided to me that she was a happy woman."

His comment made heat creep up Devon's neck. He was uncomfortable discussing his grandfather's, and his, sex life. He changed the subject. "How did she die?"

"Suddenly. It must have been her heart. She passed on in her sleep right there beside Kirkeby in bed. He was distraught. I attended the death of your parents and his wife. I've never seen him like he was that day over Arrie."

Devon asked the question most on his mind. "If he begins to eat and follow your directions, will he recover?"

"I don't see why not. True, he's not a young man. His heart or liver or kidneys could go at any time. But he could also live another ten years or more. Certainly he is stubborn enough to do that."

"That's an understatement." Devon held out his hand. "Thank you, Doctor."

"You are welcome, my lord."

The footman opened the double doors to the marquess's room and stepped out into the hall. "Dr. Partridge, Lord Kirkeby has asked me to tell you, and I quote, to stop jawboning and get yourself in here pell-mell."

Partridge smiled. "Kirkeby is *vastly* improving." He walked down the hall to answer his patient's summons.

Devon watched him go, realizing he had another problem. He wanted his grandfather to improve. Ben's presence made Devon hungry for a connection with his family—especially if both he and his grandfather passed to a stage where they might be able to understand each other better.

However, that meant that Leah must be willing to keep secrets—something Devon wasn't certain she would do . . . unless he gave her something else to worry over.

He opened the door to their bedroom.

The drapes were still pulled tight. The fire had died. His wife slept in the middle of the bed, Ben cradled close in spite of the crib being close at hand beside the bed.

Her worn, bedraggled petticoat had been slipped over one shoulder as if she'd fed Ben and fallen to sleep. Devon's full view of the exposed breast was blocked by his son's head.

"Lucky, lucky little Ben," he whispered. He pulled the sheet up over his wife even as a knock sounded on the door.

He opened the door to let in the footmen, who were carrying buckets of water. One of the footmen removed a copper tub from a closet, while another rebuilt the fire. Then they filled the tub with fresh warm water.

"Is there anything else, my lord?"

"No, that is enough," Devon answered. He waited for the door to close behind them before walking over to the bed. Leah must really be tired to sleep through that. He leaned over and softly called her name.

She frowned, wanting to push him away. "No, no, Leah, it is time to wake up and start to keep your end of the bargain."

"What bargain?" she mumbled.

"The one where you offered to be the willing wife." He carefully picked up Ben and transferred him to the crib.

Leah rolled over, giving him a tantalizing glimpse of brownish red nipple, before shrugging her chemise strap back up so that it didn't interfere with her movement. "I'm tired," she murmured. "I can't get up."

"But you must, Leah. We agreed."

She opened one disenchanted eye. "I can't do *that* now. My body isn't healed. Besides, doing *that* is the furthermost from my mind right now. I want to sleep."

"Charming euphemism, *'that'* " Devon answered. "You make it sound like a disagreeable chore instead of a slice of heaven."

She grunted her response.

Obviously Draycutt had been a clumsy lover, a thought that did not displease Devon. Gracing her with an eye-opening thump on the rump, he said, "Doing *that* isn't what I had in mind."

"What did you have in mind?" She sounded irritated, grumpier.

"Why, wife," he said cheerfully, "I wish you to wash my back."

He had her attention now.

CHAPTER 14

Leah didn't understand why Devon was so wide awake—or expecting her to do the inane and wash his back, which she wouldn't.

She frowned. "I *need* sleep," she argued. And it was all his fault, too. That kiss he'd given her had kept her awake most of the night. Who would have thought a simple kiss could have such power? Even now, the thought of it spread through her sleep-deprived limbs and set her blood humming.

"You can sleep this afternoon," Devon replied, yanking the careless knot out of his neckcloth. He tossed the article of clothing aside and started pulling the hem of his shirt up over his head. "I need my back washed now."

Leah tossed her head proudly. "I am not your valet." She picked up her feather pillow and puffed it up a bit. "I'm going to attempt to go back to sleep, if you will be courteous enough to let me," she added with a hint of sarcasm.

"I can't," he said easily. He threw the shirt over

the footboard. She frowned at it. He was usually tidier.

But then she had another concern as he began unbuttoning his breeches. She hugged the pillow protectively in front of her. "Can't you do that behind the privacy screen?"

"Then I'd have to walk naked to the tub and I'd catch cold. You don't want me to be cold, do you?" He unfastened another button.

Leah averted her gaze, finding something very interesting in the weave of the bedspread. "What I meant is that you should move the privacy screen over to the tub. That way the heat from the hearth will keep you warm."

"Well, I'm not *that* cold." The mattress gave as he sat on the edge of it.

She slid a horrified glance in his direction, suddenly concerned that he might pounce on her. But all he was doing was pulling off his boots and—thankfully!—he still wore his pants.

She clambered to the other side of the bed and put her legs over the edge. "It's time I got up anyway. I should take Ben into the nursery." Of course, she realized belatedly, Devon was between herself and the crib.

"Don't worry," he said, standing up. "Ben is happily asleep right where he is." With those words, he pulled his breeches down.

Leah feared she would swoon. She whirled around, but not until she'd had a glimpse of a generous expanse of flesh. "You don't wear small-clothes," she whispered.

"Why should I?"

"To be decent, and here—" She started to turn, thought differently of it, and stared instead at a point on the wall. "Think of the baby, Devon. You can't let him see you naked."

"Ben doesn't care. He's sound asleep, dreaming whatever dreams babies have. Besides, I've seen his bum several times over the last few days. It's only fair that he can look at mine."

The next Leah heard was the gentle splash of bathwater as Devon stepped into the tub. At last, she released her breath. "I'm going to take the baby into the nursery," she repeated. She turned and started around the bed, careful to keep her gaze on the floor lest she glimpse something she'd rather not see.

"Ben is fine," Devon told her firmly. "However, *I* need the soap. Will you hand a bar to me? It is in that basket in front of the fire. Grandfather always insists on warm towels when he bathes, and the servants do a nice job with it."

It was on the tip of Leah's tongue to tell him he could get his own soap, but then he would probably climb out naked to do it. With as much ill grace as she could manage, she stomped over to the basket and pawed her way through three warm, carefully rolled towels to find a complement of scented soaps. She grabbed the first bar and held it out to him without going around the privacy screen.

"I can't reach that," he complained.

Lack of sleep made her irritable. She'd had

enough games. With a boldness she didn't know she possessed, she stepped behind the screen and dropped the soap into the tub.

"Ow!" Devon complained without heat.

"Did I hurt you?" she drawled, so frustrated with him that his nakedness no longer mattered.

"No, you splashed water in my eye." He pretended to squint. "Now I can't see the soap. You'll have to find it for me."

"You're joking." She would have marched away, but he reached out and wrapped his wet arm around her legs. The water started to seep through her petticoat as he pulled her back toward the tub.

"You seem to see well enough now," she noted, relieved to discover that the water hid the embarrassing parts of his body from her view.

He set aside all pretense. "Come, Leah. You promised last night that if I met your conditions, you would be a wife to me. It is not much I ask. Just a little lather, a little caress. Or did you not mean to keep the promise you made last night?"

"I meant it, but I didn't think you would expect me to bathe you."

"Not *all* of me," he replied reasonably. "Just my back."

It didn't sound like such an outlandish request.

"Please," he added.

There was a flash of mischief in his eye, one she found particularly endearing. When she'd been alone and frightened and had wanted to think of other things, she'd remembered Devon's roguish twinkle.

"All right," she agreed. "But *just* your back." She knelt down.

"How about a kiss?" He found the bar of soap in the bottom of the tub and offered it to her.

The reminder of last night brought sudden heat to her face. "No kisses."

His hopeful smile flattened into a comical frown. She couldn't help laughing at him, and he smiled. He leaned forward, offering his back.

Leah lathered the soap. She sniffed the air. "What is this scent?"

"Sandalwood. I import it from India. Did you know," he said conversationally, "it takes thirty years for one sandalwood tree to produce a growth that will yield the oil in the soap?"

"No, I didn't know that," she said. She began rubbing her soapy hand over the warm skin of his back.

His eyes closed, and he practically purred with satisfaction. Beneath her fingers, she could feel the strength in his muscles. Draycutt had not been as strong. Or had shoulders as broad.

"Why do you act like you've never seen a man naked before, Leah?"

She froze. Had he the ability to read her thoughts? "I don't know what you mean."

"*That's* what I mean. Your missishness. One would think you'd never seen a naked man before."

Leah slowly swirled the soap across his back. "I haven't," she admitted reluctantly.

Devon leaned back to stare her in the face. "What about Draycutt?"

"I never saw him—" She paused. "Completely naked. Well, except for halves of him."

If Devon had laughed, she might have thrown the soap at him and vanished for good. But he didn't. Instead, he gently pulled her around, his hand on her shoulder. "You've never held your lover in your arms? Or felt the simple pleasure of having his flesh against yours?"

The image his words conjured was something completely different than what had happened to her. In fact, the picture Devon created seemed almost wicked . . . in a good way. Leah swallowed. "No."

"Then how did he make love to you?" he asked bluntly.

"The first time?"

"There was more than once?" Devon asked, a tinge of jealousy creeping into his tone.

"Three times. But I only liked it once because . . ." Maybe she shouldn't discuss this. She wasn't proud of the memories.

"Because why?" he prodded.

"Because I thought I should." Her face glowed with hot embarrassment.

"Leah," he chided. "Don't be ashamed. Not with me. Remember, we agreed we've both made mistakes. You caught me by surprise, that's all. I would have thought that Draycutt would have shown you what it means to make love."

"We did that," she answered abruptly.

"Where?"

"Why do you want to know?"

"Because it confounds my imagination. There is a way of doing these sorts of things. Don't tell me he cornered you in a garden. Not even a dairy maid deserves that treatment."

Scandalized by the rude way he'd described it, she could only nod. That is exactly what had happened. Suddenly, she wanted to go hide, to escape the humiliation of the moment, but Devon caught her wrist before she could run and wouldn't let her leave.

"Wait," he ordered. "It's not your fault, Leah. You didn't know. Is that the only way the two of you ever made love?"

"No," she confessed miserably. "I mean, twice we did it that way. I did not mind the first. In fact, I'm afraid, I enjoyed it. It made me feel as if I was taking my own fate into my hands. I told myself I was in love and that everything would turn out like one of those romantic novels. The second time was not pleasant at all, especially when I saw him flirting with another woman. I started to avoid him, but then Meg, my maid, realized I was pregnant so I had to see him to tell him."

Ashamed, she had trouble looking Devon in the eye. "I asked him to meet me at Whitney's. I arranged for us to use the back room we used to meet in. He thought I was looking for another tryst—" She drew a deep breath and released it before saying, "And it happened there."

Devon's eyes narrowed angrily. It was as she

had anticipated: He was disgusted with her. Her hands gripped the edge of the tub. She leaned forward, hiding her face from view.

"Are you sure he is dead, Leah?"

She nodded. It hurt to speak.

"Good. Because otherwise, I'd have to kill him." His hand rested on her shoulder. His voice close to her ear, he said, "Now I understand why you jump like a skittish colt at the thought of intimacy. You shouldn't feel that way. The bonding between a man and a woman is a joyous thing. At no other time are you more alive than when you find yourself in your lover's arms."

She responded to the conviction in his voice and turned her head to look at him. "I didn't feel alive."

"That's because you weren't made love to."

Her hair still hung tangled and wild around her shoulders. He pushed a lock of it back with one hand, carefully tucking it behind her ear. "Making love is like being on a quest. It's discovering what the French call *le petit mort*, when all the forces in the universe center on that one moment of ecstasy. One day soon, I will introduce you to that moment. And we will find it together."

She nodded, mesmerized by the conviction in his voice.

"We are man and wife," he continued. "You are never to feel shame with me. I vowed to protect you, to honor you—and as unconventional as our wedding was, I meant those words."

She wished now that everything had been different, that she had not let Draycutt have her. That she could be unsullied for Devon.

"Ah, Leah," he whispered. "When you look so sad, you turn my soul inside out." His lips covered hers.

Last night, the kiss between them had been an education. But now she knew how to kiss. He had taught her.

Even more important, she had a reason to kiss him.

She offered herself with shy eagerness, and Devon took full advantage. His arm pulled her close, his mouth became more demanding, and when his tongue first stroked hers, she thought she could melt from the pleasure of it.

He kissed her lips, her cheek, her neck. The tickle of his hot breath against her ear almost sent her to the ceiling.

"Touch me, Leah," he whispered. "Feel how much I want you."

She ran her hands, still soapy and wet, over his back and his shoulders. But that wasn't what he wanted. He guided her hand under the water, running it along his thigh. His skin felt like raw silk beneath her palm. Her fingers brushed what seemed like steel wrapped in velvet.

He was hard, and she understood what that meant. She couldn't touch him. She didn't want to. It was too soon after the baby. She attempted to pull away . . . but his voice gentled her.

"Don't be afraid. I won't jump on you or do anything you don't want. I just need to feel your skin against mine. Can you understand that? I want to know your touch."

She relaxed. He kissed her again, urgently. Her hand wrapped around him.

Devon groaned against her mouth. She started to retreat, afraid she'd hurt him.

"No," he begged and brought her hand back.

He kissed the line of her neck down to her shoulders and across the bodice of her gown. The heat of his mouth against her skin was delicious.

She moaned with happy pleasure. David Draycutt had never given her this.

Devon covered her mouth, his hand covering the place his lips had just explored. Her nipples pressed against his hand, begging for his touch.

At that moment, Ben started crying. In response, her breasts filled to overflowing. She felt the sudden heat and the leaking.

She was mortified—until Devon started laughing, his mouth still covering hers, his hand still covering her breast. The next thing she knew, she was laughing with him. Joyful, carefree laughter. They laughed so hard that she fell back onto the floor and he almost rolled under the water.

"I'm sorry," she managed to gasp out.

He turned serious then. "Don't ever apologize." His hand caressed the side of her face, his fingers lightly touching her brow and her cheeks. "I think at this moment, you are more beautiful than I've ever seen you."

"You said that when I had the baby."

"Yes, and I will say it tomorrow and the next

day and the next—" He kissed her hard and fast one last time. "You make me happy."

Tears pooled in her eyes. Happy. Yes, that was the word to describe how she felt.

Ben was showing a bit of temper. His cries were angrier than she'd ever heard them. "You'd best see to him."

Leah nodded, rising. She looked down at her chemise and petticoat. Worn and washed so often that they were almost gray, they hadn't handled this morning's dousings well.

"I'm going to buy you a dozen undergarments," Devon declared. "The best London has to offer. They will be trimmed with lace and ribbons and . . ." He paused. "Whatever else you want."

She laughed at his clowning and went to her son. Ben was very wet. Fortunately, she had two more nappies, but the wash would have to be done. She began changing him, pulling off his nightdress first.

Devon rose from the tub completely at ease with his nakedness. She still wasn't ready for it. He reached for a towel to wrap around his waist and stepped back behind the screen.

He'd still been aroused. His "stick" was larger and appeared much bolder than Draycutt's. But instead of fear, she felt pride. Something deep and primal reacted inside of her at the sight of him . . . and at the image of their bodies joined together. Someday. Someday soon.

Devon dressed, taking his time with it and gifting her with lingering kisses as she changed Ben.

"I'm going down for breakfast. Do you wish to join me or have a tray up here?"

"A tray will do. These are my only undergarments, and I need to dry," she reminded him pointedly.

He laughed. "I'm sending for Madame Nola." He referred to London's premier dressmaker. "I'll have her here this afternoon."

"Madame Nola won't come running," Leah answered. "She is in constant demand. You have to book fittings weeks in advance."

"She will come running for me," Devon assured her. "I supply her silks."

Leah marveled at the pride in his boast. Perhaps if more noblemen, like her brothers or father, found self-esteem and respect in the fruit of their own labors instead of gambling, they'd all be much happier.

Devon kissed her forehead. "You relax this morning. If you need anything, ring for the maid. And don't worry about Venetia. I will talk to her. Understand?"

She nodded, and he left the room.

Leah stared at the door long after he'd left. Finally, she whispered what was growing in her heart. "I love you."

Devon found Venetia in the Morning Room, clearly enjoying a cup of tea while Rex read the morning newspapers.

He greeted Devon. "Congratulations, coz, your name is on everyone's lips."

"I live to entertain," he answered curtly. "Venetia, we must talk."

"We have nothing to say to each other," she replied, pouring more cream in her tea. Her hair was perfectly coifed, every pin in place—but he knew Leah had not fabricated her story.

"You have ruined your family," she continued. "You have only to look at the papers to know how thoroughly."

"The papers? What do you mean?" Devon snapped. He practically grabbed the paper out of Rex's hands.

"Look on page three," Rex advised.

Devon didn't have to look hard. "Mystery Beauty Is Found" read the headline.

He swore softly. Carruthers had been quicker spreading the story than Devon had anticipated. The information came from Carruthers. There were several paragraphs about the discovery of a Lord C that Lord H—"a noted favorite with the ladies"—had succumbed to the parson's knot with none other than the lovely Miss Leah Carrollton, "last Season's Reigning Debutante."

He tossed the paper down on the table. "It had to be announced."

"Have you no pride?" his aunt declared. "We are the topic of every table all over London."

"And tomorrow there will be some other gossip and scandal to occupy the ton's narrow minds."

"The Marshalls have never been the object of gossip. Not until you."

Devon threw himself down in the chair opposite hers, stretching his long legs out to infringe on her space, something he knew from boyhood she didn't like. "Aunt, you may recite all my faults until the moon falls from the sky and it won't replace the fact that I will be the marquess of Kirkeby before Rex has a chance at it."

The color drained from her face. She used rouge. It showed up now as two bright spots on her cheeks. "You are unworthy."

Devon placed a fist over his heart. "You wound me." He sat up, leaning toward her. "And you may say whatever you wish to me or about me," he said almost pleasantly. "But you will leave my wife and my son alone. When you and Leah are in public together, you will be all that is good and gracious. Am I clear?"

"I won't. I can't."

"You have no choice," he said silkily, "unless you wish to be cut off." Vainhope had not left her in good financial straits, and, knowing Rex the way he did, Devon doubted if his cousin was more generous. Plus Venetia wanted to live at Montclef. She had lived most of life here, even while she was married. Devon knew she would do as he wished.

She threw down her teaspoon with such force that it bounced off the table. The action would have seemed comical except that she was so angry. "I've no feeling for you."

"That's been obvious. But after Grandfather, my word is law, and if you expect to continue to live off the generosity of the Kirkeby title, then you will accept my conditions."

Her eyes went cold with fury, and he had a

glimpse of the woman who had threatened Leah.

He continued. "Grandfather is going to make a recovery."

She blinked, surprised at his change of subject and its import. The thought flitted through Devon's mind that he had forgotten to tell Leah. His "distraction" had apparently worked for him more than it had for her.

Rex sat up straight at the news. "You are certain?"

Devon nodded. "Grandfather will be with us for a good while longer. We must live in peace, Venetia, for his sake."

Her jaw tightened. Her frown grew even more fierce.

Devon softened his tone. "I know how proud you are, and for most of my life I have avoided your path. But I can't any longer. I won't." His smile included Rex as he said those final words. His cousin's face was a study of bored interest.

"Devon." Leah's voice surprised him from the doorway.

He turned, rising to his feet. She was dressed in the blue velvet he had purchased at the inn. Her hair was styled in curls that fell down around her shoulders. Pride swelled in his chest at her regal bearing. Venetia would be wise to learn a lesson or two from Leah.

"Are you here to join us for breakfast?" he asked.

She shook her head. A sleeping Ben was cradled on her shoulder. Her eyes looked like they were ready to swallow her face whole. A maid waited anxiously behind her.

Intuition warned him that all wasn't as it seemed. "Is something wrong?"

"I have visitors." She glanced anxiously from Rex to his mother and then said, "My parents are here. They want to see me."

"Here?" Venetia said, her tone rising. "They've come here?"

Devon ignored her. "Where are they?"

The maid answered. "In the ivory receiving room, my lord."

Good. That was the room reserved for special visitors. He nodded to a footman. "Prepare some refreshment for our guests. Have Wills himself serve us."

"Yes, my lord."

Devon ushered Leah out of the Morning Room and away from Rex and Venetia's interested hearing. She was shaky. "It will be all right," he assured her. "Perhaps you would like the maid to take Ben upstairs—"

"No."

Devon glanced at the maid. She was not one of the older servants that he knew. "You may go. We will be fine."

The maid curtsied and left. Devon escorted Leah toward the Ivory Room. "If you don't wish to see them, you don't have to."

Leah was too panicked to think straight. "But I did tell them I was in London. It's what I wanted, but it's so soon . . . They know Ben is not your

child. At least, Mother does. I don't know whom
else she may have told. Thinking about it, she
probably didn't tell Father. Oh, Devon, what if he
doesn't even know about the baby?"

Devon stopped, his claim for his son his first
concern. "Is there anyone else, anyone in the
whole world who also knows the truth?"

Leah thought a moment. "Old Edith."

"She won't say anything. But what about
friends? Did you confide this to anyone?"

Her lips twisted into a rueful smile. "The com-
petition is so fierce during the Season no one trusts
anyone else. I can count my true friends on one
hand. Tess Hamlin is one, and she is off in Wales.
Anne Burnett is another. Her aunt hired her out as
a companion in Sussex before I knew I was pregnant."

"Then let us go meet your mother and hear what
she has to say."

He started forward, but still she hung back.

"What is it, Leah?"

"I just—" she started and then broke off.

"What?"

Leah didn't speak for a moment. When she did
find her voice, it was tight with suppressed emotion. "My mother. I trusted her. She was my closest friend. But it is because she wanted to take my
baby from me, to make me marry a man who is
repulsive to me, that I ran from the marriage. How
can I face her now?"

"You don't have to. I will send her away now."
He would have turned and done exactly that except

her hand caught his arm and held him back.

"She's my mother," Leah explained to his un-asked question. "She's the grandmother of our child."

Devon understood now. Deep in her heart, Leah needed reconciliation. Had he not come to London to do the same with his grandfather?

"Then see her."

Leah drew a breath and released it before nod-ding agreement. "I think I would like to see them alone first."

"Of course. Whatever you wish. I'll wait out-side."

Together, they walked to the Ivory Room. Out-side the door, Devon asked, "Do you want me to hold Ben?"

Leah started to hand him to Devon and then changed her mind. "No. I want her to see that what I protected from her plan was worth my giving up everything."

Devon leaned down, taking her face in his. "You are the boldest, most courageous woman I know. I am here for you."

She smiled then. "I know." She took two steps toward the door where a liveried footman waited, but then paused. She came back to him, reached up, and gave him a kiss. "Thank you." Before he could comment, the footman opened the door, and she walked inside.

Devon brushed his finger against his jaw where she had placed the kiss. "I love you," he whis-pered.

* * *

Back in the Morning Room, Venetia confronted her son. "Have you no sensibility? How can you just sit there, while Devon ruins the family? Father would have a fit if he knew Richard Carrollton was under this roof. This would kill him. It would!"

"Then perhaps we should tell him," her son said calmly.

Venetia stared at Rex. "But he is growing stronger. You heard Devon, and Dr. Partridge has not been down here the way he usually is when Father is sleeping."

Rex shrugged. "I'm merely suggesting that he should be made aware of what Devon's disastrous marriage is costing this family."

"He should," she agreed.

Rex rose from the table, putting the folded paper aside. He looked down the hallway. "I wonder what they were discussing?"

"Who?"

"Didn't you notice, Mother? Devon and his wife were having a heated exchange, and they didn't want anyone to overhear them."

"I don't want to discuss Devon," she complained. "One of my headaches arrived almost the moment he did. I confronted that Carrollton chit last night. I was so angry and overwrought that Devon could sweep in here and cheat you out of what is yours. You were trained for it. Father trained you himself. I can't believe after all this time, Devon fathered a child. I can't."

"I don't think he did."

"What?" She looked up expectantly. "What do you know?"

"Nothing yet. I visited my club last night. The last I or anyone had heard Devon was up in Scotland hunting with McDermott. I mean, he hasn't been in London for what? Almost a year? And it wasn't as if his path didn't occasionally cross that of people we know. Someone would have mentioned a wife to us." He nodded to the papers. "Especially one that causes this type of furor. We would have heard well before now if Devon had married Leah Carrollton nine months or more ago."

"What are you saying? That she really isn't his wife?" Venetia found that beyond belief.

"Or that the child isn't really his."

"But that would be incredible behavior—even for him."

Rex sat down in the chair across from hers. "What is *credible* behavior, Mother?" He leaned forward, an arm resting on the table, his voice low lest a servant should chance to come in and interrupt them. "My cousin has always envied me, especially when my first son was born. He pretended to be happy, but he almost choked over the words of congratulations. What if he and Miss Carrollton had planned an elaborate ruse? They could be passing off some crofter's child as Devon's."

"But the baby looks like Devon."

Rex shrugged. "Why? Because it has black hair? Under that definition, half the babies in England could be Devon's."

Her eyes brightened with anticipation. "He always wanted to cut you out of your inheritance."

"He won't. I won't let him."

"This is beyond the pale! Huxhold has crossed the line. I've talked to Father over the years about setting Huxhold aside in favor of you, but Father said it is impossible. Even if he agreed to such an idea, which he doesn't, he claims it couldn't be done."

Rex nodded. "But what if we caught Devon doing something so offensive to Grandfather's sense of honor that he was moved into petitioning Parliament into letting him set Devon aside?"

Venetia went still. "Parliament would do that?"

Her son shrugged. "Anything is possible with Grandfather's influence and money."

"Do you really believe Huxhold is up to something?"

Rex smiled. "I watched Leah Carrollton last night when Huxhold presented the baby to Grandfather. She was tense, not triumphant. And consider the way she ran out of the room later. Something is afoot."

Venetia tapped the side of her teacup thoughtfully. "So what do you propose we do?"

"I'm going to ask a few questions."

"Of whom?"

"Wills told me that Huxhold arrived in Ruskin's coach. I will start there." He pushed the top newspaper toward her. "And I will pay a call to Lord Carruthers, who is the source of much of the information in today's papers."

"What shall I do while you are out and about? Shall I take her to heart and introduce her to my friends and my acquaintances?" She wanted so much to play a part.

He grinned. "Be yourself, Mother. No one would believe you would be at all gracious toward a Carrollton or Huxhold's wife. Continue to behave exactly as you are. It will make Huxhold angry, and he won't be paying attention to what I'm doing."

"Father will be angry if he discovers you've been asking questions that could embarrass the family."

Rex pushed his chair back from the table. "I'm wagering he will be even angrier at Huxhold if we uncover a fraud."

She had to agree that her son was right. Either way, considering the stakes, it was worth the risk. Rex deserved the title, not Devon.

"Mother," Rex said thoughtfully, "perhaps you should pay a bedside visit to Grandfather. Let him know the house is full of Carrolltons. He may be furious enough to toss Devon out."

"Or he could suffer a setback."

"Yes," her son agreed without concern.

Venetia did not question his motives. Instead, she hurried to do his bidding. Anything for her son.

CHAPTER 15

Regina Carrollton had been a noted Spanish beauty in her day. Leah shared her mother's exotic features—black-as-night eyes and thick, glossy hair.

Regina's family, one of the oldest in Spain, had sent her to London for a rich English husband— and also because there had been a whisper of scandal attached to her name. But in London, she had again made a mistake. She'd fallen in love with a charming, penniless nobleman who'd wooed her with a host of promises that he could never have kept.

Leah knew her mother's history. She had been her mother's confidante, her closest friend, because even after all her years in England, Regina had always felt like a foreigner.

The footman closed the door behind Leah. The curtains were open, and white winter light filled the room, where her parents stood in a window alcove.

Her father might technically be the head of the family, but in truth, her mother was the dominant partner. She took care of the money and staved off creditors. She ran the house and raised the children and worried about the future of her family.

Silence stretched among them as they stood on opposite ends of the room, her parents with each other, she with Ben. So much could be said—words of anger, recrimination, betrayal. And yet, she could not bring herself to speak.

She waited, afraid and fearless. A daughter and a mother.

Then, her mother shifted away from her father and came forward. She stopped when they stood no more than an arm's width apart. Leah stared at her mother, unable to move or speak.

It was her mother who spoke first. She fell to her knees. "*Cara*, forgive me."

At that, Leah broke down. Sound escaped her body in a great, heaving sob. Slowly she bent until she was beside her mother on the floor.

Her mother's arms came around her. "I was so wrong," she confessed in Spanish, a language her father had never learned but Leah had. "I worried every day. I feared you dead. I am so sorry to have chased you away." Her hold tightened, and Leah was happy to be in her mother's arms once again.

The two women cried, their tears mingling as they hugged each other. Her mother pulled back, pressed a hand against her cheek to dry tears. "What is this?" she asked in English.

Now Leah found herself smiling through the

tears. She held Ben so that her mother could see his sweet face. "He is my son."

Her mother drew in a soft breath of exclamation. Her hands opened as if she would embrace the child. Fresh tears poured from her eyes. "He is beautiful." She would have said more, but her lower lip trembled, and Leah understood. Between them were regrets so deep that mere words could not describe them.

Leah wrapped her arm around her mother and kissed her cheek. "It will all be fine. From now on, everything will be fine."

"Oh, *cara*, I pray it is so. I beg your forgiveness."

"You always had it, Mother," she answered, understanding so much more now than before she'd left home. She had learned what it meant to worry about money. "Here, hold him. Hold your grandson."

Her mother's hands shook as she took Ben into her arms. Immediately, her face softened with wonder. She looked to her husband. "Richard, come here. He's perfect. He looks so much like you."

Her father had been standing stiff and alone in the background. There was an aloofness in his manner, and Leah anticipated his refusing the request . . . but then her mother knew him well. She had said exactly the right words, and Ben did look much like his grandfather. Almost in spite of himself, Richard Carrollton had to come forward to see if it was true.

"He's so little," he murmured.

"He's only two days old," Leah explained.

"Yes, but he looks exactly like my Julian and William. Can you not see the resemblance, Richard? It's in the nose and the chin."

Her father took a step back. "He looks too much like Huxhold," he replied tightly.

Leah glanced at her mother with the unspoken question. Her mother met her gaze with an unwavering one of her own, and Leah knew the answer. Her father did not know about Draycutt. He assumed Leah had run away with Devon, it was he who had fathered her baby.

She rose to her feet. "Devon is my husband," she said formally. "I ask you to accept our marriage."

"How could you?" he asked. "Especially after what he did to Julian?"

Before she could answer, the door opened. Devon's keen gaze went from Leah to his son and to her father's angry stance.

"I grew worried when you didn't call me in," he explained, inviting himself into the room. He signaled the footman to shut the door.

After a wary glance at Leah's father, Devon crossed to her mother. "I'm Devon Marshall. We haven't met before." He offered his hand to help her up.

Her mother accepted the offering, rising gracefully to her feet. She ignored her husband's fuming silence and said quietly, "I welcome you to my family."

That was more than her father could take. He took an angry step forward, his fists clenched. Frightened, Leah grabbed his arm. "Papa!"

Devon turned. "It's all right, Leah. Your father should express what he is thinking. I don't want any secrets amongst us."

"No secrets? Well then know this, I would have chosen any man but you," her father ground out.

"What happened between Leah and myself was not a matter of choice," Devon said.

"No, it was a matter of revenge!"

"Papa!"

"How could you, Leah?" her father demanded, the words bursting out of him as if he could no longer hold them back. "He crippled your brother. He has disgraced us all."

Leah stood between her father and her husband. She sensed her mother calmly watching, waiting for what decision she would make. "Papa, Julian challenged Devon, but the duel was no affair of honor. He would not accept Devon's apology and attempted to murder him. I am sorry Julian can no longer use his hand, but I will not be an excuse for him to hate. As for disgrace, Devon is my husband. I feel no disgrace in that."

Devon came to her side, his hand resting on her waist. Her father noticed his action and he looked to his wife.

For a moment, Leah expected him to charge out of the room. His honor had suffered so much over the years, and here was yet another blow. She wanted to embrace him, to weep with him as she had with her mother—but theirs had been a different relationship.

Then her father said, "What is the child's name?"

"Benjamin," Leah replied weakly, fearing the name would add fuel to her father's temper.

"Benjamin Marshall," Devon corrected proudly.

Her parents exchanged glances, her mother's expression pleading, her father's rigid. A silent exchange passed between them. Then, slowly, her father's stance softened. He faced Devon. "I would have chosen any other man but you."

"I am aware of that, sir."

Her father was about to reply, when the door opened.

"Wills, I said—" Devon started, and then further words died in his throat as two footmen carried Lord Kirkeby into the room in a sedan chair. Dr. Partridge hovered anxiously behind them.

Leah hadn't seen the marquess since the night before, and she was surprised by his robust color. His glow of health was highlighted by his red velvet jacket and breeches. He wore a matching red fez atop his head. The impact was startling and somehow intimidating.

Her father straightened like a soldier coming to attention.

"Carrollton," Lord Kirkeby barked in a raspy voice. "Mrs. Carrollton." He nodded at Wills. "Bring in those trays the footmen have lined up." He explained to Leah's parents, "Huxhold ordered refreshments, and the servants have been waiting.

I hope you don't mind. I could do with a bite of something myself."

Her mother stepped gracefully to fill in the stunned silence. "It is good to see you, Lord Kirkeby. I hear you've not been well."

"My great-grandson is the best tonic a man can have." He motioned toward Ben with one finger. "What do you think of him? Is he not a fine, healthy baby?"

He'd directed the question almost defiantly toward her father, but it was her mother who answered. "Yes, he is. A beautiful child."

"He is the image of a Carrollton," her father added.

"With the Marshall good looks," her mother enjoined, daring to defy her husband for peace.

Lord Kirkeby gifted her with a crooked grin. "You are a clever woman, madame. Like your daughter. It is hard to believe that a petite thing like Leah could produce such a good-sized boy." He chuckled at his own small joke. The servants finished laying out trays of buns, cheese, fruit and small cakes. "Eat, eat," he ordered. "Partridge, pour some of that wine over there. There's a Spanish one. Pour a glass of it for Mrs. Carrollton."

Her mother's lips parted in surprise. "*Gracias*," she murmured as she took a seat on the striped settee.

The marquess glanced at Leah's father, who still stood apart from the rest of them. "Wills, you and the servants leave us now," he said to the butler.

The servants obeyed him immediately. Lord Kirkeby waited until the door closed, the catch clicking in place. He fixed her father with a hard stare. "I have only one question for you, Carrollton. It is one I've never asked. Perhaps I should have."

"What is that?"

"Did you break the lynchpin on my son's phaeton the day of the race?"

"No."

"Why should I believe you?"

For a moment Leah feared her father would not answer from a sense of outraged pride. But then he said, "Because he was my friend." He stepped into the circle around Lord Kirkeby. "Neither one of us wanted anything to do with the feud. I would never have harmed him. Someone tampered with his equipment. Your accusation was not wrong, my lord, but misplaced."

The marquess studied him a moment and then slowly released his breath, seeming to shrink a bit in the chair. "I may have been wrong to blame you."

It was a moving admission.

Leah was so proud of her father. She glanced to her mother, wanting to share the moment, but her mother stared at a point in the distance, silent tears running down her cheeks.

Leah slipped over to sit next to her. She understood her mother's feelings, but she was a little nonplused when her mother didn't acknowledge her comfort with a small smile. It was almost as if she were lost in a world of her own.

"Then we may never know," Lord Kirkeby said sadly.

"Someday perhaps, the truth will come out," Devon answered. "Who knows what twists and tangles life will bring us?" Leah met his gaze in understanding.

Lord Kirkeby sat up in the chair, coming to grips with this new information. "I owe you a debt, Carrollton."

"You owe me nothing," Leah's father answered.

"I will give you a marriage settlement," the marquess responded.

"I will take care of that," Devon said.

"No," his grandfather said firmly. "You set your house in order. This will be my wedding gift, a joining of two families. Arrie would have insisted upon it, and I can afford it."

"I'm not a pauper," Devon said.

Lord Kirkeby chuckled. "I'm aware of that." At Devon's look of surprise, he said, "What? You thought you could quietly do anything in your life and I would not know? I've been following your business fortunes for years, Huxhold. At first I was amused. Now, I am amazed. Don't worry, Carrollton, my grandson can take good care of your daughter."

"Then that is all I ask," her father said, but her mother had a different opinion.

"That and a marriage settlement," she interjected smoothly. She caught Leah's eye and added, "A woman must be practical." And her mother always considered the financial aspects.

Ben looked up at the sound of his grandmother's voice, apparently agreeing.

"Come see me on the morrow," Lord Kirkeby told her father. "I will have my man of business and secretary here. You will find me to be very generous. I have much to account for."

"My lord—" her father started to protest, but her mother cut him off.

"We are grateful."

A looked passed between them, and then her father smiled.

Ben started crying, demonstrating his healthy set of lungs. Her mother handed the baby back, while Leah excused herself from the room.

"Yes, go on," the marquess said. "We'll discuss plans for the christening. The party will be here, of course."

Devon offered to escort Leah back to the room, leaving the plans for the religious ceremony to the grandparents.

Upstairs, he waited for her until she'd nursed the baby and put him down. "Well, are you happy? I told you it would all work out, and it did."

"Yes," she agreed. "Of course, I understand what you mean about his autocratic ways. But I am happy to let him make any plans he wishes in return for what he has done for my father."

Devon nodded, obviously well pleased with himself, but Leah wasn't ready to let him off the hook. Had he really thought she wouldn't have noticed? "We do have one problem," she said. "Your grandfather looks very healthy."

"Well, he's still weak," Devon hurriedly corrected her.

"Yes, but he looks much better than he did last night. And you didn't seem worried about him this morning."

Devon frowned, and she knew she'd caught him. Then he grinned. "I meant to say something to you, but I was distracted."

"Because you distracted me. Devon Marshall, I'd wager you had me wash your back on purpose."

He laughed. "Of course, but the purpose wasn't what you thought it was." There was so much heat in his gaze when he said that that she immediately pictured him gloriously naked and dripping with water.

His hand slipped around her waist. His mouth brushed her ear. "I enjoyed this morning. I want you to wash my back every morning."

She caught his face in both her hands. "You are tempting me, but it's not going to work this time. Devon, what are we going to do? I don't want your grandfather to suffer a setback, and yet we must tell him the truth. Already, the story is growing. My father believes you to be Ben's father."

"So, now you have a reason to continue the story."

"I hate doing it."

"I don't mind at all," he whispered before he kissed her. It was a pleasant kiss, full of hope and promise.

"Oh, Devon, when you kiss me, I lose all common sense."

He murmured, "See? Everything is fine."

"I have to worry about Ben and the future."

"No, *you* don't have to worry. I'll take care of it, Leah. I'll always take care of you."

Suddenly, Leah was tired of doubts and worries. She loved Devon. She had no choice but to follow his lead and trust him.

Fiona, her maid, interrupted them to say that the Carrolltons were staying for luncheon and would Leah and Devon join them? "I'll watch the baby, my lady."

Downstairs, they found everyone assembled in the dining room. Lord Kirkeby was starting to pale a bit, but he seemed determined to sit with them through the meal. Leah was surprised that Venetia joined them.

Her disapproval was obvious, but she did not make a scene. Considering her behavior the night before, Leah found it strange that she would even deign to eat with the Carrolltons.

Of course, when Devon suggested that the marquess host a ball to announce that the feud was over between the two families, Venetia's face paled considerably. But she did not protest.

Lord Kirkeby agreed that it was a good idea. "We'll be the first ball of the Season. When should that be?"

Her mother said something about six weeks.

"Good, plenty of time for planning." Lord Kirkeby looked to his daughter. "You plan it, Venetia. Spare no expense. I want this ball to be the talk of the town for years."

"I will see what I can do," was Venetia's tight-lipped reply. Leah found herself wondering why the woman hadn't refused outright—and what it could mean.

CHAPTER 16

Over the next few weeks, Madame Nola designed an exquisite wardrobe for Leah. Devon urged the dressmaker to spare no expense. She used the silks that he supplied. The jewel-bright colors were perfect for Leah's coloring.

They asked Fiona to be Ben's nanny. The young maid was happy to have such an important role. At Devon's urging, Leah then hired a lady's maid.

"It feels silly," she told him. "You don't have a valet." So, he hired a valet, completely dumbfounding his wife.

"Why after all this time?" she asked.

"Because everyone is watching us," Devon answered. "I want them to see that married life suits me." And it did. He'd never been happier.

Leah grew lovelier every day. He hadn't thought it possible, but the transformation was amazing. The hollowness left her eyes. Her skin took on a happy glow. Her hair was glossier and shinier than ever before.

He'd catch sight of the sway of her hips as she moved past him, and he couldn't think of anything else for the rest of the day. Or she would wet her lips, and he'd practically fall all over himself to be close to her.

He loved the graceful movement of her hands. They were always busy soothing, encouraging, nurturing. Touching. She touched him often. Little pats, a hand on the shoulder, a brush against his thigh, a light kiss coming and going—which always led to something deeper, needier . . .

Devon felt very needy, even though she no longer hugged her side of the bed but let him pull her into his protective arms.

She made it part of her morning routine to always wash his back, which led to more touching, more kissing . . . but she was also careful to hide her nakedness from him. Her reserve more than anything else signaled to him that she was not ready for intimacy, and without intimacy did they really have a marriage?

He was almost mad with frustration. He ached with the wanting of her. Another woman would not do. He'd learned that lesson during their year apart. He wanted Leah. Leah, Leah, Leah.

And through it all was a fear that she didn't want him. He was sensual. What if his wife was not?

Devon told himself that he should be content. But the contradictions in their relationship nagged at him. He felt closer to her than to any other woman he'd known. And also more distant. Each day they became closer—discussing the household, Ben—even his business dealings. But he couldn't talk about this important facet of their marriage.

Sometimes, he would catch her with an expression so sad that it was painful to see. He'd ask her what she was thinking, but she wouldn't answer. One time, though, she'd whispered, "I wish I could be whole for you."

He had long since come to terms with Draycutt. The man had been a ham-handed lover. He was confident he could banish his memory from her mind.

Given a chance.

"You haven't touched the money I put in an account for you," he observed. He and Leah had just gone to bed. They often talked quietly at this time of day. Ben slept in the nursery now that Fiona was there to guard him.

"No, I haven't," Leah answered.

Devon rolled over on his stomach. "Is it because you don't know what to spend it on?"

"No."

He considered her answer a moment and then asked, "Will you tell me when you do?"

She didn't answer.

He assumed she had fallen asleep, but he was awake for a long time after that, thinking of reasons why she would want money and not touch it. He did not like the answers.

*   *   *

The next day, he decided to visit Baroness Charlotte de Severin-Fortier before he drove himself to madness with suspicions about his wife.

Charlotte greeted him effusively. "It has been too long, *cher*, and look at you." She stepped back to admire the shine of his boots, the cut of his new coat. "You look most handsome. Marriage agrees with you. And everywhere I go, I hear people sing the praises of your new wife's beauty. And you are a *papa*! That news was very much a surprise to me."

They stood in the walled garden of her town house, away from prying eyes. It was the beginning of April. The sun was shining, and Devon remembered a day much like this a year ago that boasted blue skies, a mild wind, and a young woman walking to church with her maid.

He came to the point. "Charlotte, I need a woman's opinion."

She sank gracefully onto one of the wrought iron benches in the center of the garden. "About your wife?"

"Yes."

Charlotte frowned, shaking her head. "I don't think this is wise."

"Why not? If I had a business question, I would go find an answer from someone who might know. Now I have a, um, wife question. I need to talk to someone who understands the female nature."

"Women are not like your precious silks and spices, Devon. We are not all alike."

He sat down on the chair across from her, his

elbows on his thighs. "I know that. But she's a riddle I can't solve, and I must."

"Then ask *her* the questions," Charlotte advised.

"I do, and I don't get answers." He sat back in the chair, stretching his long legs in front of him. "For example, she asked me for her own money. I assumed it was pin money, you know, to buy the things women like. I started having money put aside in an account, a generous amount, every week."

"What did she spend it on?"

"She hasn't spent it. She hasn't touched it. In fact, she's the most undemanding woman I've ever met."

Charlotte smiled. "This is not something most men complain about, Devon."

"Most men don't pay attention to what their wives do or think."

"True." She shrugged. "But why do her actions bother you?"

Devon released his breath in exasperation. "It's a feeling I have." He decided to tell Charlotte of their secret trysts, the duel, the parting, and discovering Leah pregnant, but he let her believe Ben was his. After all, he had turned to Charlotte in the beginning.

She listened to his story, her arms crossed, her face expressionless.

"Well?" he said. "Is there something I am missing? Some reason she would want money and not spend it?"

"It is not the money that troubles you, Devon."

He hunkered down in the chair. "What is it then?" he asked reluctantly.

"Let me ask you a question first. Do you love her?"

"I married her."

Charlotte's laughter rang in the air. "You of all people know that love is the last reason people marry. From your story, it sounds as if you had no other choice but to wed."

"But I did have a choice," he said without thinking. "I could have walked away."

"From your own child?" She frowned. "That would not be in your character, Devon."

Apparently it hadn't been in his character to walk away even when the child wasn't his. He immediately recoiled from such a thought. He couldn't imagine his life without his son—or without Leah.

"She is my life," he said.

"Then you should tell her so," Charlotte gently advised.

Devon wasn't sure. "If I knew why she was hoarding money, I would feel better."

"Because you wish to know all her secrets?"

"Because then I could trust her," Devon said and paused. The import of his response struck him between the eyes. He sat up, suddenly uncertain.

"So, perhaps you have discovered a wall between you, Devon."

He couldn't speak. He'd believed he'd forgiven Leah everything, but he hadn't. Still lingering in the back of his mind was the sense that if she had spurned him once, she could do so again.

Charlotte crossed to him. The air had grown cooler, and she hugged her shawl around her shoulders. "There is something you are not telling me. That is fine—but whatever it is, you must let it go. It is not enough to give love, you must also give trust."

"I thought I had."

"You may have, but remember, *cher*, a woman is not like a man. A caring, compassionate woman does not give her favors easily, and she falls apart a little when she discovers she has put faith in an unworthy man. Even I have always been very careful about the men I choose."

"*I* wasn't the unworthy one," he countered stoutly and then stopped. "How did you know?"

"What? That perhaps there was someone else in her life? Why else would you not trust her? Men are simple, Devon. They have only one issue, and that is faithfulness."

"I fear she could leave me again," he admitted quietly. "It hurt, Charlotte, when she refused me. The pain was real. I fear that is why she wants the money . . . in case she decides to leave."

Charlotte knelt in front of him and covered his hands with hers. "Then you have discovered a wall between you."

It was true. It made sense, especially when he remembered when Leah had asked for the money. "What do I do?"

"Tell her what is in your heart, Devon. It sounds as if the two of you barely knew each other but there was always something special there. I have been your friend for a long time. You are a man with a true depth of emotion, and you have found someone special. Don't lose her, Devon. Worse, don't drift away from her and let these wonderful feelings of love you have now die from neglect."

"And let her hoard all the money she wants?"

"Maybe she needs that right now. She has fears, too." Charlotte rose. "It is frightening to be a woman without money. The world is not kind to us. Be patient, Devon. Give her time."

He came to his feet, took her hand, and kissed it. "What you are suggesting is not easy. I am not a patient man."

"It will be worth it, *cher*."

"I want the two of you to meet. You will be at the ball tomorrow night?"

"The event of our age?" Charlotte asked with mock reverence.

Devon laughed. "Venetia is not taking well to Leah's presence. However, when Grandfather suggested Leah help with the planning of the ball, it motivated Venetia to take it all over herself and plan the grandest ball of the Season. Grandfather has given her carte blanche."

"How is your wife handling Venetia's over-bearing ways?"

He shook his head. "The further away Leah is from my aunt, the happier she is."

"A wise woman," Charlotte said.

"I will see you tomorrow evening." He kissed her hand again and took his leave.

*   *   *

While Devon was at Charlotte's, Leah had taken Ben to her parents' house. Her mother played with Ben. She cooed at him. He cooed back.

"He is so precious," she said.

"Devon can make him laugh. He becomes so excited when he hears his papa. Even Lord Kirkeby acts silly in Ben's presence. This baby will be the most spoiled child in the kingdom."

"And is that so bad?" her mother asked Ben. He gifted her with one of his rare smiles, and she laughed with joy.

Leah and her mother had grown close once more. Relations were good with her family—with the exception of Julian.

"Have you heard from Julian?" Leah asked.

"No," her mother said curtly. "He is better off in Spain, Leah. Away from here, he will have a chance to think and perhaps realize that no good comes from hate."

Hate. It was a brutal word. She'd had more than her fill from Venetia, and she didn't trust Rex at all. He smiled to her face, pleasant, charming, occasionally delightful—but she sensed he was biding his time.

"Will it ever end?" she asked.

"It has been going on for centuries," her mother answered. "It is unrealistic to believe the distrust and animosity would end because we have settled our differences. It is enough of a miracle that Lord Kirkeby can set aside the sword. Ah, now, please, don't worry. Think of the future. Of your son."

"I do . . ."

"But?"

Leah shook her head, uncertain whether to continue.

"What is it, *cara*? What makes you so sad? You should be happy. You have everything a woman could want."

"Yes," Leah agreed, the regret of her doubts lingering in the word. She bowed her head. "What I don't understand is how to live with the weight of my past mistakes. They haunt me. I wake in the night and can't sleep, wishing I had done things differently. But if I had, then there would be no Ben. I seem damned either way."

Her mother hugged her close. "There isn't one of us who doesn't have regrets. Some of what we fear is that our sins are so heavy there can be no atonement. But there is. You forgave me, and even more of a blessing, you have been returned to me safe and unharmed." She paused. "And wiser."

"I believe it much easier to forgive others than to forgive myself."

"You are correct," her mother agreed sadly. Her voice carried the regret of experience. "The hardest part, Leah, is forgiving ourselves. Those who love us go on, and we should too. Do not linger over events you cannot change. Worse, sometimes there are mistakes of judgment that are not public knowledge. Secrets that we carry in our hearts. We fear confessing them because the consequences of atonement might cost more than we are willing to pay."

A hollowness in her mother's voice caught Leah's attention. She had not meant to burden her mother with her worries. Covering her mother's hand with her own, she attempted to lighten her tone as she said, "Thank you. I will try to leave the past behind."

Her mother nodded. "You must. For the sake of those you love. They are all that is important. In Devon's arms and in the lives of your children, you will find peace."

In Devon's arms.

There was another question she had wanted to ask. She knew of no one else she could turn to. "Mama, how do you let a man know it is all right to use *his* stick with you again?"

Her mother blinked. "Stick? Your Papa loves me. He would never beat me. Has Huxhold beat you?"

"No," Leah said hurriedly, "but I'm not talking about a stick but a *stick.*"

"A stick that is not a stick?" Her mother's accented English made the question sound inane.

Leah raised her hand to her forehead. She wasn't doing this well. She tried to explain. "Remember Mae, my maid? She explained to me about men and women. She called that part of men a stick." She made a harried gesture with her hands to explain herself, unable to use words.

"Ahhhh," her mother said with understanding.

She inched closer to Leah on the sofa. "You have questions about the marriage bed?"

"Yes," Leah said, relieved. "The marriage bed. That sounds better than stick."

"And you have not asked Huxhold these questions?"

"After the baby I feared asking in case he thought me well enough to, well, *you know.* The idea of a man doing *that* to me in the weeks after Ben—" She broke off with a shiver.

"Understandably, *cara.* But now you are starting to wonder?"

"Yes." She was more than starting to wonder. Devon paraded himself nude in front of her all the time. She had grown accustomed to the sight of the male body, but lately she had been feeling something else. Something called *desire.* It was becoming increasingly difficult to lie in his arms at night and not want more. Especially when his kisses had the power to turn her inside out. But Leah had turned shy. How did a woman ask her husband to make love to her? Especially when she feared the act itself?

There had been pain with David Draycutt, but she was willing to suffer the small discomfort for Devon. She wanted to please him.

Her mother laughed softly. "It is not difficult, Leah. Tell your husband what you just told me, but leave off the part about a stick. It is too confusing."

"I don't think I could say anything like that to him." Her face overheated just at the thought of discussing such a subject with Devon.

"Well," her mother said thoughtfully, "perhaps you can tell him without words." She whispered in Leah's ear some of the ways a woman could express herself—if she were bold enough.

Leah waited for what seemed like an eternity for her husband to return home. She knew he'd arrived when she heard the sound of his voice in the nursery. He had stopped to see Ben. He then asked Fiona about Leah's whereabouts, which was not surprising, since she usually was in the nursery every evening at this time.

But tonight would be different.

A single knock on the door was her only warning before he entered the bedroom. "Leah?"

Her heart slammed against her chest. "I'm here," she called softly from the other side of the privacy screen. She swallowed. "How was your day?"

"Fine." She could almost picture him yanking at the knot in his neckcloth. It was the first thing he always did when he came home. He'd even banished the fastidious valet from attending him at any other time than in the morning. It was not a problem, since both she and Devon preferred the quiet of home.

Leah closed her eyes, praying for courage. What she was about to do was the most outrageous thing she'd ever done. She only hoped it wasn't the most foolish.

Silently counting to three, she stepped out from behind the screen wearing a large linen towel, her hair, and not anything else. She just wished her legs didn't feel like water.

Devon had started to shrug out of his coat when she made her appearance. He froze, his arms still in the sleeves. He stared, dumbfounded.

She waited. Her mother had assured her she wouldn't have to do much, not with her husband's reputation.

But he didn't move. She wet suddenly dry lips. *Why didn't he move?* Perhaps she had to be bolder. Or perhaps she was wrong and he was perfectly happy with everything between them exactly the way it was.

She was just preparing to apologize and hop behind the screen and get decently dressed when he said her name.

"Leah." His hushed inflection made the word sound like a prayer.

Now she must do the second part of her plan. The part her mother assured her would invoke a response out of Devon. Closing her eyes, she released her hold on the towel.

She couldn't look. She was afraid to. What if he laughed? What if he frowned in disgust at her? Her body had still not returned to its prepregnancy form. She feared it might never return. Her hips seemed wider, her breasts heavier. Panic coursed through her. She shouldn't have done this. Her head lowered to hide her deep embarrassment, and she reached for the towel lying in a heap around her ankles.

Then he was there. He'd thrown his jacket to

the floor. His hand took her arm. "No, don't."

She was thankful her hair covered her breasts. She wished it reached lower. "This is silly. I shouldn't have done it."

"No," he emphatically denied. "This is anything but silly."

She still didn't have the courage to look at him. His hand slipped up to her hair and he pushed it back, exposing one tightly puckered nipple. He rested his hand on her rib cage, his thumb brushing the curve of her breast. "In fact," he whispered, "you are beautiful this way. I almost regret buying clothes for you."

His words made her feel hot and moist. She raised her gaze to his. "Do you think I am beautiful enough to kiss?"

Devon didn't disappoint. "Oh yes." His kiss drank deeply. Her full breasts pressed against the material of his shirt. The sensation made her lightheaded. She felt wanton to be naked while he was clothed.

She also felt safe. Devon couldn't do what Draycutt had — with his breeches on.

The realization startled her. She pulled back. His hold tightened. "What is it?"

She couldn't tell him. Everything inside of her, the emotions, common sense, rational thinking, it was all jumbled and confused. "I don't know," she admitted.

"Leah, don't be afraid. This is right. It's the way we are meant to be."

"I know. I won't jump. I promise. I'll stand still."

Her words stunned him momentarily. Then he drew back, swearing under his breath.

"I've made you angry." She started to turn away.

"No," he said quickly, his hold tightening. "I'm just frustrated. Draycutt is like a ghost in our past."

"I don't think about him," she lied.

He lifted a dubious eyebrow, but he didn't challenge her. "Leah, are you sure you are ready to consummate our marriage?"

She nodded miserably.

"Or is it that your body is ready but your mind isn't?"

"Does it matter?"

"Does it matter?" he repeated incredulously. "Oh, Leah, let me show you." Before she knew what he was about, Devon lifted her up in his arms and carried her to the bed.

She stiffened. "What are you going to do?"

"Banish ghosts."

CHAPTER 17

The coverlet felt cool beneath her naked skin. Leah lay back. Devon tugged off his boots. She waited for him to undress . . . but he didn't.

Instead, he climbed beside her on the bed, his weight on the mattress rolling her toward him. He kissed her. Lightly at first, but then with growing intensity. His tongue entered her mouth. Slowly, her embarrassment was forgotten and her body no longer felt chilled but warm, fevered even.

She ran her hands along his shoulders and pulled at his shirt, wanting to feel his skin against hers. He caught her hand and held it away. His body covered hers.

"I want to show you passion, Leah," he whispered. "I don't want you to ever be afraid again."

"Just kiss me," she answered, and he laughed and did exactly as she ordered.

Leah was lost in the kiss. The weight of his body across hers felt good. Suddenly, he rolled her over. She found herself sitting astride him. The kiss broke as he positioned her over his hips.

She could feel the length and force of his erection pressing against her intimately, separated by one layer of warm leather. The heat between their bodies startled her. His hands rested on her thighs, pressing lightly to keep her in place.

"Do you feel it, Leah?" he asked, his eyes gleaming with a wicked light.

Oh yes. "Feel what?" she asked half in jest and half with a tremble of fear.

"This." He moved his hips, lifting up. Desire spiked deep within her. He moved again, and she cried out in pain and pleasure. Where had this come from?

His eyes closed, his lips curling with satisfaction. "It's going to be good between us, Leah. You are so amazingly responsive. I knew it the first time I kissed you."

His hands stroked her thighs, his fingers moving higher each time.

"Devon?" She shivered in anticipation for something she did not yet understand.

In answer, he raised up to cover her breast with his mouth. At the same time, his thumb circled and touched what seemed the very core of her. The caress of his thumb was like a jolt of electricity; only the energy was different. Instead of backing away, she pushed forward.

His lips moved hungrily against her breasts. She wrapped her arms around his head, needing to be grounded. Sparks danced and leapt inside of her. She no longer controlled her own actions. Her body moved and pressed against his hand.

Devon rolled her over again. He covered her with his body, his legs along hers, his hands capturing hers at the wrists.

"You are so beautiful," he said under his breath. "So very beautiful."

She closed her eyes. Her body glowed with warmth and well-being and a vaguely unsatisfied need.

"Leah?" He nudged her with his nose, teasing her into opening her eyes. "That was just a taste. I want to take you to the top of passion. I want you to see what it is like when you fall over the edge. Will you trust me?"

At this point, she would follow him anywhere. He read her answer in the dazed expression of her eyes and smiled. He kissed her then. First the underside of her chin, then the pulse point of her neck. He nuzzled each breast, his tongue circling the nipples.

His hands shaped and stroked her waist, before running down the smooth skin of her hips. "Your skin smells of honeysuckle," he whispered. "It reminds me of spring and sunshine. It even tastes sweet."

As if to demonstrate what he meant, he tracked a line of kisses along her belly. Playfully, he dipped his tongue in her belly button. Leah gasped, then laughed at the ticklish sensation, burying her fingers in his dark, glossy hair. He resisted her efforts to pull his face back up where she could kiss him.

And then his mouth went lower. Her breath caught in shock and delight. She'd never imagined he would dare do such a thing. His lips covered the point of pleasure his tongue had teased.

Wicked, delicious desire flashed through her. He couldn't, he shouldn't! She started to protest, but when she opened her mouth it was to sigh. Her hands ceased their resistance. Instead, she grabbed handfuls of the bedcovers, searching for sanity. Her whole being centered on where his lips teased.

Leah was lost in incoherent yearnings. They all whirled madly inside of her, spiraling upward and upward, carrying her with them.

This was pagan, madness. It was glorious.

And then, suddenly, she discovered the pinnacle. He'd wanted to take her to the top. She'd reached it. A point so fine, so sharp, so sweet, it made her delirious. The sensation of it whipped through her with the speed of a shooting star.

"Devon!" she cried, right before she felt herself begin to fall over an imaginary precipice. But this wasn't anything dangerous. Instead, she descended with the lilting dance of a leaf falling to the ground. Downward, downward, where she found peace.

Her heart pounded against her chest, and yet inside, wave after wave of radiating warmth flowed through her arms, her legs . . . and her heart.

Devon eased up beside her to kiss her nose. She returned his smile with a dreamy one of her own. "That was amazing."

"Wait until you see what it is like when we do it together."

"I can't wait."

He laughed and flipped the bedcover over her nakedness, his arms hugging her close. "Tomorrow, Leah. Tomorrow."

"I think you are the wisest, most handsome man in the world," she enthused.

Devon's smile turned wolfish. "I have my moments."

He would have kissed her, but a knock sounded at the door. "Damn." He raised his voice. "Who is it?"

"Rex. I need to talk to you."

Their time alone had ended. "Give me a moment," Devon called. Then he lifted his eyebrows in askance toward Leah. She gave a small shrug. She didn't know what he wanted. She and Rex barely spoke to each other when he was here. Lately though, he'd spent a great deal of time visiting his children at his country estate, although he rarely discussed them except to answer the most perfunctory of Leah's questions.

Leah slid off the bed and disappeared behind the privacy screen. Devon took a moment to straighten himself. He opened the door. "Yes, what is it?"

"Grandfather wishes to see us," Rex answered.

"All right," Devon said reluctantly. "I'll be right there."

"Wait," Rex said as Devon started to close the door, "I believe you should know, I overheard Julian Carrollton talking about you the other day."

"Where was this?"

"I'd taken the children to a horse fair. Julian was there with friends. He is very vocal about his sister's marriage."

Leah felt all the happiness drain from her. She had thought that Julian was in Spain.

"Be careful, Devon. He wasn't sober, and he looked as if he'd been in his cups for days. He's angry at his parents, too."

"I'll watch for him," Devon said.

"Thought you would want to know. Didn't want to say anything in front of Leah. Especially with Mother being so aggravating over the ball."

"Yes. Thank you. I'll see you in Grandfather's rooms in a moment."

Leah came out from behind the screen. "Perhaps if I talked to Julian—"

"You'll do no such thing. I'm the one he is angry with, and I will settle the matter." He tucked in his shirt. He appeared pleasantly mussed. Her body still hummed with contentment. It was hard to worry about Julian when she felt so relaxed.

Devon started fiddling with his neckcloth. She reached for her robe.

"Devon?"

He struggled with the knot. "Yes?"

"When are we going to tell your grandfather the truth about Ben? It has been six weeks."

His fingers went still.

Leah looked away. "Your grandfather is feeling much better. He grows stronger and stronger, Devon. The more time that passes, the harder it will be. And I must confess, I don't want Venetia's hostility. It isn't my place to say so, but I almost wish you could give Rex the title and we could put both of them behind us and create a world of our own."

"I know. But I can't do it yet. I mean, he seems stronger, but Dr. Partridge warns that his heart is weak. Maybe after the ball."

"Maybe you are not being fair to your grandfather. He dotes on Ben, and I think he really has changed."

Devon seemed dubious. "Not even a Mrs. Oswald can change the basic nature of the man. What if we tell him and he turns from Ben?"

"Or you? Perhaps that is what you are afraid of? That he will reject you again."

Her observation must have struck its mark, because he withdrew, saying, "Leah, you don't understand—"

"I do, Devon. You feel you must do this in your own way. But remember, Ben and I are involved, too."

"I know."

She placed her hand over his heart. "Then trust us. Ben and I will be here for you, no matter what."

He covered her hand with his own. "I do trust you, Leah."

He kissed her then, and left to answer his grandfather's summons. Leah hugged herself, wanting to believe that what he'd meant was that he trusted her enough to forgive Draycutt. For a second, she closed her eyes, remembering the feel of his touch on her body.

Devon. He knew her soul. He was her life.

She went to check on their son.

Devon stayed late with his grandfather. Leah had intended to wait up for him, but she hadn't been able to keep her eyes open. When she rose for the middle of the night feeding, he was still not in bed beside her.

However, he was there at six. He rubbed his face sleepily when she accidentally woke him as she rolled out of bed to feed Ben.

"Where have you been?"

Devon hugged his pillow. "Looking for Julian."

Her heart stopped. "Did you find him?"

"No."

Leah leaned forward, placing her hand on his shoulder. "Devon, you didn't go alone, did you?"

"Yes." He yawned.

She took his hands. "You must not look for Julian by yourself. Promise me you won't."

"Leah," he drew out the syllables of her name with tired irritation.

"Promise. Please."

"Whatever."

She stood. "I will talk to Papa. He'll find Julian."

But Devon had fallen fast asleep.

Leah lay awake beside him. Today was the day of the ball.

Hours later, she left Devon sleeping and went

downstairs to find Venetia a whirling dervish of activity.

Since any offer of help she made was rebuffed, Leah decided the wisest course was to stay out of Venetia's way. She took Ben to visit her mother, who again assured her that Julian was in Spain.

"If he had returned, he would have come to us first. We are his family. We have not heard a word from him. You can't trust what Lord Vainhope said."

Her mother changed the subject. She was excited about the ball. "Think, *cara*, everyone will be there. They will all see how beautiful my daughter is and how much her husband loves her and they will all be envious."

"Loves me?" Leah laughed even as her heart skipped a beat. "Mother, what makes you think that?"

"It is there in his eyes. And he loves you too," she told the baby. "You are a lucky woman. Very lucky."

"Mama, he married me for the baby."

She frowned. "You are more naïve than I imagined."

"You don't know," Leah said sadly. "I love Ben, but I wish I'd never made that mistake with Draycutt. I wish I could still have Ben but be pure for my husband."

Her mother hugged her. "One mistake does not ruin a life."

"But the size of the mistake—"

"There are those of us who have done worse.

It's the past, Leah. You cannot change it."

"I wish I could."

"*Cara*, forgive yourself," her mother said with exasperation. "Look at how you have forgiven me for chasing you away. If I'd had my way, Ben would not be alive."

"You only wanted to do what was best for the family," Leah murmured.

"No, I wanted to save face." She took Leah's hand. "I should have told you this before now. Years ago, I gave up a baby. It is painful not knowing where your child is. My aunts took it from me and my family sent me to England."

The admission stunned Leah. "Does father know?"

Her mother nodded. "He is such a good man. He really is. I love him to the depth of my bones, but he has a weakness. Julian and William have it too."

She took Leah's hand, her squeeze conveying fear, regret. "But I have done worse. Their weaknesses are nothing compared to mine."

"Mother, you have been the strength of our family. We all love you. There is nothing you could do that we would not forgive you."

"I pray it is so. Because someday, I fear I will have to atone for the sins I have made, even those I did in innocence."

"Perhaps you should remember the advice you gave me and forgive yourself. I am finding it hard to do."

"It is," her mother agreed. She forced a smile. "But don't worry about us, especially today when we have such a ball to anticipate. Everything is better now, *cara.* Lord Kirkeby has been more than generous, and your father has promised to quit gambling. The duns no longer knock on our door."

"Perhaps we Carrolltons have no choice but to learn our lessons through hard experience. It seems to be our destiny." In spite of the element of truth in her comment, she'd meant it to be taken lightly.

"Perhaps," her mother agreed, finally smiling. "You have grown wise, daughter." The praise pleased Leah. She had to leave then. The hour was growing late.

Instead of immediately dressing for the evening, she turned Ben over to his nanny and went in search of Devon. She found him in the study, going over papers.

He was happy to see her but immediately sensed something wasn't right. She told him what her mother had confessed.

"It is to your credit you can forgive," he said when she'd finished.

Leah nodded. "But I will not treat Ben in the same way. I will let him have his own life and become his own man—just like you. No son could ever ask for a better father."

To her surprise, Devon blushed, and before she realized it, she said the words she'd held back, the ones she'd feared he'd reject again. "I love you, Devon."

He jerked his head up as if he scarcely believed what he'd heard. "What did you say, Leah?"

"I love you."

"Again." He stood and came around the desk.

"I love you." She rose to her feet. This time she said the words louder and with more conviction.

He stopped in front of her. "One more time. Please, Leah."

She shouted then. "I love you!" The "you" was smothered by his mouth. It was a greedy, hungry, joyous kiss.

"And I love you," he answered when they both had to pause for a breath.

"You do?"

"Oh, Leah, from the moment I first laid eyes on you."

Before she could make comment, Lord Kirkeby's gruff voice said from the doorway, "We know! We know! You love him too!"

Startled, they turned to discover they had an audience. Lord Kirkeby's wheelchair was surrounded by Dr. Partridge, and Wills, and several chambermaids stood gathered around him. They all broke into grinning applause. Now it was Leah's turn to blush hotly, and Devon laughed, placing a kiss on her forehead.

There was no more time for confidences. The family ate an early dinner, and then everyone had to hurry to prepare for the ball. It was going to be crush. No one had refused the invitation.

Later that evening Leah was in a panic. She'd spent the last hour trying to get dressed and couldn't seem to make any headway.

Then Fiona brought Ben in for a feeding. Leah sat at her vanity table, dressed in her undergarments, holding her baby. One stocking was tied with a garter, the other hung down around her ankles.

Devon walked into the room and started laughing.

"Stop it," she commanded. "Or I won't come down at all."

He sat on the end of the bed. "I'm not certain we want you to."

Ben stopped nursing long enough to give Devon a smile and then went back to his business.

Devon reached over and brushed the back of his fingers against Leah's cheek. "I'm going to tell Grandfather tomorrow morning."

"Oh, Devon." Relief washed through her. "It will be best."

He didn't respond but went behind the screen set up in front of the fire to bathe. Soon his baritone voice was raised in a rousing song.

Leah laughed. His silliness took the edge off the moments leading up to the ball.

Fiona claimed the baby. Devon was still splashing, and Leah slipped behind the screen. "Do you want me to wash your back?"

"Later." He slid down in the tub, and she noticed he was aroused. "I don't wish to spend all evening downstairs. Do you?" he asked.

Desire sparkled through her. "Oh, no."

He grinned. "That's the right answer and for that, you are going to win a prize, viscountess."

"What sort of prize?" she asked with suspicious humor.

"Grab my jacket hanging from the corner of the screen."

She did as he said.

"Check the pocket," he said.

"What am I looking for?"

"You'll know when you find it."

Her fingers closed around a small box. She pulled it out. "This?" She drew a sharp breath. The box lid bore the crest of Rundell and Bridge, London's leading jeweler.

"Open it."

She lifted the lid and thought she'd faint. Inside was a huge ruby ring surrounded by diamonds and sapphires.

"I should have given it to you earlier in the study," Devon confessed, "but I didn't have it. I'd planned on dropping it in the tub, like the soap that day, and make you search for it. But then I started to fear we might get diverted," he said with a roguish twinkle, "and forget about the ring. Then the servants would throw it out with the bathwater and—"

She silenced him with a kiss. "It is the most glorious ring."

"Here, let me have it." Taking the ring, he pulled her left hand forward. He paused a moment, thinking before saying, "I pledge my heart, my worldly goods, but most of all my soul to you, my wife, Leah Marshall." He slid the ring on her finger. It just fit.

She threw her arms around his neck. "Maybe we don't need to go downstairs at all," she whispered in his ear.

Devon moaned. "We must go downstairs. The party is in honor of your parents. Imagine what would be said if we didn't make an appearance. Plus, I have particular friends coming I want you to meet."

"Like whom?"

"Lady Dorchester," he said, and she smiled, remembering the masquerade. "And my good friend the Baroness de Severin-Fortier. They are anxious to meet you, since they had a hand in our courtship." He told her the story behind the masquerade. "They are both convinced you are a sorceress."

"I am." She leaned against the tub. "Devon, hold out your hand."

He did as she asked. She raised her hand, their palms inches away from each other—and there it was, the magic. Their hands met, their fingers lacing with each other's, and they smiled at each other, as deliriously happy as children.

The moment was interrupted by a knock on the door. It was her dresser. With a sigh, Leah came to her feet.

Devon frowned. "This house is so ridiculously old, it's not even worth modernizing."

"What do you mean?"

"It would be nice to have a separate dressing

room and water pumped upstairs. Or how about a water closet on this floor?"

"It sounds delightful," Leah answered, pulling on her dressing robe. "But what can you do? Montclef is the Marshall family home."

"Perhaps not after I tell Grandfather the truth tomorrow," he responded seriously. "I've been thinking that it may be best for us to find our own home. A clean break perhaps. But something with modern conveniences."

"A home of our own," she enthused. "Mother was telling me of a new home being built in Mayfair."

"We could look there or build a country estate. We could do anything."

"Yes, yes, I would like that. A clean break from the past." The dresser knocked on the door again, this time with more insistence.

Devon sighed and sank down in the tub, ready to remain a prisoner behind the privacy screen while Leah dressed. "Go on, let her in and tell me when you are done."

When she'd finished dressing, Leah felt she sparkled like the stones in her wedding ring.

She wore an off the shoulder dress of rich blue silk. Paste jewels trimmed the sleeves, and her hair was piled on top of her head and held in place by diamond studs. The studs had been loaned to her by Lord Kirkeby, as was the diamond collar around her neck.

It took far more time for her to dress than

Devon. He played with Ben in the nursery while she finished. When at last she opened the door, he gave a low, appreciative whistle. "Madame, you look spectacular."

Devon himself appeared a true nobleman in his black velvet evening clothes. The starched white of his shirt and neckcloth made an elegant contrast.

He offered his arm, and together they made their way toward the stairs. Devon paused halfway down the stairs. "Nervous?"

She considered the question and then shook her head. "I've been more concerned that you loved my son more than you loved me."

"And have I convinced you otherwise?"

"Yes," she said softly. "I believe you love us equally."

"I'm sorry that you discovered that," he said with a wink. "I was hoping to be more convincing later."

Deep within her, she felt the heat of anticipation. "I beg you to do your best."

"I will," he assured her, and she was suddenly overwhelmed by her good fortune. All the pain, fear, and insecurity she had suffered were now firmly buried in the past.

As they joined the receiving line, she found herself filled with renewed confidence. Her opinion of herself no longer rested on the thoughts of others. She held herself with pride. After all, a viscountess answers to no one.

Her parents stood between her and the marquess, in his sedan chair. He was dressed in sartorial splendor. His black evening clothes were embroidered in a silver thread and trimmed in gold braid. His eyes burned with intelligence, but he seemed drawn and pale to Leah. The excitement of the ball might be too much for him.

On the other hand, her parents looked radiant. For the first time in a long time, she was certain her father was completely sober. Pride filled her chest and she leaned over to Devon, standing beside her, and placed a quick kiss on his cheek.

"What was that for?" Devon asked, surprised.

"For being the wonderful man you are."

Devon smiled, pleased to be worshipped.

Soon, the rooms were so crowded that it was hard to move. She and Devon joined Rex and Venetia and her parents for the opening dance. Her mother was a vision in blood red silk, which brought out her Spanish coloring. Men openly admired her and rushed to claim the next dance, but she would not leave her husband's side. They looked so happy together that it almost brought tears to Leah's eyes.

Devon introduced her to a husky, broad-shouldered gentleman. "Leah, you remember the earl of Ruskin. Rusky has been taking care of my noble Gallant," he said, referring to his horse with obvious affection.

"That animal is a disgrace," Rusky declared.

"That animal is my pride and joy."

Leah arbitrated peace between the two men by offering her gloved hand. "We met last Season, and thank you for the use of your coach. It was appreciated."

Rusky bowed over her hand. "I am happy to be of service, my lady." He then frowned at Devon. "How do you do it, Huxhold? You managed to capture the Season's reigning beauty without even being in town."

"It's my charm," Devon answered. His words were met by a chorus of guffaws from those around them.

Of course, all was not perfect. Leah caught the hint of whispered gossip, but she didn't care. Nothing could spoil this evening for her.

Devon caught sight of something past her shoulder, and nodded. "There is Rex and my aunt."

They were standing separate and apart from the other guests. "I would be interested in knowing what they are discussing with such passion. I would wager my horse it isn't decorations or guest lists."

"Devon, are you truly worried?" she asked with surprise.

"Let's just say, I'm cautious. They are probably discussing nothing of importance."

"Don't worry. Not tonight," she whispered. "This is our night."

The musicians struck the first chord of a spirited reel. "Oh, come," she said, tugging his arm. "Let's dance."

There was a commotion coming from the front door. Someone must have fallen or stumbled. She hesitated, wondering if she should investigate.

Then a man shouted.

Leah frowned. Perhaps one of the guests had already had too much champagne, but Wills would take care of it. She moved to the dance floor, Devon following. Couples were skipping to the happy music. Concentrating on the pattern of the dance, she and Devon took their places at the end of the line.

However, during the pause in the next beat in the music, the man shouted again. He called, "Huxhold!" Leah heard him clearly, and the voice was frighteningly familiar.

Devon heard, too, as did all the other guests and the musicians. A woman screamed, and people started moving away from the door, where her brother Julian stood.

It had been almost a year since she had seen Julian. He'd put on weight, and his face was bloated and blotchy. She realized he'd been drinking. He swayed on his feet, nursing his bad hand by holding it close to his side. In his other hand was a loaded pistol.

The musicians stopped playing.

"Huxhold," Julian said in the sudden quiet. "I demand satisfaction." He then raised the pistol and aimed it at Devon's heart.

CHAPTER 18

"Julian!" Leah cried. She stepped forward even as Devon pushed her toward Rusky and out of harm's way.

The earl caught her by the arms. "Let Devon handle this," he warned.

She ignored him, twisting to release his grip. "Julian, why are you doing this?" she cried.

"Come outside, Huxhold," Julian demanded. "We shall settle this in the middle of the street with *many* witnesses this time."

"I don't want to fight, Julian," Devon said.

"No!" Julian held up his mangled hand. The fingers curled like claws, permanently frozen. "I believed you when you said that once before, and look what I have to show for it. This time you will meet me like a man."

The guests eased away from Devon, lest the pistol Julian held went off and the ball struck them instead.

Her father stepped forward. "Julian, you do not

come into a man's house and in front of guests demand satisfaction. Hand me the pistol and we will take this into another room, one more private."

"I'm not going with you," his older son announced. "You've sold yourself. You have no pride."

Her father's eyes blazed with a fury the likes of which Leah had never seen before. "You will obey me!"

"Aye, I will obey you, Father, once Huxhold is dead," Julian vowed. "He has shamed my sister. Disgraced my family! The Marshalls and their false accusations have ruined you and ruined me. It's time one of them paid."

Leah strained against Rusky's hold. "Julian, please, you don't know!"

"I know everything!" He practically spit the words out. "He was seeing you, having you lie to your parents while he used you. I know he had to be forced to honor you with marriage. I know when the marriage took place, Leah. You didn't run away to join him the way everyone thinks."

Leah went wild at his apocalyptic words. Where had Julian got this information? "You don't understand," she said desperately.

But Julian had dismissed her in his mind. "Meet me, Huxhold. Now!"

Her father started forward, but Devon motioned him back. "It is no use talking to him. He isn't interested in the truth. And I'm bloody tired of the accusations. Let us give him what he wants."

Leah wasn't certain what Devon meant. His expression was so composed that it could have been set in stone. He began walking without fear toward Julian.

Julian watched him approach, taking a step back and then another. The gleam in his eye grew more reckless.

"Take the gun from him!" Leah shouted to the bystanders, wanting someone to grab Julian and wrestle him to the ground, but they held back.

"Let Huxhold take care of it," Rusky whispered furiously.

Leah rounded on him. "You don't understand. I can't risk this. I can't live without him!"

Then to her horror, Julian stopped, but Devon kept coming until the bore of the pistol pressed against his jacket, aimed straight at his heart.

"Go ahead, Julian. Fire."

Leah screamed in outrage. She'd had enough! Her brother was not sane. Did Devon not realize the danger? She brought her heel back and kicked Rusky's shin with all her might. The sudden pain surprised him, and she was free. She ran across the floor to her husband, hurling herself at him to push him out of the way.

But Devon didn't move. Instead, his arm circled her, holding her safe. She could feel the tension in his body. He could break Julian if he wanted, and he would to protect her. If something didn't happen, there would be fresh blood and no end to the fighting between the two families.

"Kill me, Julian," she begged. "I am the one you are angry at. Take my life."

"No, not you, Leah. Huxhold." Julian's hand shook. Sweat beaded his brow and upper lip. The scent of fear was in the air.

"If you kill him, you are killing me," she pleaded. "I love him, Julian. He is my life."

Her brother's eyes widened. "How can you? After all that the Marshalls have done to our family? His grandfather has ruined us, Leah, I have proof. He blames us for deaths we never caused."

"Julian, you don't understand, it's over. *No one wants this.*"

"I understand that we will never know peace until the Marshalls are dead. All dead." He pushed the gun against Devon, and Leah felt Devon tense, ready to spring on her brother.

Then her mother's voice cried, "No, wait!"

Everyone but Devon and Julian turned to her. She stood a step apart from Leah's father. "I broke the pins."

It took a moment for her words to sink in. Her father was the first to understand. "You, Regina?"

Her mother raised her hands as if to stave him off. "You have taken the blame for too many years and I've let you because I was afraid of what would happen if the truth was learned, but I can't let this go on." She turned to her oldest son. "I did it, Julian. I was responsible."

"But why?" Julian demanded, his expression growing confused. "Why would you kill them?"

"I didn't mean for them to die. I just wanted to hinder Lord Huxhold's rig so that your papa could win the race. We needed the money, Julian. I did it for the money." Her lower lip quivered and her hands were clasped tightly, but she did not cry. Instead, she turned to the marquess. "I did not think they would be harmed. I just wanted Richard to win. Then there was that terrible accident—"

Her voice broke off with a choked sound.

She stood in the middle of the room, surrounded by her peers, and Leah's heart bled for her. But there was nothing she could do. This was the terrible secret she had carried all these years. This is what she had alluded to.

Her mother turned to her father. "I even took the money you won for finishing the race. I know you had refused it, but we had no choice. We needed it . . ." Her voice trailed off.

No one moved. The shocked silence was more damning than any recrimination. Leah didn't know what to do. The marquess turned away from her mother, and she stood there all alone, a broken figure.

Then her father held out his hand. "Come, Regina."

She shook her head. "You should send me away. I've disgraced you, but I'm sorry, Richard. I'm so sorry."

"I know."

The tears came freely now. They rolled down her mother's cheeks as she whispered, "It has been so hard to live with it."

Her words hung in the air. But when the answer came, it was Lord Kirkeby who spoke. "It was an accident. Caused by foolishness," he responded gruffly, his own voice full of emotion. Still, he found it difficult to look at her.

"Richard?" she whispered.

Leah's father came forward. He placed his hands on her shoulders. "I am guilty as you are, Regina. I should have been more help. Let us go home."

They started slowly for the door, but her father paused in front of Julian. "Come. We've all done enough for tonight."

His words had a sobering effect on her brother, who suddenly seemed to realize he had an audience. His gaze followed the line of the room, and he gaped at the guests who stood in frozen tableaux, their expressions curious, angry, indignant. His arm holding the pistol dropped to his side. Without a glance at Devon, he turned and left the room. His parents followed him out.

Silence echoed their departure.

Leah stood beside Devon, but she felt alone. Slowly, the numbness gave way to a great weariness.

Devon whispered in her ear. "Release it, Leah. It isn't worth it. Come. We've all had enough for tonight."

She nodded mutely, but her world had been destroyed. All these years, she had believed her family unjustly accused.

He walked her toward his grandfather as Venetia swept forward and signaled the musicians to begin playing again. Her efforts were in vain. The atmosphere of the ball had been destroyed. Already, guests were taking their leave, anxious to share such juicy gossip.

Lord Kirkeby looked ill.

"I'm so sorry," Leah said.

"It's done." The marquess turned to his footman. "I am ready for my bed."

Leah watched him leave. He barely moved as the servants lifted his chair and carried him out of the room with stately elegance.

She sensed Venetia's angry glare, but that didn't bother her. Not as much as the knowledge that all these years, her mother had known.

Leah escaped upstairs using the excuse that Ben needed her. It was half past twelve. She was exhausted. The night had taken its toll.

A fire burned in the hearth. It was the bedroom's only light, making it seem a safe place to hide.

The door opened. She sensed Devon's presence even before he spoke. "Tired?"

She shook her head. "Don't pretend it didn't happen, Devon. All my life, I've had people around me pretending. We can't pretend anymore."

He sat on the edge of the bed. She couldn't look at him.

"Leah, it wasn't your fault."

"It's *my* family, Devon. People will never forget what happened here tonight."

"Leah, family is important, but each of us is separate and apart. Your mother's actions are no reflection on you."

"She murdered your parents." The sound of those words made her shudder.

"Murder is too harsh a word. She cheated, and her actions had tragic consequences. She didn't intend for my parents to die."

"So you think it is all right?" she lashed out and immediately wished she could call the words back.

"No. But I also don't believe you are your mother."

There it was. She lifted her head and looked at him. "I idolized her, Devon. Even when I knew she was being unreasonable or wrong, I tried to please her. It was only when she threatened Ben that I knew I had to run away—and I was still so eager to forgive her." She broke down crying.

Devon rubbed her back. "Your mother is a weak person, Leah. She wanted things that maybe she couldn't have. I'm not making excuses for her behavior, but people do reprehensible things out of jealousy and greed."

"Like wanting to destroy your own grandchild?"

He didn't answer. There was no answer for it.

"Oh, Devon." She turned to him, needing his arms around her. They embraced. "Do you know what the worst part is?" she asked in a low voice, her face against his neck. "It is that perhaps if it hadn't been Tiebauld they wanted me to marry, I might have let her take my baby. I think about that often when I'm holding Ben in my arms. I was tempted, Devon. Tempted. I wanted to please her that much."

His answer was half laugh, half sound of exasperation. "Leah, you made your choice. Don't second-guess yourself. You did what you were meant to do. Otherwise, I would not have found you."

The fear, hurt, and anger balled up inside of her slowly began to relax. "There will be a dreadful scandal."

"No," he corrected, "there will be the rehashing of old scandals. But they can't touch *us*. We are not our parents. You are no more your mother than I am my autocratic grandfather. We are something better, something finer."

"Why is that?"

"Because we've already come to grips with what is important in life. I'd take you and Ben over titles or drafty old houses in desperate need of modernization—"

His words made her smile.

"—It isn't money either. I had money, but when I thought I'd lost you, I was miserable."

"I don't know if I will be able to see my way through this without your confidence." She gave a watery smile. "And your love."

"We will face whatever happens side by side."

"You are still going to tell your grandfather about Ben tomorrow?"

"Absolutely."

"It could cost you your birthright."

"I can live with that." He paused. "But I can't live without you."

Leah pressed her lips against his. At last, she released the doubts, the remorse. This kiss was gentle and yet demanding. It was a promise, more binding than wedding vows or the symbol of the ring on her finger. She would always be beside him.

Devon drew her to her feet. Slowly, he began undressing her. She pushed his coat off his shoulders and began untying the knot at his throat. There was intent purpose in their tasks.

As her dress fell to the floor to pool around her feet, he rubbed his palms back and forth across her shoulders. "I love the smoothness of your skin."

She placed her hand against the wall of his chest. "You are hard where I am soft. Strong where I am weak."

His hand covered hers. "You are a piece of my soul that I have been missing."

She leaned forward and pressed her lips against his chest where his heart beat. She could feel his blood race in his body. She rubbed her cheek against his muscles and the soft hair. "A piece of my soul," she repeated. "Yes, that is what we are to each other."

"And no amount of scandal can make us separate."

The fears and burdens of her family. Together they made a whole. He was her family.

She raised herself up on tiptoe and kissed him, offering herself fully to him.

They didn't waste time. Devon's eagerness was obvious. She pushed the satin knee breeches down over his hips. Her fingers brushed along naked skin. "Do you ever wear smallclothes?" she asked, laughing.

"Never." He guided her hand to where he was already hard and strong for her. Velvet and steel . . . but no longer something to dread. Her fingers studied the line and shape of him, circling the tip.

His reaction delighted her. He covered her hand with his. "Gentle, Leah, or we'll be done before we start, and I have plans for you. Big plans."

"I could think of nothing else all day."

She slipped her arms up around his neck. Her breasts pressed against the fine hair of his chest. She could feel it even through the fine lawn of her chemise. His bold arousal jutted against her flat stomach. They would fit together now. He would shove himself into her. There would be pain.

She must have involuntarily flinched, because he chided softly, "No, not yet. You are not ready."

"Ready?"

"Remember how it was yesterday. It will be better today," he promised, and she relaxed.

He lay her back on the bed, untying the tapes of her petticoats. He pulled them off and then rolled her stockings, garters down over her legs, his lips following their path.

Leah shivered with anticipation, remembering the sensations those lips had inspired last night. He finished one leg and then the other, and all she could do when he was done with her was purr with satisfaction.

"Am I ready yet?" She wore nothing but the thin, almost transparent material of her chemise.

His teeth flashed in his smile. "Almost."

He finished undressing then, glorious in his nakedness. She propped herself up by her elbows, focusing on his arousal. She had seen the tip of Draycutt's stick. It had appeared red and overeager. Devon's was magnificent. Bold, proud, masculine. "You are beautiful."

He laughed, pleased by her compliment as he stretched out on the bed beside her. She couldn't stifle a small moue of anticipation, which turned to a soft cry as, without preamble, he covered her breast with his lips. The heat of his mouth, combined with the damp material, made her blood sing.

He took his time with each breast. She reached out, needing to touch him. Her hand found the muscular curve of his hip and traced the hard lines of his thighs.

He nudged the strap of her chemise aside. First one, then the other. His mouth followed the trail of her clothing, and as he lowered the delicate material over her breasts, his tongue flicked the sensitive points.

He knew her body better than she did herself. She arched up against him, wanting more. Daringly, she traced the path up the inside of his thigh until she could stroke and caress his hard length.

Now it was Devon's turn to be ensnared, to be teased and coaxed and loved. He thrust himself forward, giving her full access—and she took it.

His hand slipped between her legs. His fingers teased her, creating the same magic she had discovered only the day before. He touched that sweet spot that seemed to paralyze her with pleasure.

Her legs opened, granting him further access.

Devon kissed her neck, brushing her hair back with his tongue. "I'm going to enter you, Leah," he whispered. "If I do anything you don't like, you have only to say so and I will quit."

The movement of his fingers had robbed her of the power of speech. She could only nod, and then caught her breath as his fingers moved even lower. She felt them slip inside.

She tensed . . . and then slowly relaxed.

"Do you like this?" he asked, his lips only inches from hers.

Lost in a haze of sweet emotion, she nodded. She was moving against him now. Her body copied the teasing strokes of his hand.

"Leah." He moved his hand. She noticed its absence immediately and gave a small sigh of displeasure.

"Wait," he cautioned her as he shifted himself up and over her. He slid his hands under her hips, raising up slightly. She felt the probing hardness. A flame of sensation skittered across her skin when he touched that sensitive little place. He eased himself back and forth against her.

Leah moaned, reaching for him. She wanted him. She parted her thighs, opening herself fully to receive him.

Devon hesitated for a moment, and then he thrust into her.

Leah loved the feeling of his body joined with

hers. It felt right. She tightened around him, wanting to hold him and keep him to her.

Devon gave a shaky laugh and then began moving against her. Leah stared up at the ceiling in wonder.

"My love," she whispered over and over as her body moved in rhythm with his. Her arms held him close to her. This was the way it was supposed to be. Not hurried and furtive but passionate and joyful.

She buried her fingers in his hair, her body shifting to bring him closer. Every inch of her tingled with the feeling of him inside of her.

It was so clear. Joined together, they created a whole.

His heart pounded against her chest. He lifted her, going deeper and deeper. Filling, stretching her.

Then Leah felt it. Oh, yesterday had been fine— but tonight, a million sparkling crystals seemed to all shatter at once. She pressed his hips to her, wanting all of him.

Devon held her tight. And then, with one last deep thrust, she felt his release. She cried out, feeling the life force inside of her.

At last, they collapsed, their arms and legs wrapped around each other.

Their breathing echoed in the room. "Devon?"

"Yes."

"I didn't know it could be like that," she said.

He smiled against her breast. "I didn't either."

*   *   *

They slept then until she had to rise and feed Ben in the early hours of the morning. When she stumbled back to their bed, Devon had thrown back the covers. He lay waiting for her, stretched out on the bed, hands behind his head, hard and ready.

What followed was playful, teasing, and satisfying.

Her husband knew everything there was to know about what pleasured a woman. "You *are* everything they said about you," she cooed before drifting off to sleep in his arms.

But he wasn't done.

The next morning, she woke to find him inside her. Her back was against his chest, his hands covered her breasts. Her body ached in places she didn't know existed, but when he moved, she was so sensitive that she came immediately and again and again.

By the time Devon had finished with her, Leah couldn't lift a limb. He brought the baby to her. The two of them lay facing each other with Ben, nursing, between them.

Devon's hands lightly touched her hair, her cheek, the curve of her jaw. In this way, they drifted off to sleep. For the next two days, they refused to leave the room. Everything they wanted was defined within those four walls. Other commitments, other promises could wait.

Devon had never realized that marriage could be so deeply satisfying. His wife had turned into a sensual creature. There was nothing she feared doing. She fascinated and delighted him.

But more important, making love with Leah was more fulfilling than it had been with other women.

His wife and child were his world. He questioned how other men, those who had never discovered the joy of love, found any measure of happiness in their lives. Leah made his heart sing.

They talked about everything and they talked about nothing. Time passed quickly. Their favorite topic was planning the perfect house. They designed it in their minds from the ground up and pretended to make love in every one of those imaginary rooms.

But the real world had to intrude sooner or later. The knocks on their bedroom door with messages from his grandfather or his business associates came with increasing frequency. Finally, his grandfather sent word complaining he was lonely. Venetia was still pouting over the social disaster of the ball and had locked herself in her room. No one knew where Rex was.

So, Leah and Devon had to leave their haven.

As they were dressing for dinner, Leah was reminded of something they hadn't done. "Devon, we need to tell your grandfather about Ben."

Devon, who had banished his fussy valet forever from the room the morning after the ball, pushed his foot into his boot and nodded. "You're right." He paused. "I just pray he takes it well."

Together they went downstairs. Since they were late, about fifteen after the appointed dinner hour, they went directly to the dining room. The table was set and the servants were in place, but the room was empty.

"Do you know where Lord Kirkeby is?" Devon asked a footman.

"He hasn't come from the library yet, my lord."

"Well, let us go fetch him," Devon said to Leah.

But in the library, they discovered his grandfather wasn't alone. He sat in a leather chair in front of the hearth. His face was abnormally pale.

Rex stood by him, obviously pleased with himself. Venetia sat ramrod straight on the edge of another chair. Across from her was a woman Devon thought looked familiar but whose face he couldn't place.

Leah recognized her immediately. "Mae? This is a surprise." She turned to Devon. "You remember my maid, Mae."

Mae had started shaking when Leah first entered the room. Almost desperately she frowned at Rex. "Please, my lord, may I go now? I've told you everything I know."

"Oh, no," Rex said lightly. "You must repeat it all for my cousin's benefit. He may already know the story, but I'm certain he will enjoy hearing it again."

Leah stepped forward. "What is the matter, Mae?"

The woman crumpled into tears. "I'm sorry, Miss Leah, but I had to tell him about the baby. About how it wasn't Lord Huxhold who was the father."

CHAPTER 19

Leah wished the floor would open beneath her and she could disappear—especially as Lord Kirkeby turned to Devon. "Is what she said true?" he asked heavily.

"That I am not Ben's natural father? Yes," Devon answered without compunction. "But he is *my* son."

Lord Kirkeby nodded absently, physically shrinking in size from the disappointment. Leah took a worried step toward him, but he held up a hand, warding her off. "Not now. Not now," he repeated.

"I had no other choice but to tell Lord Vainhope the truth," Mae declared loudly. "Please believe me, Miss Leah. Your mum turned me out after you ran away. She said there was no money for my wages. She wouldn't give me a reference because she blamed me for your bolting. Remember my cousin? I went to live with her but she's taken sick. Her landlord was going to throw both of us out into the street if I didn't pay the rent. I needed the money. Needed it bad, I did."

Venetia shook her head with a world-weary sigh, but her concern was not for the plight of the maid. "I am sorry, Father, that Devon has played this terrible hoax on you. I think we all owe a debt of gratitude to my son, who discovered the truth before it became public knowledge. There has been too much scandal already."

Leah stood between her husband and his grandfather. Lord Kirkeby had aged ten years in a minute, and Devon was so still, so silent, that she feared another estrangement between them.

Angry, she confronted the maid. "I hope Lord Vainhope is paying you well, Mae. You deserve a fortune for this night's work."

"I'm sorry, Miss Leah. So sorry." Tears rolled down the maid's face.

Lord Kirkeby's eyes burned with anger as he half rose from his chair and said, "Get that sniveling woman out of my sight! Now! This instant!"

Mae didn't need to be told twice. She ran from the room. The door slammed shut behind her.

He sat back in his chair, his expression stricken.

Venetia tisked softly. "This is terrible, just terrible. What some people will do to cut others out of their rightful inheritance."

Leah ached to box her ears.

"I must say I'm disappointed," Rex agreed. "I thought we had a better relationship, coz. An understanding of sorts."

Devon didn't respond. Instead, he focused on

his grandfather. Leah's heart went out to him. There was nothing he could say now that would undo the damage.

Lord Kirkeby stared with unseeing eyes into the hearth. His hands, tightly gripping the arms of the chair, were his only show of emotion.

Venetia, unable to stand the silence lest it bode well for Devon, said, "This is very serious. An absolute flaunting of tradition and the value of the title. I wouldn't be surprised if you aren't *disinherited*, Huxhold."

"Nonsense, Mother," Rex answered. "Parliament would have to be petitioned for such a thing. Do we really want our name whispered in those halls?"

Leah would have wagered her soul they did.

The marquess jerked, finally hearing what was being said around him. Leah prayed for him to set Venetia and Rex in their places. Instead, he looked to her husband. "Why?"

"He's my son," Devon said simply.

"But is he your blood or is the curse of that fever still on you?"

Devon's gaze shifted to Leah. Suddenly, she knew that whatever he claimed, she would maintain.

"It is still with me," Devon answered.

It had taken courage for him to admit it. Her heart was going to break. She reached for his hand.

"You lied to me," his grandfather accused.

"I let you believe what you wished to believe,"

Devon corrected. "You were ill. You needed a reason to live. There is a difference."

"Not according to my code." His words rang with finality. "You patronized me, Huxhold. I'm an old man, but I'm not senile. I no longer want you under my roof."

Devon didn't so much as flick an eyelash, but his hold on Leah's hand tightened. "It will be as you wish." With a curt bow, he turned. Together, they left the room.

Outside the door, he started toward the stairs. Leah pulled back. "Devon, isn't there something else you can do? Something that will soften his heart?"

"Like what? Say that I'm sorry and beg his forgiveness?" He shook his head. "I'm not sorry, Leah. Ben is mine as certainly as if he came from my own flesh. I will not apologize for being his father."

"But these last few weeks . . . you and your grandfather enjoyed each other's company."

"No, my grandfather enjoyed what he thought I was."

"Which was?"

"His definition of a *complete* man. His love comes with conditions, and I'm tired of lying to myself. I'm done with them all, Leah. Rex, Venetia, my grandfather," he said with sudden bitterness. "I've spent years with their simmering jealousies. It's a wonder they didn't hire someone to pop me off."

"They wouldn't!"

"Would you have thought they would do this?" He frowned. "It's all about money and prestige. I want nothing to do with the lot of them. Come, let us pack. I will put us up at Grillon's."

She followed, holding back her doubts. Such disappointment reaped bitter fruit. She had only to think of Julian to recognize that fact.

"Devon, it is just as well. Mae merely told the truth, something we should have done."

"And if we had, Grandfather would probably be dead," he threw over his shoulder as he charged up the steps.

She hurried to catch up with him. "Then tell *him* that."

"You heard him, Leah. He has his code! He's right back to being the man he was before. He'll never change."

Leah slowed her pace. This morning, she had been content. Now those she loved were being ripped apart, and she lacked the wisdom to make everything right again.

Up in their room, Devon had already rung for a maid to help with the packing. He sent a footman to Grillon's Hotel to see about rooms. Leah went in to Ben. Her baby was asleep.

"We are leaving, Fiona," she told the nanny. "You may wish to stay with the household or join our employ. It is your decision."

She knew she'd caught the girl by surprise. Fiona's aunt and sister worked for the marquess. She might not leave. "Why don't you go below stairs and think about it," Leah suggested tactfully.

"Yes, my lady, thank you." Fiona left.

Devon came to the doorway. "We will build our own house now. A modernized one like we discussed."

"That's true," Leah said. "Of course, it rankles that Rex and Venetia will receive Montclef."

"It never was a contest, Leah."

She nodded absently. "But it was your birthright."

"Perhaps my birthright was lost to me when my parents died. Whatever. I know I will not allow Ben to grow up thinking he is less than a whole man."

"Is that how I made you feel?" came his grandfather's voice from the bedroom doorway. Leah turned in surprise. The marquess had let himself into their room. No servants accompanied him.

"You know you did," Devon said stiffly.

Lord Kirkeby walked with difficulty toward his grandson. "You have already started packing. Wills said you've ordered a coach."

"Grandfather, you don't have to ask me twice to leave. I am not a hanger-on." He faced the marquess and said proudly, "I'm my own man."

"Devon, I—" Lord Kirkeby started apologetically and then stopped. Leah realized that he couldn't go on. It was impossible for him to admit he might have been wrong.

The set of Devon's face hardened as he waited. Finally, he broke the silence. "It's all right, Grandfather. I understand you better than you believe I do. I've waited all my life for your approval. I can wait longer. I just don't want to be like you."

Lord Kirkeby jerked as if Devon had hit him.

A maid arrived at that moment to help with the packing, a footman carrying two large trunks behind her. She knocked on the still open door.

Without another word, Devon pushed past his grandfather to supervise the servants. The footman lost hold of one of the trunks and dropped it. It bounced on the floor, knocking over a table and crashing a glass vase. The sound of the accident startled Ben awake.

He cried. Leah picked him up, quietly calming him. Lord Kirkeby watched her, even as she changed Ben's nappy.

Finally, she could take it no longer. The man was miserable. She glanced at her husband, who, in the other room, seemed completely occupied by the task at hand. And yet, she knew Devon would have regrets, too, if he parted in this manner.

"It isn't easy, you know," she said to the marquess.

"What isn't?"

"Forgiving."

The corners of his mouth dropped into a huge frown. His jaw tightened, just as Devon's did whenever he was angry. "I probably could go on and ignore it if Arrie was alive. She would have helped me. Made it easier." He was practically pouting.

"Well, now you have no one," Leah answered.

"Oh, wait, I forgot, there is Rex and Venetia." She lifted Ben to her shoulder. "They will take care of you because they want something of you."

She started for the bedroom. "Wait," Lord Kirkeby said, his voice weak and gravelly.

Leah turned.

"Huxhold shouldn't have played me for a fool."

"He didn't," she insisted. "He just wanted you to approve of him. He knew what you wished for more than anything else and he wanted to grant that wish and it worked. You are better."

"I thought I had something to live for."

"You do." Devon had come to stand in the doorway behind her. She turned Ben so that Lord Kirkeby could see his sweet face. "Look at him. You have the opportunity to influence him. To have an impact on his life."

"He's not my blood."

"Oh, bollocks on your blood!" she said in a swear that would have made Old Edith proud. "Did you *marry* Mrs. Oswald?"

"I couldn't. I would have, but it would have driven Venetia wild."

"But did you love her any less because you *weren't* married? Was her company, her counsel less valuable to you?"

"It's not the same—"

"It is," Devon answered. He came into the nursery, shutting the door behind him. "Grandfather, Rex can have the title. All I want is your respect. It's all I've ever wanted."

"But you lied."

Devon sighed heavily. "Maybe I was wrong and for that, I ask forgiveness . . . but the other night at the ball, did you notice what the Carrolltons did after Mrs. Carrollton confessed what she'd done? They left *together*. In spite of everything, including public humiliation, they walked out the door with each other."

"I bet there were fireworks once they were alone!"

"No, Grandfather. Leah's family is returning to their country estate where they believe Julian will grow better. They are all still close. You and I, on the other hand, have not been together for years until these last months. I've enjoyed it. I liked believing you needed me. When I received word that you were dying, I came back to London not as your heir but as a grandson hoping to reconcile with his family. But it won't happen, will it? Ever. To my aunt, I'm in the way, and to my grandfather I'm useless because I can't father a child." He straightened. "I won't come back next time. We've had a second chance, and one of us was too stubborn to take it. I apologize for not telling you the truth about Ben's parentage sooner, but it doesn't matter. He's my son with or without your blessing."

Devon placed his hand on the door handle and would have left, except Lord Kirkeby said, "Devon." He held out his hand. "Ben can't inherit."

"I know that," Devon answered.

His grandfather took a step closer. "You betrayed me."

"I was angry growing up. Your rejection after the fever was a betrayal."

"Is there no end to it?"

"Yes." Devon came forward. "We just stop judging each other. All I ever wanted was your acceptance. Your approval."

The words rang in the air. Ben swung his head in the direction of his papa's voice. He smiled, kicking his feet happily, but the two men were absorbed in their own drama.

Leah sensed that at last Lord Kirkeby understood, but it was still a struggle. Old habits die hard, and he was more stubborn than most.

Then, suddenly, he grabbed his chest in pain. "Dev—" he started before collapsing.

Devon caught him before he hit the floor. "Grandfather? No! Wait, don't do this. Not now."

Leah started for the bedroom to send the maid for Dr. Partridge, but Lord Kirkeby weakly called her back. "No. Don't . . . get anyone."

"We must," Devon said.

Lord Kirkeby shook his head. "Give . . . a minute."

"No," Devon replied emphatically, lifting his grandfather in his arms. He held the man as if he weighed close to nothing, and the image of Devon gently carrying Lord Kirkeby in his arms burned into Leah's brain.

She hurried to open the door leading to the hallway.

Wills had just come up the stairs to check on the packing. Devon ordered, "Send for Dr. Partridge. Have him come here immediately." He carried his grandfather to his room, where he carefully laid him on the bed.

Leah turned Ben over to the maid with instructions for her to find Fiona. She then followed her husband.

Lord Kirkeby was deathly pale. His eyes were closed, his lips pressed tightly together. Devon knelt by the bed, covering his grandfather's hand with both of his own. "Don't leave us now," he whispered. "We still have to finish that argument."

That comment inspired a small smile on his grandfather's face.

Venetia appeared in the doorway. "What did you do to him?" she demanded before running in and throwing herself dramatically across the bed. Even Rex appeared. He stood at the edge of the bed, staring. Leah wished she knew what he was thinking. Did he care about the man's health? Or was he damning him because he might pass away before disinheriting Devon?

Dr. Partridge arrived within fifteen minutes. "He collapsed," Devon explained.

The doctor nodded. "It was to be expected. He's been suffering pains off and on, but he didn't want me to say anything. He weakened his heart when he went into a decline last month. I had feared the ball would be too much for him."

"It's Huxhold's fault," Venetia declared. "He was with Huxhold when it happened."

"It could be a number of things," Dr. Partridge said with good common sense. "Lord Huxhold's presence was no more a factor than your own would have been, Lady Vainhope."

Venetia was dissatisfied with that answer. She wanted Devon to be guilty. In a fit of outrage, she marched from the room.

Rex leaned against the bedpost. He waited until Dr. Partridge went downstairs to mix some powders. "Well, it looks as if you are going to be a marquess, coz. You win again."

Devon didn't answer him. Leah understood. What could he say? Rex would have twisted his words to suit his purpose either way.

Dr. Partridge returned, and the bedside vigil of prayers and comfort began. Eventually, Rex wandered off, bored by the sickroom.

Leah sat in a chair next to Devon, who kept guard over his grandfather even after Dr. Partridge had gone off to sleep in a guest room. A yawn escaped before she could stifle it.

It brought his attention to her. "You don't have to sit with us," he told her.

"I want to be here."

"I know," he said, rubbing her fingers with his thumb, "but think about the baby. Go on to bed. I will be there when I can."

She hesitated, and then he said the words that made up her mind. "I need to be alone with him, Leah. I need time."

She nodded, yawning a second time and left. In the bedroom, their trunks were all neatly packed and stacked against a wall, a symbol of the efficiency of the Marshall household.

Leah was so tired that she pulled the pins from her hair, climbed out of her dress, and slept in her undergarments.

Devon prayed. His grandfather couldn't die. Not when they'd been about to finally reach an understanding.

He placed his hand over his grandfather's heart. Over a month ago, he'd felt Ben's heart start beating. Would he feel his grandfather's stop?

At half past two, when all was quiet, his grandfather opened his eyes. He released his breath. It rattled in his throat, and Devon feared the very worst.

Slowly, his grandfather rolled his head to face him. "Where were we in our discussion, Huxhold?" he asked. His voice was feathery soft, but he was completely lucid.

Devon reached for his hand. "You gave us a fright."

"Yes, but I'm not dead yet," came the labored answer.

For a second, Devon couldn't speak. Then he said, "I'm sorry."

The older man's smile was in his eyes. "No, I'm sorry." He paused, considering the words before saying heavily, "That was easier than I imagined."

"It was easier than I imagined, too."

His grandfather stared up at the canopy over the bed. "Sit with me. I don't want to die alone."

His words put a chill in Devon. "Dr. Partridge says you will fully recover," he lied. "You just need rest."

"No. This is different." He drew a breath. Again there was the rattling sound. He searched blindly for Devon's arm until he found it. "I dreamed." He paused, his gaze dreamy. "I saw Robin."

"Father?"

He nodded. "He was with that pretty young wife of his. What was her name?"

"Delia."

"Yes. Delia. Silly name. I never could remember it." His gaze slid toward Devon. "I was joking."

Devon shook his head. "You will never change."

"Oh, I have." He rubbed his lips together.

"Here, let me give you a drink." Devon didn't wait for an answer but tilted a glass of watered wine to his grandfather's lips. He drank deeply.

For a time, they were silent. Devon had almost begun to think his grandfather had fallen back to sleep when he spoke.

"Robin is proud of you."

"In your dream?"

"No. He's here."

Devon feared his grandfather was hallucinating. He wondered if he should wake Dr. Partridge, but then his grandfather fixed him with a steady gaze. "He wanted me to tell you that, Devon. That sweet wife is proud too."

"They are both here?"

"Yes. Along with Arrie. She's never far from me, Devon. Never far. Don't let Leah go far from you."

Tears stung Devon's eyes. He struggled with them.

His grandfather patted his hand. "I am proud of you too."

"I should have come sooner. I shouldn't have been so stubborn."

"You can't help it. You're a Marshall." There was a hint of a smile in his voice, and then he tensed, a shudder running through his body. He spoke with more urgency now. "Take care . . . family. All of them. All." He closed his eyes.

One moment, his grandfather was in his body, and in the next, his spirit left him. It transpired in the blink of an eye.

Devon looked around the room, wondering if they were all still here. Was his grandfather with them?

He sat quietly. Waiting. His grandfather's presence had loomed large over his life. What would he do without him?

Then, from down the hall, Devon heard Ben cry. It must be time for his feeding. Or did he know of his great-grandfather's death?

Devon bent his head and wept.

The marquess of Kirkeby lay in state for four days. The brisk spring day of the funeral boasted rare April sunshine, drawing a huge crowd to pay their respects.

The service was long. Devon and Leah, the new marquess of Kirkeby and his marchioness, were the perfect hosts. The Carrolltons and the Marshalls stood together. Even Julian was present—and sober. Many noticed that Lady Vainhope appeared pinched and worn out in her black bombazine, but that was to be expected. After all, everyone knew how devoted she was to her father.

For Devon, the most difficult part of the funeral was when he was called forward to throw the first handful of dirt upon the casket. The dirt hitting the lacquered coffin made a hollow sound.

His mind flashed to his boyhood and the ceremony for his parents. He'd been afraid then of being left alone.

Now, he heard his grandfather's voice assuring him his parents were proud. He knew his grandfather watched.

Venetia stepped up next, but broke down completely before she could perform the ceremony. Rex stepped up for his turn, and then the priest commended their grandfather's soul to his Maker.

It was time to leave the rest to the gravediggers.

The guests began leaving. Many would return to Montclef for the wake. While they ate and drank, the family would gather in the library to hear the will read, although Mr. Brewster had assured everyone there would be no surprises. Devon was the heir.

Leah had already gone to the coach. Devon lingered to press a coin in the gravediggers' hands and to spend one last moment saying good-bye to his grandfather.

He was not surprised, though, when Rex approached him.

"You are going to get it all, you know," Rex said.

Devon shrugged.

"That's what irritates me about you," his cousin snapped. "You never appreciated it."

"Never appreciated what, Rex? What exactly is it you want?"

"Besides the title and the money?"

"You'll have that someday."

"I will insist it is stated in writing that Ben cannot inherit," he responded stiffly.

Devon frowned. "I'm more than happy to do that. I know you won't believe this, Rex, but my goal was never to cheat you out of what you think you deserve."

Rex shook his head. "Oh, being a marquess will be nice, but I have a title, I have money. All I ever wanted was Montclef. Now it is yours. Mother and I will both be moving."

"You want Montclef?" Devon asked with disbelief.

"There is no finer house in all England!"

Devon was dumbfounded. He looked to the coach where Leah stood, waiting. Leah, his life and his mate.

"So all you've ever really wanted was Montclef?" he repeated to Rex.

"Is that so surprising?" his cousin answered.

"You can have it."

"What?" Rex said in disbelief.

"You can have Montclef."

Rex's gaze narrowed suspiciously. "Why would you give it to me?"

Devon searched his own motives and then said, "Because we are cousins. We are family. It will make Venetia happy and give you what you want. That is enough. I will tell Brewster to arrange it this afternoon."

"But where will you live?"

Devon smiled. "Oh, Leah and I will manage. Don't worry about us." He started walking toward his coach and his wife. Now it was Rex who hurried to catch up.

"Will you include a maintenance allowance?"

"That is negotiable," Devon responded, laughing, and the two of them argued good-naturedly in the coach all the way back to Montclef . . . but in the end, Devon thought he'd made a very good deal.

AFTERWORD

1817

ℒeah and Devon built a lovely villa in the country—but not too far from London to be a nuisance. It had every modern convenience.

Devon delighted in learning about new mechanics and better construction. He'd taken such an interest that he also financed a number of housing schemes that turned a pretty penny.

In an amazingly short amount of time, he lost his reputation as a rake. In fact, he was often referred to as a stunning example of a devoted husband, which Devon laughingly said demonstrated just exactly how fickle people were.

But he *was* devoted. Leah believed the love between them grew stronger every day—as did their passion for each other.

She knew for a fact there were *many* good reasons for marrying a rake!

Ben adored his father. The two were inseparable. Devon carried a laughing, chattering Ben on his shoulders when he visited the wharves. The two become such a familiar sight that the silhouetted image of a man carrying a child on his shoulders soon became the sign for the company of Marshall and Son.

Leah blossomed with marriage. The former debutante who had so jealously struggled for acceptance was replaced by a compassionate woman at peace with the world. She surprised everyone when she started a charity for foundlings. She funded it with the money she had asked of Devon. Originally she had wanted that money in case she and her son had been forced back into the world alone. Now, she knew the bonds between herself, Devon, and Ben were unbreakable.

Even her parents were eventually accepted back into society. Julian surprised everyone when he decided to stay in the country. At first, Leah worried it was his way of evading her and Devon, but when his betrothal was announced to a squire's daughter, she heaved a sigh of relief.

Rex and Venetia were not happy.

In spite of receiving Montclef and a reasonable maintenance allowance from the Kirkeby estate, Rex and his mother didn't hesitate to tell everyone that Ben was not Huxhold's natural son. Few cared. What concern was it of theirs—especially since the marchioness was such a kind and considerate creature? Ben would not inherit; the world would go on. Soon people of consequence and distinction grew tired of Vainhope's carping and began avoiding his company.

It was the third day of September when Leah went in search of her husband. She found him in his study. The book-lined room was his special haven. Ben played with a ball. He'd roll up on the desk, right on top of Devon's papers, where his father would have no choice but to throw it, and Ben would happily chase it.

As Leah entered the room, Devon looked up. He'd taken off his jacket and tossed it over a chair. His valet would not be pleased, but Devon didn't care. He'd already caused four to leave his employ in an artistic huff. What was one more?

"Hello," he greeted her, his smile still having the power to make her heart beat faster.

"Hello," she answered.

"Hello," Ben echoed, tossing the ball in her direction. She rolled it across the India carpet before standing by the edge of her husband's desk.

Devon scratched his head, lost in thought. "These figures are incredible," he said. "The percentages are all in our favor." He looked up suddenly. "I may be buying my fourth ship."

"Good. We must maintain Madame Nola's goodwill at all costs," she teased.

He smiled absently and returned to his column of figures. He loved adding and subtracting, scribbling out percentages, and considering new ways of making money. Sometimes, Ben would sit on his knee with his own pen and paper and pretend to do the same.

She remembered the day on the wharves when Devon had boasted to her of the business empire he would build. It was now a reality. Furthermore, his prediction of it being a new age had also been correct. His business acumen was now envied among their peers, who often solicited his advice.

Trailing her hand along the smooth mahogany of the desk, she worked around to where he was sitting. Her movements disturbed his papers. He didn't even blink but patiently put them back in order and kept working.

She decided she needed to try something else to capture his attention. Placing her hands on his shoulders, she began kneading the muscles of his neck the way he liked it.

Now she had his attention. Devon leaned back in the chair, a smile crossing his face.

"You work too hard," she chided softly.

"Not always. But right now, Rusky wants to invest in a tin mine. The markets are in a devil of a state. I'm wondering how we can do it and make good money."

"Oh, I'm sure you'll manage," she said. She ran her thumb up and down the back of his neck.

"That feels good."

"Ummm," she answered.

Devon turned. "Something is not right here."

She stopped the massage. "What do you mean?" she asked, innocence itself.

"The expression on your face." He studied her

a moment. "You look like a cat that has been in the cream."

Leah laughed. "I have."

"Oh?" He sat forward, his voice dropping. "Any cream in particular?" Ben rolled the ball up on the desk. Devon caught it before it fell off the other side and tossed it for him. The toddler charged after it, his body almost getting ahead of his feet.

Leah sat on the edge of the desk. "I have a secret."

"One that includes me?"

She nodded.

He ran his hand up and down the top of her thighs. "*These* are my favorite secrets," he told her with a sleepy leer.

She caught his hands. "I'll wager one week of backscrubbing every day that you can't imagine what my secret is."

He grinned, intrigued. "Does it have anything to do with Ben?"

"Maybe a little" She reconsidered. "Actually, quite a bit."

"So it is about Ben and me?"

"Especially you."

"And it is good news?"

"Oh, very good news." She practically sang the words, adding, "Unless you are Rex or Venetia."

He mouthed her last words. "What could it be that Rex and Venetia wouldn't like?" He laughed, lifting his hands heavenward. "What wouldn't it be? They are turning into absolute fustians."

She smiled her agreement before offering, "Would you like a hint?"

Relentless, Ben walked up at that moment and threw the ball. Devon caught it with one hand and tossed it. "We do this all day," he admitted dryly. "And yes, I want a hint."

Leah placed his hand against her abdomen. "Do you feel anything?"

"Should I?"

"Oh, Devon. Think of miracles and wishes and dreams and the almost impossible."

"Almost impossible," he repeated. "That doesn't make sense—? Wait." He caught her meaning. "Leah?" he asked incredulously.

She nodded, happy tears coming to her eyes. "Yes. We are going to have a baby."

His reaction was everything she could have imagined. With a loud whoop, he scooped her up in his arms and twirled her round and round.

Laughingly, Ben chased them, begging for his turn at a ride in Papa's arms.

Alexander Marshall, who the family called Alec, was born seven months later. It was an easy delivery, although Devon did not attend this birthing. He and Ben were perfectly happy to pace back and forth outside the bedroom door as the very professional doctor took care of matters. Ben was overjoyed to have a brother, someone who would be pleased to play toss and fetch all day.

Devon held his newborn son in his hands, fearful that he would feel more for this child than he

did for Ben. But in truth, he discovered he loved
Alec and Ben equally. They were both children of
his heart. Yes, Alec would someday be Viscount
Huxhold, heir to the marquess of Kirkeby, but
Leah and Devon would insist that both their sons
learn to be men of the world.

And so they were.

Benjamin Marshall and Sons Names New Head
London Financial Express 15 APRIL 1999, SEC. C: 6

One of Britain's most influential and established money houses, Benjamin Marshall and Sons, named a new president this morning. Delia Marshall will step in to fill the position left vacant since the departure of Sir Scott Carrollton due to illness last month. International markets rose 1¾ across the board in reaction to the news.

Considered by some to have the keenest financial mind of this century, Miss Marshall was groomed personally for her new role by Sir Scott. In a statement issued from his home in Sussex, Sir Scott said, "Delia is an energetic visionary who will successfully guide Benjamin Marshall into a new millennium."

Miss Marshall is the first female head in the almost two hundred years of the bank's history. She assured this reporter she has no plans to change the company's logo of a silhouetted man carrying a small boy on his shoulders, considered by many to be one of the most trusted and recognized trademarks in the world.

A direct descendent of bank founder Benjamin Marshall, she is also the cousin of Britain's ambassador to France, Vincent Marshall, Lord Kirkeby.

DO YOU REMEMBER
THE FIRST TIME...

...you saw him? Perhaps your eyes met across a crowded room... and you knew he was the one destined to change your life. Or was the last person you thought you'd fall for... the one all your friends warned you about. Infuriating, fascinating, and ultimately irresistible... he's the man who can rouse your passions as no other.

Now, come meet six unforgettable men... cowboys and rakes, both honorable and scandalous (and some a bit of both!), as created by your favorite writers: Barbara Freethy, Cathy Maxwell, Christina Dodd, Lorraine Heath, Susan Andersen and Kathleen Eagle.

Turn the page—you could be meeting the man you've been waiting for all your life....

Katherine Whitfield thought she'd found herself a cow-boy on the wrong side of the Mississippi. There she was, stranded on a Kentucky roadside, with no one to help her but lean, sexy Zach Tyler. Trouble is, Zach might be easy on the eyes, but he had the most annoying habit of telling her what to do. And although it soon became clear that he had a gentle hand with horses and a slow hand with women, Katherine sure didn't want him to get the upper hand with her!

ALMOST HOME
by Barbara Freethy

COMING IN JANUARY 2000

𝕶atherine shook her head, trying to figure out where she was and who was yelling at her. There was a man—a tall, dark-haired man with burning black eyes standing next to her car window. He was pulling on the door handle and yelling all sorts of absurdities that seemed to have less to do with her and more to do with a horse.

She roused herself enough to unlock the door. She pushed on it as the man pulled on it, sending her stumbling into his arms.

He caught her with a sureness, a strength that made her want to sink into his embrace and rest for a moment. She needed to catch her breath. She needed to feel safe.

"You could have killed my horse," he ground out angrily, his rough-edged voice right next to her ear. "Driving like a maniac. What were you thinking about?"

Katherine could barely keep up with his surge of angry words. "Let me go."

His grip eased slightly, but he didn't let go.

They stared at each other, their breaths coming in matching frightened gasps. Dressed in faded blue jeans and a white shirt with the sleeves rolled up to the forearms, the man towered over Katherine. His eyes were fierce and his thick dark hair looked like he'd run his fingers through it all day long. His face was too rugged to be handsome, but it was compelling, strong, stubborn, determined . . .

Good heavens—she had the distinct feeling she'd found herself a cowboy.

Forced to rusticate in the country to hide the disgraceful results of her elopement, Leah Carrollton is utterly dismayed to see Devon Marshall striding toward her across the English countryside. The beautiful debutante had fled the wagging tongues of London's ton and an arranged marriage to another, but could marrying Devon truly save her from scandal?

A SCANDALOUS MARRIAGE
by Cathy Maxwell

COMING IN FEBRUARY 2000

Leah had been standing a step apart from a group of other debutantes. They'd all worn pastels and smelled of rosewater. Their claim to conversation had been self-conscious giggles. She was one of them, and yet alone.

He instantly recognized a kindred soul. He understood. She wanted, no, *had* to be accepted by the group but exerted her own independence.

She sensed him staring at her. She turned, searching, and then looked straight at him.

In that moment, time halted. He even stopped breathing, knowing he still lived only because his

358

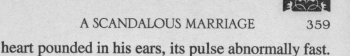

heart pounded in his ears, its pulse abnormally fast. Cupid's famed arrow had found a mark.

For the first time in his adventurous life, he felt the sweaty palms and the singing in his blood of a man smitten beyond reason by the mere presence of a woman. The poets had been right!

Oh, she was lovely to look at. Petite, buxom, rounded. He could have spanned her waist with his two hands.

Her heavy black hair styled in a simple, elegant chignon held in place by gold pearl-tipped pins emphasized the slender grace of her neck. He imagined himself pulling those pins from her hair one by one. It would fall in a graceful, swinging curtain down to her waist. Her eyes were so dark and exotic they reminded him of full moons, Spanish dancers, and velvety nights.

But it wasn't her beauty that drew him. No, it was something deeper. Something he'd never felt before. He wasn't a fanciful man but he could swear he'd been waiting for her to walk into his life.

She smiled. The most charming dimple appeared at the corner of her mouth and his feet began moving of their own volition. He wasn't even conscious that he was walking until he stood in front of her.

"Dance with me." He held out his hand.

Carefully, as if she, too, understood the importance of her actions, she placed her hand in his. It was a magic moment. He felt changed in some indefinable way.

Lady Ruskin had a twinge of guilt in hiring Charlotte, Lady Dalrumple, also known as Miss Civility to the members of the ton. *Though Charlotte was well-connected and highly recommended, she was working as a governess, of all things. But it wasn't Lady Ruskin's grandchildren who needed lessons in manners. No, it was her handsome, incorrigible son, leaving the fearful mama to dread the moment the two would meet and Charlotte to give her real lessons in . . .*

RULES OF SURRENDER
by Christina Dodd

COMING IN MARCH 2000

Adorna, Lady Ruskin, could scarcely contain her fascination. She knew the current marquess of Avon, and he had both children and wealth. Why his niece was working as a governess, Adorna could not imagine. Nor, because of the restrictions of refinement, could she inquire. "Sit down, Lady Dalrumple. Let us have tea."

Lady Dalrumple sat, but with such rigidity Adorna would have sworn her spine never touched the back of the chair.

Adorna picked up her tea and confessed the least of her problems. "My grandchildren have lived abroad all their lives."

"Abroad?" Lady Dalrumple arched her brows.

Adorna ignored the delicate inquiry as to the place. "They are, I'm afraid, savages."

"Of course they must be," Lady Dalrumple said. "The lack of a stabilizing English influence must have worked against them. As the eldest, I suppose the son is the worst."

"Actually, no." Words failed her.

Lady Dalrumple set down her cup. "So let me understand you, Lady Ruskin. If I train your grandchildren to behave like civilized English people in three months, your plan is to keep me on as their governess until the youngest makes her bow ten years from now?"

"This first three months will irrevocably try your patience."

Lady Dalrumple allowed the slightest of a patronizing smile to touch her lips. "With all due respect, Lady Ruskin, I believe I am capable of handling two small children."

Lady Ruskin knew, as a decent matron, a respectable grandmother, she ought to tell the rest. She ought to. But really, this attractive young woman would find out soon enough.

But in order to salve her guilty conscience, she did offer a magnificent salary. "And you guarantee your complete discretion?"

"Absolutely."

Lady Ruskin rose. "Send a bill to my town

house. I will instruct that it be paid at once. Lady Dalrumple, how much time do you need to prepare for a trip to my country house?"

"I can be ready tomorrow morning. There is no time to waste."

"I will send a carriage for you at eleven." Adorna pulled on her gloves with a sense of accomplishment and looked around the room again. What would this young woman do when she discovered the real savage that need taming was not one of her grandchildren, but her son.

Saucy Jessye Kane knew from the get-go that Harrison Bainbridge, the second son to an English earl, didn't belong in a sun-baked place like Fortune, Texas. He was a mysterious scoundrel, an aristocrat who managed to keep her riled up whenever he came near. Jessye told herself that she wished he would sail on the first ship home . . . but she knew she was just lying to herself . . .

NEVER LOVE A COWBOY
by Lorraine Heath

COMING IN APRIL 2000

Jessye saw the pale lamplight spill out of a window—Harry's window. The intense heat swirled through her like flames bursting to life. She didn't want to think about what Harry might be doing— but she seemed unable to stop herself.

He'd take off those fancy clothes he wore, clothes that would make any other man look like a dandy—but they only provided Harry with the appearance of sophistication.

Whenever she joined him at a table, she felt like a sow's ear sitting next to a silk purse. Sauntering through the cotton fields had bronzed his skin. When he shuffled those cards, his deft fingers mesmerized her.

She enjoyed their verbal sparring, was challenged by his ability to always win with the hand he was dealt. Out of deference to her suspicions, he played with his sleeves rolled up so she knew he wasn't cheating. He swore he never cheated when he played her, but she knew that was an outright lie—otherwise, she'd occasionally win a hand. She wasn't that poor of a poker player.

Now he needed her—or more accurately, he needed her money. She might have given it to him with no strings attached if he didn't always call her "Jessye-love." She trusted the endearment as much as she trusted the man. She knew he didn't love her, and using the word made a mockery of an emotion that could wound unmercifully and heal unconditionally.

The light from his window faded into darkness, and she realized he'd gone to bed. She dared not contemplate what he might *not* wear while he slept. Every time she changed the sheets on his bed, she wondered if they'd known the touch of his bare back . . . stomach . . . buttocks . . .

Squeezing her eyes shut, she spun around. She'd sworn never again to become involved with a man until she was a woman of independence, although Harrison had a disconcerting way of making her regret that vow . . .

Daisy Parker had never forgotten Nick Coltrane. She'd been sixteen, he'd been twenty-two . . . and he'd driven her crazy! Nine blissful, Nick-less years had passed since then, when suddenly he was back in her life as gorgeous and self-assured as ever . . . and he still had the nerve to call her by that awful nickname "Blondie." But if she really thought Nick was so awful, why did she feel so curiously wonderful whenever he came near?

BABY, DON'T GO
by Susan Andersen

COMING IN MAY 2000

𝔇aisy Parker glared at her secretary. "For Tom crying out loud, Reg. I may not be wearing dress-for-success pinstripes, but my clothes are eminently suitable for guarding this guy's butt. Why should he care what I wear, anyway? Is he the crown Prince of England?"

"Close," said a cool voice from the doorway behind her.

No. Oh, dear God, please, no. Her heart pounding an erratic tattoo, Daisy slowly pivoted, hoping

against hope that her ears had played a trick on
her.

They hadn't. It was exactly who she'd feared it
would be: Nick Coltrane. The last man in the
world she wanted to see.

He was as gorgeous as ever, too; damn his blue
eyes. That tall, beautifully formed body looked as
hard and fit as she remembered, even covered by
an old pair of jeans and a V-neck sweater. Nick
had always looked like he was born in tennis
whites. He had an air of casual sophistication, of
belonging, that was as natural to him as breathing.

But then, why shouldn't he? He did belong; he
always had. It was she who had been the outsider.

Nick gave her a thorough perusal. "How are
you, Blondie? You're looking good."

"Don't"—she took an incensed step forward before she caught herself—"call me Blondie," she
finished with a mildness that burned her gullet.
The nickname was a hot button and he damn well
knew it, which was undoubtedly why he'd pushed
it. She'd been sixteen years old to his twenty-two
when he'd first started calling her that, and fish that
she was, she never quit rising to the bait. Feeling
heat radiating in her cheeks, she drew in a deep
breath and held it a moment before easing it out
again, perilously close to losing her composure.

She would eat *worms* before she gave him that
satisfaction. And certainly before she'd allow him
to see that when he looked at her with those cool,

casually amused eyes, she felt the ache of rejection all over again.

"I take it you two know each other," Reggie said when the silence had stretched thin.

"My father was married to her mother for a while," Nick said.

Daisy froze. *That's* what he saw as their strongest connection? It shouldn't hurt—not after all the other ways he'd managed to hurt her. But damned if she'd let him see he still had the power to get to her.

"Yeah?" Reg demanded, giving her a distraction to focus on. "Which marriage was that?"

"Her third," she said.

"It was my dad's fifth," Nick offered.

"So, what's it been, Coltrane, six, seven years since we last saw each other?" Daisy asked coolly. As if she didn't know to the minute.

"Nine."

"That long? My, time really flies when you're not being annoyed. What brings you slumming in my neck of the woods?"

"Uh, he's our two o'clock appointment, Daise."

Slowly, she turned to look at her secretary. "He's what?"

Reggie held his palms up in surrender. "When I made the appointment I had no idea he was your step—"

"I am *not* her brother," Nick cut in peremptorily, his voice flat.

Daisy turned her attention back to him. "No,"

she said, "you certainly never wanted that role, did
you?"

He met her angry gaze head-on. "No, I didn't.
And if you haven't figured out why by now, you're
not half as bright as I always thought you were."

*Helen Ketterling had never forgotten Reese Blue Sky . . .
he was her first real love, the one she compared all the
others to. He'd left her breathless, filled with anticipation . . . and when she discovered she carried his
child she was determined never to force him to settle
down. Now, Helen has another chance to rekindle
their passion. It's a dream come true, but what will
happen when Reese discovers the truth?*

WHAT THE HEART KNOWS
by Kathleen Eagle

COMING IN JUNE

Helen spotted him immediately. Surrounded by
people, he stood above all of them, easily seeing
over their heads. He looked straight at her when
she came in the door, but there was no change in
his face, no sign of recognition or welcome or displeasure. He simply looked at her, kept on looking
at her in a way that drew her directly.

She made an attempt to smile, then let it slide
away. She'd thought about what she would say if
he didn't recognize her right away. Something
witty and flippant. A casual quip, some sweet, pri-

vate little joke to jar his memory and maybe throw him slightly off balance. Then she'd have the upper hand. But he was still looking at her, his dark eyes still completely unreadable, and she couldn't think of a single clever thing to say.

So she offered a polite and collected handshake. "Helen Ketterling."

"I remember." His big, warm hand swallowed hers up completely. "It's been a long time."

"Yes, it has."

"Ten years?"

"More than that. You're looking—" Casting about for her wits had left her suddenly short of breath.

"Yeah, I'm looking." His smile was slow in coming, but finally his eyes befriended hers. He wasn't releasing her hand. She wasn't drawing it away. "You haven't changed."

"Yes, I have. I'm really very . . ." She shook her head and glanced away. She was going to say *sorry*, but it felt like a pale, simpering word, and it had little to do with his comment.

He'd changed, too. She'd known him when he was raw-boned and edgy, when his everlasting hunger burned in his eyes, but now she beheld a cautious, confident man who had made his mark. "I've only been back for a short time," she said quietly. "But your father had become a friend."

Reese looked surprised. "To you?"

"He remembered me from . . ."

His surprise turned to expectancy. Would she say it? From the time he'd introduced her as *his girl* and she'd teased him about using a school-boy's term? She'd used his greenness against him at times, embarrassed him in a shameless attempt to gain the upper hand in their impetuous courting game.

Unable to look him in the eye, she sidestepped, withdrawing her hand. "He invited me to ride his horses anytime, and of course, I jumped at the opportunity. We visited about politics, history, folk-lore, all kinds of things. He had so much life in him, so many stories."

"What brings you back?"

"A job. The quest for the perfect job."

"And you came back here to Bad River?" He chuckled, shook his head in disbelief. He'd always worn his hair long, neatly trimmed, touching his shoulders in back. "Well, it's good to see you."

"Not like this, though."

"Why not? It's good that you came to say good-bye to your friend. You forget to do that some-times."

"We said good-bye. In the rain that night. Re-member?"

As soon as it was out she was sorry she'd said it. She could feel the cold rain on her face, his wet shirt beneath her hands, his warm, promise-making breath in her ear. He'd said he figured he had one shot and now was the time to take it. He would call. He would be back. He would catch up with her.

Cold rain, she remembered, shivering inside as

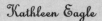

she noted the cooling in his eyes. "It was a long time ago," she said quietly.

"And I didn't realize it was meant to be a final good-bye."

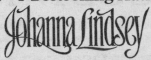